NO PLACE TO HIDE

SOFIA SAWYER

No Place to Hide
Copyright © 2019 by Sofia Sawyer

This novel is entirely a work of fiction. The names, characters, and incidents portrayed in it are the work of the author's imagination. Any resemblance to actual persons, living or dead, events, or localities is entirely coincidental.

Printed in the United States
First Printing, 2019
ISBN (Paperback): 978-1-7332090-0-7

Developmental Editor: Megan Records
Copy Editor: Suzanne Johnson
Proofreader: Salt & Sage Books
Formatting: Uplifting Author Services
Cover Design © 2019 Louisa Maggio

To my parents, who always encouraged me when it came to writing. And especially my mother, who kept every horrible poem from grammar school and proudly printed off entries from my blog.

To my husband and dog, for being supportive during my neurotic periods and patient during times when I was lost in my work.

NO
PLACE
TO
HIDE

CHAPTER 1

I stared at the packed bag on the worn pine floor of the apartment. It was his overnight bag—the expensive one made with the finest Italian leather—that he'd been using for his sporadic work trips lately. I eyed it curiously over my steaming cup of coffee. My mind, still foggy from sleep, struggled to remember whether he had upcoming travel. I squinted, trying to get the wheels in motion. They were sluggish this early but I knew there were no out-of-town trips. So why was his bag sitting in the foyer stuffed to the seams?

"I've been thinking..." he started. "This isn't going to work anymore."

My eyes flashed to him. "What are you saying, Trevor?" Despite my croaky voice, the question was clear. But even as the words left my mouth, I had a sinking feeling. The bag placement by the front door was a strong indicator and, if I was truly oblivious, his body language confirmed it. His eyes darted uncomfortably between me and the door.

"The last four years have been amazing, Em. But I

think we're going in different directions. Different life paths."

Even as he gave me the cliché speech, he looked perfectly collected. I took stock of him and then myself and realized it was a tangible representation of what he was trying to say. Here I was standing in the foyer of our apartment in my pj's, which included a worn t-shirt from my eighth-grade "Battle of the Classes." My hair, knotted from a restless sleep, was thrown up in a messy bun. Yesterday's leftover mascara was currently smudged under my eyes, making me look like a deranged raccoon. I thought one of the perks of being in a committed relationship this long was not having to be perfectly made-up all the time. I was human, after all.

But as I took in Trevor standing before me in his tailored suit, shined shoes, and expensive watch at six in the morning, I started to wonder if maybe I'd gotten it wrong. Maybe I had let myself get too comfortable. I was never that put together so early in the day, even as a café owner who was regularly at work before daybreak. Knowing him, he'd probably also done a morning run and caught up on emails before he gave this speech.

It was funny to think that only four years ago he was a law school graduate struggling to get ahead. He'd be swimming in ill-fitting suits that were off the rack and usually out of season. He'd work long hours on crappy cases, which meant never having time to focus on his appearance, let alone having a routine that involved daily exercise. His car was usually littered with fast-food wrappers thrown haphazardly on the floor. He was a mess. Despite it all, I stood by him as he struggled to make a name for himself.

Because that's what you do when you love someone. Or so I thought.

Then, a year ago, his hard work and our sacrifices paid off. He landed a high-profile case that paved the path straight to partner at his firm. The transformation from harried henchman to polished professional happened almost overnight. And now here we were, me still apparently stuck in the past while he was looking for bigger and better things that didn't include me.

"Are you breaking up with me?" I finally asked the obvious, gripping my mug while I waited for his response.

He gave an exaggerated sigh like this was the hardest conversation he'd ever had, although it looked like it was more of an annoyance than anything else. "I just don't see how this will work. We're two different people now, Emily," he said as if I were dense. "I will always love and appreciate you, but I don't think we're doing each other any favors by dragging this out." His patronizing tone made this unexpected speech sting more.

I stood there, speechless. The warm glow of the rising sun filled the apartment, and the scent of my freshly brewed coffee had seemed like the makings of a pretty good day. Instead, I was being forced to watch a big part of my life grab his bag and walk out the front door.

He ticked off his last checklist items. "I left a check on the counter. It should cover the next six months of rent. I'll send someone to get the rest of my things later this week. You can keep the furniture we bought." He started for the door handle before turning back to me. "You can also keep the ring," he added before making a swift exit out of our apartment.

Well, just my apartment now.

I calmly put down my coffee mug on the breakfast bar, concentrating hard to keep my hands from shaking, and walked through the living room to peer out the front window. Down on the street below, I saw Trevor walk straight to Melissa Maher, another lawyer at his firm, who was waiting by her Mercedes convertible. It was all sleek and flashy, just like the redheaded beauty herself.

But it wasn't the car I'd never be able to afford that caused my blood to run cold. It was Trevor, who possessively grabbed Melissa around her waist while he passionately kissed her. She smiled at him adoringly. The embrace looked familiar, as if this kiss was just one of many they had shared. I watched them as they got into the car and drove off without a backward glance.

So this is what it felt like to have all your life plans come crashing to the ground.

• • •

An hour later, I was stuffing another mini cupcake into my mouth. Maybe it wasn't the well-balanced breakfast I should have been eating at thirty, but it was my way of pushing down my feelings and delaying the inevitable. The breakup hadn't hit me yet. It still felt like a normal day. I'd take over the late shift at the café and wrap up just in time for Trevor to come home for dinner.

Only this time he wouldn't be.

"I made your favorite flavors," Joanna cooed as she handed me another cupcake, enabling my avoidance tactic. That was how I knew I had picked the right best friend. Rather than forcing me to talk about my feelings, she was there to provide the goods while I still processed what happened.

Joanna Locklear was both my best friend and the co-owner of our coffee shop, Crafty Café. She was also a baking goddess. It was times like these that having my café right below my apartment came in handy. Within thirty minutes of calling Joanna, she was at my door with an endless supply of mini treats in hand.

I inspected the cupcake I was holding and ate the thing whole in one fell swoop. "Mint chocolate chip isn't on the menu today," I attempted to say with a full mouth, accidentally spitting out pieces of cake in the process. God, no wonder Trevor left me.

She settled in next to me on the loveseat and wrapped an arm around my shoulders for a quick hug. "I know, but I figured I'd make you a special batch. It seemed like that kind of day."

Joanna, the most thoughtful girl in the world. I didn't deserve her but was glad she hadn't come to the realization herself yet. "You didn't have to, Jo."

She cocked her head to look at me, her beautiful black hair cascading past her shoulders. "Well, Trevor's a bastard," she declared.

For as long as I'd known her, it always shocked me when she cursed. As a Native American descendant, Joanna was beautiful with her flawless tan skin and high cheekbones. But the thing that made her truly special was her soft voice and sweet way of talking, almost as sweet as her delectable baked goods. So in the rare instances when she did say something profane or raunchy, I couldn't help but laugh. It was the equivalent of a fluffy puppy threatening to bite your face off. You felt compelled to pick it up and squeeze it.

"He *is* a bastard, isn't he?" I agreed after I was done laughing.

"Yeah. And a dick!"

I gave her a face. "Let's not get carried away. I think you hit your cursing quota for the day."

"What? He is. Who leaves their fiancée like that? No warning. No opportunity for discussion. He just left."

I sighed while I debated whether I should eat another cupcake. "I may have left something out when I called you this morning." I bit my bottom lip.

"Well?"

"I'm pretty sure he was cheating on me with Melissa from his office," I said quickly. Saying it out loud to someone else made it feel real. My stomach sunk as I let the admission settle over us.

Jo's jaw dropped. "Pretty sure?"

"Well, he didn't exactly give me a chance to ask him in his one-sided conversation with me this morning. I barely had a chance to ask anything, really. He blindsided me, said his piece, and left as if whatever he said was final. But when I say I'm pretty sure, it's because I saw him kiss her outside the apartment before he left."

She slapped her leg. "How did I miss that? They would have been right outside the café's window." She folded her legs under her and turned to me. "Wow, Em. I don't know what to say. How are you not a blubbering mess right now?" She rubbed my back in big circles to soothe me.

"I don't think it has sunk in yet. Thankfully, I have today off to deal with it. Hopefully, I can cry it out before I work in the morning. It might be bad for business if I wept into our customers' lattes." I pushed myself off the couch, padded barefoot to the kitchen, and poured myself another cup of coffee. Joanna waved it off when I offered her some.

I leaned against the counter as we both mulled over everything. Then she made a face, one I recognized as her I-want-to-say-the-truth-but-the-truth-hurts face.

I let out an exasperated breath. "Come on. Get on with it, then."

"Emily, honey. Maybe this is for the best. He's been kind of a jerk to you since he landed that big case."

"What are you talking about? He was fine," I protested. "He was just busy proving he deserved that promotion to partner. It's not like I wasn't working like crazy too, trying to make the café a success."

She shook her head. "Even now you're making excuses for him, after he left you for another woman, no less."

I shot daggers at her. "What's that supposed to mean?"

"Remember the time he forgot your birthday?" she asked cautiously, sensing my bubbling anger.

"He had a big case."

"It was your thirtieth birthday. It was a big deal."

"But—"

"You were supposed to go on that romantic trip to Italy together. You dreamed of going there for as long as I've known you. Don't you remember how excited you were to explore the vineyards of Tuscany and dine seaside on the Amalfi Coast? You missed your own birthday trip because he forgot about it and you couldn't get ahold of him. You were crushed when I had to get you from the airport because he never showed."

I tried to think of an argument, but I didn't have time before she shared another example. She was on a roll.

"How about the time he embarrassed you at your family's Christmas? Or when you overheard him saying something pretty hurtful about you to one of his colleagues?"

"They were just being guys. You know, 'Arg, my woman is such a nag,'" I said in my deepest voice while shaking a fist. "That sort of stuff."

She gave me a frustrated look, one that only a best friend can do effectively. "You know it was much worse than that. Stop making excuses. Maybe things were good between you for the first few years, but he's been treating you like crap for at least a year. You let his proposal overshadow his treatment of you."

She walked over to me and leaned against the counter. "I know you were committed to making Crafty the best ever," she said in her soft voice. "And I couldn't be prouder to work with someone like you, especially with everything you do for us and the café. But all that hard work made you miss some pretty important signs when it came to your relationship with Trevor. It's like you avoided it by throwing yourself into work."

"You know how important it is for me to make sure our café works. We put all our savings into it. I can't let us fail."

"Maybe I'm not the business-savvy part of this co-ownership, but you could have relied on me. You don't have to shoulder it all."

I looked at her. "If you knew Trevor was treating me so poorly, why didn't you speak up?"

"I tried, Emily. You just didn't want to hear it."

That sounded like me, all right. I looked at the gleaming engagement ring on my hand. "He said I could keep the ring. Also gave me a rent check for six months."

I slipped it off my finger and slammed it on the counter. We both stared at it.

Jo rolled her eyes. "How generous of him," she replied sarcastically. "Maybe you could cash it in and take that trip you missed," she suggested.

If only. "I think the money would be put to better use for a new espresso machine. It's mid-May. We're going to be slammed with summer tourists once Memorial Day hits. We need something more reliable than the lemon we have downstairs."

Portland was a small city in Maine but attracted a ton of people in the warmer months. With a great foodie scene, craft beers, waterfront views, and proximity to the local beaches, business had been booming for us ever since we opened four years ago. And it just got busier year after year.

There was something about the salty sea air and squawking seagulls that made things feel right in the world. At least, that's what I believed when I moved here after Trevor got an offer at a family friend's firm in the city, the one where he was now a partner. I fell in love with this city the moment I arrived. I guess I lucked out, because I was committed to following him wherever he needed to go for work. We could have ended up in a dying city with no potential for the café.

Joanna rolled her eyes again, no doubt to mock my overbearing quality of being sensible. "I have to get back to work. I left Meg alone at the counter and the morning rush will be starting soon. But first, I have another idea to make you feel better."

"And that is?"

She crossed the room and grabbed my laptop off the coffee table. "I think it's time to revisit your favorite pastime."

I groaned.

She placed the laptop on the counter and plugged in the password before spinning it to face me. "You *love* to research. You were our go-to girl in school when it came to writing papers or stalking crushes. Why not put those skills to good use and cyberstalk Melissa?" She gave me an encouraging smile. "I bet she has some embarrassing photos on social media. Everyone does. Maybe she was super frumpy or had horrible highlights in college or something."

"Lawyers aren't usually on social media. Trevor said something about making sure nothing could get kicked them off the bar or whatever."

"I have a hard time believing she doesn't have *something* on the internet. What about MySpace?"

"Likely deleted."

"Is yours?"

I bit my bottom lip. "I don't know. I think I just stopped

signing in one day and kinda forgot about it."

Joanna pointed a finger triumphantly. "Exactly. I tried to delete my account like five years ago and it was such a hassle that I just gave up. Our old profiles are floating out there in cyberspace. I'm sure we're not the only ones who forgot all about it."

I gave a snort.

"C'mon, you know it will make you feel a little bit better, if only for a moment." She gave me a wink and walked out the front door.

I watched the cursor blink on Google's search bar. Would going down this rabbit hole only make me feel worse? What if Melissa had always been perfect? Knowing her, she probably never went through that awkward adolescent stage us mere mortals did.

The cursor egged me on. Just doing a few searches wouldn't be the worst thing. Joanna was right. I was a huge nerd when it came to investigating and research. I bet I could find exactly what I needed to feel slightly better in a matter of minutes.

Two hours later, I was still deep in my research. Growing up in a digital world, it wasn't hard to find information on most people. Social media, online forums, blogs, reverse phone lookup. They all made looking into someone's life that much easier. I mean, who hadn't jumped at the chance to get a Facebook account when they finally got into college so many years ago?

But then there was Melissa Maher, practically a ghost in the cyber world. No matter how hard I looked, it was as if she had never existed until six years ago.

This discovery—or lack thereof—made me feel unsettled, but I couldn't figure out why.

CHAPTER 2

It had been two weeks since Trevor left. True to his word, someone came by to gather his things. At least that was one promise he could actually keep. Too bad it came after our relationship ended.

I stood in the doorway of my bedroom after all was said and done and noted how bare it felt. The closet was full of unused hangers, and the bathroom no longer held scents of his aftershave. His side of the bed was left neatly made and untouched. Even though Trevor worked long hours and occasionally went away for business, the apartment seemed incredibly empty. And lonely.

I had spent the majority of these past two weeks purging my life of our broken engagement. I couldn't stomach the reminders of how he blindsided me with his betrayal. I wasn't sure what hurt worse: the fact that he left me for another woman or the fact that he took measures to create an exit plan before he dropped the bomb. He knew he was leaving me. He had time to prepare for it. I was taken off guard and left to deal with it.

As I removed the photos in the picture frames and

tossed them into the trash with the wedding magazines, I couldn't stop crying. It was that gut-wrenching pain, the kind where it felt like the hurt wouldn't ever stop, where I couldn't breathe. I sunk to the ground and curled into myself, allowing the tears to flow freely.

This overwhelming feeling of loss left me distraught, and all I wanted now was to let go of the pain and move on. When I could finally catch my breath and my brain cleared away some of the fogginess, I realized that moving on was going to be a long journey. I only hoped some of the heartache would ease up soon so I could endure the process and come out on the other side okay.

I grabbed a tissue from the bathroom and took stock of my appearance. My red-rimmed eyes and chapped nose were evidence that I had gone through hell these last weeks. Although I did a great job keeping it together when I was at Crafty Café, I couldn't stop the tears from falling when I reluctantly made my way back up the stairs to the apartment each day. It was exhausting to pretend things were okay for my employees and customers. And although Joanna was just trying to be supportive, her spontaneous hugs and murmurs of encouragement made it harder to not come undone.

I wasn't just crying because I was adjusting to life without him—I was adjusting to a life that no longer had a plan. Trevor used to say I was organized to a fault and that I left no room for spontaneity. I argued that those skills were the reason I was able to start my own thriving business. But now I wondered if maybe his complaints were hints that our relationship was about to fail.

Maybe my obsession with order and process had led him straight into Melissa's bed, where he could be wild and uninhibited. What man wouldn't want that?

All these future plans we had, ones we'd talked in depth about and made specific strides to work toward, changed at the drop of a hat. This wasn't the spontaneity I was open to. This was a disaster, one so unimaginable I couldn't even think of a recovery plan. The scariest part was I had no idea what to do next or how to move on. I couldn't even fathom how to plan out the next steps. My only saving grace and sense of stability now came from the coffee shop and Joanna. Hopefully, that would keep me sane while I figured it all out.

I made my way downstairs later that morning. It was a gray Monday in May, making it feel more like winter was lurking in the distance than like the balmy summer months were within our reach. I threw on an apron and grabbed a rag to clean up after the morning rush. There was something soothing about doing a mindless task like wiping down a table. The instant gratification of seeing cleanliness where dirt had been was an attainable goal. For a moment, I was able to shut off my brain and just be.

Even with the dismal weather, the café always made me feel warm inside. The large storefront windows brought in a lot of natural light that complemented the warm colors of the exposed brick walls and tables made of reclaimed wood. It was rustic and cozy, and the scents of fresh coffee elevated that. I fluffed up a couple of the teal and yellow pillows on the benches as the morning rush finally settled down.

Making my way to the kitchen, I grabbed some fresh baked goods and brought them to the front for Meg to re-stock the case while things were quiet. Suddenly, Joanna came rushing through the kitchen swing door.

"Did you hear?" she asked frantically when she reached the counter.

My eyebrows knitted in confusion. "What?"

She held out her phone and pulled up a livestream from one of the local news stations. Trevor's face was frozen on the screen. Curious, I hit the play button.

"We are doing everything we can to find her." His demeanor was stiff yet professional when addressing the field reporter who was holding the mic.

The feed switched back to the anchor at the studio. "Melissa Maher has been reported missing for five days with no leads as to where she may have gone." I let out a gasp. The woman on the screen continued. "Portland police do not suspect any foul play at this time but urge the public to call their tip line with any information about her disappearance." The woman rattled off the number that appeared on the screen. "No information is too insignificant."

I looked back to Joanna's wide eyes. "I don't understand" was all I could manage.

Before she could respond, the bell above the door dinged to announce a new patron. I looked up to see a man purposefully walking to the counter. Although he had a lean, fit physique, his imposing presence made him seem larger than life. I examined his face—a strong jaw lined with dark scruff and hazel eyes that popped under his dark eyebrows. He wasn't a regular, and judging by how his jaw ticked with determination, I knew he wasn't here for an espresso and scone.

"I'm looking for Emily Ayers," he announced in a rich baritone voice.

I chewed my lip, feeling apprehensive over the man in front of me. "I'm Emily. How can I help you?"

He slipped a strong hand into his jean pocket and pulled out a badge and ID. "I'm Detective Ben Hunter with the Portland PD."

I eyed the badge and felt my anxiety kick up. "What's this about?"

He looked at me directly. "I have a few questions to ask you regarding the disappearance of Melissa Maher."

I crossed my arms over my chest. "I'm not sure how I

can help you, Detective."

"Please, ma'am. This is standard procedure."

"Okay…"

He gestured to one of the small tables in the corner. "Mind if we sit?"

Not feeling like I had much say in the matter, I followed him to the table and sat down across from him. I gripped my hands in my lap, wringing them slowly, and threw a glance back at Jo. She gave a concerned shrug and busied herself with restocking the coffee mugs, no doubt trying to overhear the conversation.

"Listen, Officer Hunter—" I started.

"Detective," he corrected with a tight smile that didn't reach his hard eyes.

"Detective," I emphasized, not liking his penetrating stare. I felt uncomfortable with the way he was silently sizing me up. "I'm not sure what I can tell you. I really didn't know much about the woman."

He pulled out a small notebook and pen. "We can start by discussing your relationship with Miss Maher. How do you know her?"

"She was a lawyer at my fiancé's—err—ex-fiancé's firm," I shared.

He leaned back in his chair, stretching out his long legs in front of him casually while he mulled over what I said. He might have been trying to display an air of aloofness, but the determined gleam in his nearly green eyes never left. "Interesting choice of words," he finally said while leaning forward.

"I'm sorry?"

"You said she was a lawyer, past tense. Why is that?" His question was calm but pointed, as if he just backed his prey in a corner, playing with it before going in for the fatal strike.

My anxiousness had turned into irritation. I briefly wondered how much trouble I'd get in for strangling a man of the law.

"Was. Is. It's just a word," I ground out.

He looked at me for a beat. "Sure," he said passively, but I wasn't convinced he'd just let it go. "Can you tell me more about your interactions with her?"

I tucked a stray lock of hair behind my ear while I considered my response. "They were minimal, at best. She started at the firm a couple years ago and we crossed paths maybe a handful of times at company events or when I was visiting Trevor at the office. Our conversations were limited to pleasantries and small talk. Surely not enough to claim I knew the woman. I wouldn't even call her an acquaintance."

He made a note and looked back up at me. "When was the last time you saw her?"

"Two weeks ago. Around six a.m. on May fourteenth." AKA, the day my world turned upside down.

He cocked an eyebrow. "Very specific. What did you two talk about?"

"We didn't. I saw her for a moment from my living room window before she drove off in her car." With my fiancé.

He ran a hand through his thick, dark hair. His face was pensive. A crease formed in his forehead before he spoke next. "I understand your fiancé had an affair with Miss Maher and left you for her."

No empathy. Just facts.

I leaned forward so our faces were mere inches from one another. I would be damned if I would be bullied into admitting something I had nothing to do with. "Are you insinuating something, Detective?" I challenged him.

He lingered there for a moment, testing my nearly wavering bravery. When I held my ground, he made a slight move to back down. "One could say it's curious timing how you found out about the affair and then she went missing. Wouldn't you say?"

I stood up and slammed my hands down on the table, causing the tiny vase holding a single flower to rattle. "What I would say, Detective, is that I had nothing to do with the disappearance of Melissa Maher. You can see yourself out now."

My face heated, and I heard Joanna suck in a breath behind me. I didn't usually react like this, nor was I the type to get combative. But something about this man had set me off. He didn't know a thing about me, and yet he waltzed in here and acted like I didn't have the capacity to move past my ex's infidelity. That'd I'd actually *murder* someone. It was ridiculous.

Detective Hunter stood slowly and towered over me. "Stay close by in case we have further questions." His voice held a subtle threat. "Thanks for your cooperation," he added without sincerity. He nodded to Joanna and left the café.

Jo rushed over to me. "What was that? Does he think you offed her or something?

I tried to slow my racing heart. "I don't know, but this can't be good."

CHAPTER 3

The tense meeting with Detective Hunter had me feeling uneasy the rest of the morning. It was clear he knew about my recent split with Trevor and that Melissa had played a role in it, but what? Could Trevor have said anything that caused the detective to believe I had something to do with her disappearance?

As much as I wanted to avoid Trevor to give myself room to heal, the unanswered questions gnawed at my insides. That afternoon, I mustered up enough courage to leave the safe confines of my little shop on Milk Street and made my way to Trevor's practice on the corner of Congress and Exchange. Even though the gray clouds were breaking up, a slight chill in the air made me wrap myself tighter in my Crafty Café hoodie. Every step I took urged me to turn back, but I pressed on.

I entered the lobby of a historic brick building situated across the street from the iconic Press Hotel. I punched number three on the elevator panel and waited as I slowly ascended to the top floor that housed Trevor's law offices, Kaminsky and Miller.

The offices were professionally decorated with warm wood paneling, frosted glass doors, and upscale lounge area. The lobby was plastered in awards, no doubt to instill confidence in clients.

I didn't bother stopping at the reception desk once I entered the lobby. My anxiousness gave me a one-track mind. I blew through the glass door that led to the lawyers' offices and conference rooms and beelined straight to the back corner office to find Trevor.

Lois, the sweet yet edgy older woman who worked in reception, called out as she tried to gracefully power walk behind me. "Mr. Miller is busy!"

She tried to catch up but her long, flowing skirt got stuck under her pumps, causing her to stop mid-stride before the whole thing came sliding down in the middle of the office. She adjusted her skirt, giving me just enough time to make it to his office and close the door before she could stop me.

Trevor, completely oblivious to my intrusion, stood behind his chair as he peeked over the shoulder of a young man. The man, possibly in his early twenties, rapidly pounded away at a laptop. His skin was pale, as if he never saw the outside world, and his long, dull-brown hair was pulled back in a tiny bun at the base of his head. He paused and leaned in closer to read something on the screen. Trevor also squinted, hand over his mouth, as he scanned whatever was on the screen.

"There," he said while pointing.

The man sitting in the chair clicked the mouse and pushed oversized glasses up his nose while he read further. After a few seconds, he nodded. "I think we can work with that. I'll get back to you later today."

He unhooked the laptop from the docking station and gave me a polite nod as a way of telling me I was blocking the exit. I sidestepped to the right and let him leave.

Lois poked her head into the office, face flushed from chasing me. Her pixie cut showed off the colorful earrings that matched her skirt perfectly. "Mr. Miller, I tried to tell her you were busy, but she got away from me." She glared at me.

"It's fine, Lois. You can leave us. Thank you."

Lois closed the door and Trevor looked at me with a sigh. "This isn't a good time, Emily."

I crossed my arms defensively. "I met Detective Hunter today. Mind telling me what you said that caused him to grill me?" I demanded while walking farther into the room.

"Nothing but the truth," he replied in an obnoxious, lawyerly tone. It was hard to take him seriously when I knew how many lies he had told me.

"So you told him you were a cheating bastard?"

He pinched the bridge of his nose, something he did to calm himself so he wouldn't yell. "In not so many words. Is that all?"

He had been tense since I entered the room, and I wondered if what he had been looking at on the laptop had something to do with it. "Who was the kid at your computer? I haven't seen him here before."

"He's our new IT intern. He's going through Melissa's computer to see if there's anything useful to share with the police. Maybe something's on there that can give us a clue as to where she might be."

"Doesn't your firm normally outsource that? Kinda weird to intern at a place that doesn't even have an actual tech department or someone to mentor him. Don't you think?"

He mumbled something under his breath, his irritation with this conversation becoming more apparent. "Maybe so, but he's a smart kid and doesn't need much guidance. Fred was doing a favor for his wife's yoga instructor's friend. He's a good kid. Efficient. Resourceful. And a hell of a lot cheaper than outsourcing our IT needs. It worked out. Anything else?" I shook my head. "Great. Can you see yourself out then? I've got a lot to do." He gestured to the door, took a seat, and dove into the case files stacked on his desk. He didn't bother to look back up, giving me a clear sign that this discussion was over and he wanted me gone.

I started to leave but turned back with one last question. "You don't really think I could have been involved in this, do you?"

He looked up at me, and his face softened a fraction. "No, Em. I know you're not that type of person, despite the circumstances of our breakup. The police are just doing their due diligence."

"Do they have any leads?"

Leaning back in his chair, I noticed how exhausted he looked. "No. The only thing they have to go on is what I think might have happened. Sometimes she likes to go running before dawn when she's dealing with especially complex cases. I woke up that morning and she was gone. Normally, she'd be home by the time I got up but she wasn't. She didn't take her phone with her either, which isn't like her. The police can't triangulate and track the GPS. We've got nothing."

I gave a tight-lipped nod. "I'm sorry," I said simply as I left the office, eager now to get away.

Trevor spoke of her with such tenderness and familiarity, something that could have only come from spending significant time together. I tried not to drown in the sinking feeling of knowing he and Melissa already shared a home and normal routine. Were our four years together so easy to replace? Hell, I was replaced before our relationship had even ended.

I walked back to the café in a zombie-like state, not registering anything around me. I should have trusted my gut and stayed away. Now, after my chat with Trevor, I was left with more questions than answers and a lot more heartbreak. If the detective hadn't gotten under my skin, I could have left it alone. Instead, images of Trevor and Melissa playing house behind my back filled my mind. How could have I been so blind?

Thankfully, my evening would be filled with mindnumbing inventory, a task I hated with a passion but now suddenly welcomed. It was simply black and white. No gray areas. No surprises. It was something I could count on when my world was becoming murkier.

After a few hours into inventory, Joanna and I decided to take a break to grab dinner and a much-needed drink around the corner at The North Point. We grabbed our usual spot at the corner of the small bar top, and my stomach growled in response to the delicious scents wafting around me. I wished I was one of those people who couldn't eat when they're upset. Instead, my stress-induced hunger was in full force tonight. Joanna didn't even bat an eye when I ordered charcuterie, cheese, nachos, a flatbread pulled pork sandwich, and a bottle of Pinot Noir. I later added a pear salad to help even out the fat content.

"What a day," I complained as I took a healthy sip of my wine. The spicy sensation warmed its way through my body, giving me one blissful moment of relaxation.

Joanna daintily ate a piece of baguette with Havarti and jam. "I believe it. First your breakup, now this whole Melissa thing, and then your first encounter with Trevor since he left. You need a break."

I had filled her in when we were counting our supplies, and although she didn't press for details, I could tell she was hoping the wine would loosen my lips.

"I don't have time for a break. Plus, you heard what

the detective said. Skipping town would seem suspicious."

I scouted out the perfect nacho, loaded with a bit of everything, and stuffed it in my mouth. Sour cream smeared across my cheek. I wiped it off and sighed as I thought of a peaceful vacation in a log cabin away from technology and people.

Joanna thought for a moment. "Maybe we can do something different. A girls' day of pampering or something." She tugged at my ponytail. "Maybe some highlights to lighten up your auburn hair for the summer?" She eyed me up and down. "And a new wardrobe to show off that rockin' bod you like to hide under your aprons and oversized hoodies and t-shirts."

I rolled my eyes and took a big bite of pizza.

"Seriously, Em. With the way you eat, it's beyond me how you can keep your figure. Most women would kill for that. Not to mention you're successful, strong, and smart. You're the full package, girlfriend."

I stared blankly at her and ate another nacho.

"Should I mention the freckles?"

I pointed a chip at her. "Don't you dare mention the freckles."

"But they're so cute," she taunted in a singsong voice. "Guys love it."

"I'm a thirty-year-old woman, Jo. Not a little girl."

"Freckles are so in." She laughed. "But really, when was the last time you did anything for yourself? Even a simple manicure would be a step up. You're single again. It's time to put yourself out there."

"Ugh, too soon." I slumped in my chair and slurped my wine. "I can't imagine dating at this age."

Joanna shrugged. "It's really not that bad. There are so many dating apps out there now that make it pretty easy. Plus, you're the one who said you wanted to move on. Maybe you need to start easy with a rebound or something."

I gave her a playful slap on the arm. "Too soon!" I checked the time on my phone. "We should head back to Crafty. I still have to finish up paperwork and clean."

We paid our tab, took our to-go boxes, and made our way back, taking pleasure in the cool spring night air on our short walk. I took a deep, cleansing breath and, for a fleeting moment, felt like things would be okay. Maybe I'd try those dating apps sooner than I expected.

Or maybe it was the wine talking.

"I can take care of the paperwork if you want to finish cleaning up," Joanna offered when we got back to the café.

"Sure." I was thankful to take on the cleaning. My brain felt like mush and dealing with numbers didn't sit well.

I wiped down the benches in the kitchen and put the clean baking equipment in their respective places. After tidying up, all I had left was to take out the two bags of extremely stinky trash. I lifted one in each hand and awkwardly made it out the back door to the small alley that housed the dumpsters for the businesses on Milk Street.

I waddled to the closest dumpster with the heavy bags, attempting to lift them high enough so they wouldn't rip on the asphalt. I dropped one by the dumpster and used my free hand to lift the lid.

That's when I saw her.

Melissa's lifeless eyes stared back at me. Her body was resting haphazardly on the trash bags in the dumpster, and her fiery-red hair was plastered to her head with dried blood. Her pale skin contrasted against the deep bruising on her cheek and jaw.

Aside from funerals, I'd never seen a dead body before, especially one that was clearly violently murdered. I froze, unable to look away. A woman who was so full of life a few weeks ago was suddenly in front of me looking like a victim from a horror movie.

Except this wasn't a movie. This was real life.

I dropped the trash bag I was still holding and brought my hands to my mouth to smother a scream that never came. The dumpster lid crashed down, hiding her body again, but the image was burned in my brain. How did this happen? Why did this happen?

When the initial shock wore off, my legs finally decided to move. I ran back into the café and tore through the kitchen to reach the phone hanging on the wall. I nearly knocked down Joanna in the process.

"What the heck, Em!" she yelled as she grabbed the bench to steady herself.

With shaky hands, I dialed 911. "I found Melissa Maher," I nearly screamed when the operator answered. All the adrenaline made it hard to control the franticness of my voice. "She's dead." I shook as tears streamed down my face. I tried to gulp in air between my sobs. I felt sick.

Joanna grabbed the phone and took over. She put her hand over the receiver and turned to me. "Where did you find her, honey?" Her normally soft and comforting voice trembled as she asked me.

I slid down the wall and sat on the floor, holding my knees tight to my body. "The dumpster." Joanna relayed the message and confirmed we would stay put until the police arrived.

She sat down next to me and gathered me in her arms while we waited. I was grateful she was by my side and even more grateful she hadn't witnessed what I had. I liked to believe I was a tough woman, but I hadn't been prepared for something like this. I would never get the image out of my mind.

The police showed up moments later, flooding in from all directions, with Detective Ben Hunter running the show. He called out orders and members of the force, forensics, and medical examiner scurried away to do their jobs. Police tape was put up, and large flashes from a camera in the alley shone through the back door, illuminating the kitchen like lightning.

Detective Hunter made his way to where Joanna and I still sat on the floor. We stood but didn't speak. He ran a hand through his hair and let out a breath. Putting his hands on his hips, he took a dominant stance before addressing me. "Kinda strange how the mistress of your ex-fiancé showed up dead behind your shop," he accused in a low voice.

Joanna pushed me behind her protectively and spoke up. "This isn't what it looks like. She didn't do anything wrong. You couldn't really think she killed someone, placed the body behind her *own* shop, and then called it in?" she argued.

His eyes moved to my face as he sized me up. "Could be a good way to throw the police off track. A hidden-in-plain-sight situation."

I still couldn't find the words to speak. I didn't know if I was more stunned from finding Melissa's body or by the fact that the detective was basically suggesting I was some mastermind murderer.

He never took his hazel eyes from mine, as if he could intimidate me into making a confession. Joanna noticed the stare-down and popped her head in the way of his vision, breaking his line of sight to me. I squeezed her hand as a thank you.

"Don't leave town." He stalked off to the alley, leaving me both worried and angry.

The next hour passed in painstaking slowness and all I wanted to do was go back to my apartment, away from all the madness, and process everything. I half-expected the detective to come in from outside and throw cuffs on me, but he never did.

Finally, a Hispanic man with tan skin and a thick head of hair approached me with a notebook. "Miss Ayers, I need to take your statement now."

Before I could breathe a word, Trevor came barging through the door and stomped straight up to me. "You better fucking lawyer up!" he screamed in my face, spittle from his mouth spraying onto my cheek. I shrunk back behind Joanna.

An officer standing near the alley doorway rushed up to Trevor and held him back, struggling to restrain him. "Damn it, Trevor. I told you out of courtesy. You can't be here right now."

"Get him out of here!" the man interviewing me yelled out to two nearby officers.

Things had just gotten a whole lot worse.

CHAPTER 4

It was a two-bottle kind of night. Had I had more wine on hand, it would have been an even higher bottle count. Or maybe a lobotomy would be more appropriate to rid myself of the horrible memory of Melissa in the dumpster. Either way, nothing seemed enough to cope with today's events.

Joanna and I had sat on my couch, drinking our respective bottles of wine in silence for the last thirty minutes. No glasses were needed for a night like this. After some questioning from Officer Sanchez, we made our way up the stairs to my apartment and internalized what happened. Jo was always good about giving me the quiet time I needed to process, but she got antsy if the silence went on for too long. Her voice broke my train of thought, indicating the time for processing was over.

"I can stay with you for as long as you need," she offered. "I can run home tomorrow to grab some things and camp out in your guest bedroom."

The company would be welcome, especially after the deafening silence of living in the apartment alone. It was strange how living alone seemed to amplify the quiet, as if it was trying to make me insane. Between that and Crafty being closed for the next few days while the police collected evidence, I worried the idle time alone would get to me. I was even more concerned about what the closure would do to our bottom line. Memorial Day weekend always kicked off the busy season. What would a café closed up with police tape say to our prospective customers?

A knock sounded at the door, startling us both. It took a lot for me to muster up the energy to answer it. Wine aside, I felt lethargic after coming down from the earlier adrenaline high. I opened the door, using it to hold up my body, which felt like jelly. Detective Hunter stood on the other side, looking sinister. The last three hours seemed to have worn on him, making the strong angles of his face more pronounced. His light eyes seemed to have darkened under his furrowed eyebrows. More troubled. If he looked this battered, I wondered what I looked like.

He critically eyed the bottle of wine dangling from my hand but said nothing. I didn't care. He already seemed to think he had me all figured out anyway. I hoped his suspicions didn't seal my fate in this investigation.

"How can I help you, Detective?" I took a slug from the bottle while maintaining eye contact. He waited patiently while I finished.

"Are you aware the security camera in the alley was down for the last four days?" he questioned.

"No. That's not our equipment. It's our neighbor's. Delores. She owns Ambience, that scent and candle store next to ours. To be honest, she's a little on the older side and not great with technology. She's always asking one of us to help her with something. Probably didn't even know it was down." I leaned harder on the door, causing it to teeter slightly back and forth.

He cracked a knuckle and stretched his neck, his patience wearing thin. "Looks like someone tampered with it."

"Maybe there's footage of the person who did said tampering," I suggested indifferently.

He seemed to back off a bit, his tone less accusatory. "Our ME was able to place the time of death. Three days ago between the hours of three and five in the morning."

I straightened. "I know what you're going to ask me. I was home. Sleeping. Alone." I had no alibi, which didn't help me in the least.

He looked downcast as if in thought and nodded with tight lips. "We'll need you and Miss Locklear down at the station tomorrow for more questioning. Ten a.m."

"Okay," I answered, a little deflated.

He looked at me again intently, as if studying me. His jaw ticked slightly under the scruff of his dark five o'clock shadow. This time he seemed more curious than suspicious. "Get some rest." He eyed the bottle again and turned to leave without another word.

I closed the door behind him and made my way back to the couch. Before I could flop back down, another knock sounded at the door.

"Who is it this time?" Joanna asked.

"Probably the detective to torture me some more."

I stood on wobbly legs and shuffled my way back to the door to find Delores, speak of the devil. She wrapped me in a tight hug and fussed. I sank into it, enjoying the warmth and security it provided. Delores had been a great shop neighbor and also a wonderful mother figure. It was hard being away from my parents while living in Portland. I only got to see them a handful of times a year despite being so close to Rhode Island. Delores's matronly presence helped fill the void in between visits.

"Oh, honey. I heard the racket on the police scanner

and came over as soon as I could." Even at ten in the evening, she was still dressed head to toe in the vibrant florals of Lilly Pulitzer. She pulled back from me and adjusted her matching scarf before leading me to the couch.

She sat down on the loveseat that was perpendicular to the couch and fluffed up a pillow to make herself comfortable before I unleashed an epic saga. And unleash I did. Nearly an hour had gone by when I finally caught her up to the present.

Her jaw had fallen open from shock, and her hand was on her chest by the time I finished. "There are no words."

"Tell me about it."

She shook her head. "I just never woulda believed it. This area of Portland hasn't seen much crime in all the years I've lived here. Nothing in the thirty some odd years since I opened up my shop. Sure, we had some tough times during recessions and what have you, but murder? No way!" She continued to shake her head in disbelief and then stopped abruptly.

"What, Delores?" Joanna prodded.

"Um, well. Come to think of it, there was one incident that happened on this very street," she answered, deep in thought. She pointed a finger at me. "In fact, it was few apartments down from you, Emily. How could I have forgotten *that*?"

I closed my eyes, exhausted from the riddles. I circled my hand around as if to say "get on with it."

"It's been nearly fifteen years, but I can remember it like it was yesterday. It was a horrible thing. A real tragedy. A nice family who lived above one of the stores had a terrible ending. I don't know what exactly happened that led up to it. Something about the husband having a mistress?" She waved a hand as if it was a small detail and pursed her lips. "Anyway, the wife, in a fit of passion, shot her husband and then killed herself."

Joanna gasped. "Oh my goodness. That's heartbreaking."

Delores gave her a look like she had even juicier gossip and leaned in closer to us. "That wasn't even the worst part," she whispered, despite us being the only ones in the apartment. "The whole thing happened right in front of their little boy. He couldn't have been more than nine years old. Poor thing. To witness such an act of violence and suddenly be an orphan? I don't know how a young mind can come back from that. He was such a sweet boy, too."

I leaned forward too, engaged in the story, happy to talk about anything other than my current situation. "What happened to the boy?"

Her forehead scrunched together as she tried to remember. "I wish I could tell ya. I didn't see him after that. I know he went into the foster system and didn't hear much about it since. I think the community wanted to forget the tragedy, to be honest. It was just too much to fathom. But other than that, there hasn't been so much as a peep of crime around here. Makes me think whatever happened was deliberate."

I sunk back into the cushions. "That's what I'm afraid of."

• • •

The next morning, Joanna and I made our way to the Portland precinct for further questioning. I wasn't sure what was more painful: my hangover or the examination. As I sat in the dingy, stagnant interrogation room, I tried to keep down the dry toast I had eaten earlier. Officer Sanchez's cologne wafted in my direction and made it nearly impossible to focus, but I pushed through.

I went through the night's events again and my relationship with Melissa. After being battered with the same questions over and over again, I had had enough. I "politely" let the officer know that just because he was asking me the same question in a different format, it didn't mean the response was going to change. I was telling him the truth. Why couldn't they believe me?

I *needed* them to believe me. We were getting nowhere.

At least Detective Hunter wasn't doing the interrogation. I learned he wanted a neutral person running through the questions and wondered if he thought my defensive nature toward him was preventing them from finding inconsistencies in my story. Even though he wasn't in the room, I could feel his gaze through the double-sided mirror. It made me want to squirm in my seat.

As little as they found out, we learned just as much.

Melissa Maher was murdered by asphyxiation. She was hit over the head with a blunt object initially, which explained why her hair was caked with blood. Unfortunately for her, it didn't kill her. Her nails were jagged and some were missing, as if she had fought off her assailant trying to escape before she had been suffocated. There was no DNA on her and no evidence of a struggle in the alley. Once again, a dead end. No pun intended.

We left the station worse for the wear and feeling defeated. The café would be closed for another few days as the police did a final sweep for evidence.

All they'd found so far seemed to point to me, despite being inconclusive. The fact that it was speculation was the only thing working for me, but I had no idea how to get out of their range of fire.

"We have to prove them wrong," I said out of nowhere as we walked back to my apartment. I slipped on my sunglasses to lessen the blinding glare of the sun. My head was killing me.

"Huh?" Joanna responded, clearly confused by my random train of thought.

"You and I both know I'm not the killer. The only reason they're considering me is that they have no other leads."

Jo gave me a skeptical look. "If the Portland PD can't find evidence or leads with all their resources, what makes you think we can do any better?"

I shrugged. "What other choice do I have? I can't just sit back and go to jail."

She gave me a look out of the corner of her eye. "You're always the rational one. Do what rational people do and research the best lawyers in town to represent you. Let the police do their jobs and do your best to protect yourself."

"It's a small town, Jo. Trevor knows all the local lawyers. You saw how he reacted to me last night. He'll probably turn them all against me if I even try. I think I'm on my own for this one. This is my life and I want to give myself the best shot. I can't trust anyone to have my back the way I would."

She shook her head and winced, likely from a headache. "I don't think this is a good idea," she stated. Then curiosity seemed to get the best of her. "What exactly do you have in mind?"

I chewed on my bottom lip as I considered it. "I haven't really thought it through. However, I will tell you this—if even an inkling of a clue pops up, I'm going to investigate it."

"Oh, I wouldn't doubt it for a second. You're like a dog with a bone once you get into your investigative mode. No point in trying to talk you out of it, huh?"

"Maybe I'll come to my senses when I calm down and regenerate a few brain cells. But not today."

Jo and I parted ways at Milk Street to go to our respective apartments. Heading down Fore Street, she called out that she'd be back in an hour after she grabbed a few of her things. I was grateful she convinced me that she should stay at my place. As much as I liked to think I was independent, the last few days had me shaken up and I didn't want to be alone.

But alone, I wouldn't be.

Much to my chagrin, I found Detective Ben Hunter leaning against the wall in between my apartment door and the café storefront. Objectively, he was exceptionally good-looking. Long, lean, strong, with dark hair that complemented his olive skin and hazel eyes. The dark scruff that peppered his jawline had become a new attraction of mine, which surprised me because I always preferred Trevor clean-shaven. If he wasn't out to pin a murder on me, he would have been the type of guy Jo would have pushed me to rebound with.

He seemed raw and intense. That would probably translate well in bed. But I couldn't be objective. Not with him.

"Have you not finished your daily quota of annoying me today, Detective?" I asked while squeezing by him to unlock my door. A pleasant, woodsy scent floated from him and I did my best not to breathe it in.

Okay. Maybe I did, just once. It was too damn good not to.

"Just came by to let you know your shop can reopen by the end of the week." He pushed off the wall and looked down at me. Even though I was on the taller side for a woman, Ben always seemed to tower over me. I wondered if he did it on purpose or if it was his natural way of being. I stepped through the door to create more personal space between us.

"Thanks for the news, but you could have just shared that little tidbit while I was at the station," I said over my shoulder as I made my way up the stairs.

"I had to stop here to check on things anyway."

I pushed through my front door and turned, acting as a barricade from his prying eyes. "Any new discoveries?"

"I'm not at liberty to say, Miss Ayers."

"Emily," I insisted. I hated formalities even though I knew keeping my distance from him was the way to go. I hoped the casual suggestion didn't make him think I was letting my guard down.

"Emily." The way my name rolled off his tongue almost sounded seductive. I let out a breath.

"Is that all?" I asked, dropping my purse on the table in the entranceway and sorting through the mail.

He paused at the door and leaned casually against it. "For now. And, Emily?" he said, grabbing my attention so I'd make eye contact. "We will find out what happened to Melissa Maher and bring her killer to justice. I've never not gotten my man...or woman."

I pursed my lips. "And what if your evidence wrongfully accuses someone?" I challenged, not appreciating his veiled threat.

"It'll never happen," he responded confidently.

"There's a first time for everything, Detective," I said before closing the door in his face.

CHAPTER 5

It was a restless night. The events from the last few days were swirling through my mind, causing me to question everything. Why was Melissa murdered? Did we miss any clues that could have hinted at what happened? Who knew the significance of leaving her body behind my café? What was my role in all of this?

When I finally forced my eyes closed in an attempt to sleep, Melissa's lifeless face appeared. I turned on my side and punched my pillow a little too hard to fluff it up, but it was no use. The morning light was starting to creep through my blinds, and I knew it was time to give up hope for any sleep.

I grabbed a discarded hoodie on the chair in the corner of my room and slipped it over my head before padding my way barefoot to the kitchen. The oven clock read 6:07 a.m., and I inwardly groaned. I needed my wits about me if I was going to figure out what happened to Melissa. Lack of sleep and increased stress weren't a good start.

I shuffled around the kitchen to fill a teapot with water and placed it on the stove to heat up. Although I was a coffee kinda gal, I figured the antioxidants from green tea would be a healthier choice to remove the fogginess from my brain.

As I waited for the water to boil, I picked up the mail I had left on the breakfast bar from yesterday. After my chat with the detective, I had completely forgotten about it. I flipped through the pile and noted that most of it was addressed to Trevor. I resisted the urge to toss it out and just be done with it all.

Sighing, I made my way through the rest of the pile, landing on a letter I had set aside earlier in the week and had forgotten all about. "Emily" was written in black Sharpie with blocky, neat penmanship. There was no stamp or return address.

Curious, I opened the envelope to find a map of Portland. There was a location marked with an X on Morning Street by the Eastern Promenade. Another X marked Crafty Café. A red line made its way from the X on Morning Street, around the promenade, up through East End, then East Bayside, and back up Fore Street before ending at Morning Street again. It was clearly a path, but for what?

I flipped over the map to find a small note in the same black blocky letters. "Melissa Maher's running route," it simply stated.

My heart thundered in my chest. I turned the map over again and studied it. Melissa hadn't been murdered in the alley behind my café and, based on the trash schedule, she would have been dumped there within the last twenty-four hours. If Trevor was right in saying she went for a run that morning, then this map could be suggesting that she'd been kidnapped along this route. If that were the case, why did they deliberately move her body to Milk Street to be found?

The murderer could have gotten away with it. Instead, they had chosen to put her body front and center. It made no sense.

This map meant that someone knew something. But why bring it to me?

Joanna appeared from the guest room as I considered this. The unanswered questions were piling up.

"What's with the face?" she asked as she pulled out two mugs and tea bags.

I handed her the map and took the whistling kettle off the burner. I poured the steaming water into our mugs while I let her digest it.

"What do you think this means?" I asked after a few moments.

"I don't know, Em, but I think you should give this to Detective Hunter."

"I don't know who sent it. It could be a sick joke. We still don't know if she went running that morning for sure." Even as I said the words, it felt off. I didn't believe it was a joke. This had some significance; I just wasn't sure what.

Jo pulled her long, silky hair into a messy bun on top of her head and blew on her cup of tea. Even first thing in the morning, she was stunning. Meanwhile, I was avoiding the mirror.

"I still think you should give it to him. It might be a joke. It might not be true. But it's something, and right now that's all you've got," she pressed, eyeing me over her mug. "Not to mention you could be arrested for withholding evidence. What if the cops get a warrant to search your apartment and find this?"

I hated when she was right. "But—"

Jo placed her mug on the counter and gave me a serious look. "Em, what has gotten into you? This isn't like you. You're by-the-books, not some vigilante."

I let out a huff. "The detective has really gotten under

my skin." I ran a hand down my face. "All of this…it's just too much. The breakup and infidelity were hard enough. Now all of this?"

"You have to work with the detective," Joanna said sternly. "I'll admit he's been a little too hard on you, but, ultimately, you both have the same goal: find the killer. Maybe you should work together instead of against one another. You know, two heads are better than one."

I leaned against the breakfast bar. "Fine." I couldn't argue with her. She had a point. Even if it turned out to be nothing, I'd rather know for sure than miss a key piece of the puzzle. I looked at the clock again. "You think it's too early to call him?"

She gave a little shrug. "Do you care?"

Nope. I didn't. I dialed his number and told him what I found. Despite it being early in the morning, he sounded awake and alert.

"He said he'll be over in a few minutes," I told Joanna after I hung up.

Mere moments later, a knock sounded at the door. Even in the early morning hours, Detective Hunter looked like he was on top of his game. Dressed in a t-shirt and pullover fleece with jeans that hung on his hips well, he looked more ready to leisurely sail around Fore River than to spend time sorting through a lead.

"Where did you find this?" he asked as he took the map from me and scanned it.

I sidled up next to him. Awareness hit me as I felt the heat and solid muscle from his arm pressed against mine. I shook my head to focus back on the conversation. "Someone must have slipped it through the door's mail slot downstairs with the rest of the mail. It doesn't look like it made its way through the postal system." I handed him the envelope so he could see.

He looked down at me and arched an eyebrow. The look of determination was back in his eye, but for once it was directed toward the map rather than figuring me out.

"Any idea who might have sent it? Does the handwriting look familiar?"

"No to both questions." I leaned in closer to him to get a better view of the map. That intoxicating woodsy scent made it hard to concentrate.

I cleared my throat. "We need to find out if this information is accurate," I said while pointing to the red line outlining Melissa's alleged running route. "Trevor said she went for runs in the morning, right? Maybe he knew where she went, and he can confirm this. Maybe she was taken or killed somewhere along this route."

"Have you checked her phone to see if she had a running app? Sometimes they'll document your running path through GPS," Joanna suggested as she perched herself on a bar stool across from us.

I looked back up to the detective. "Did she have a fitness watch? Those usually track it, too."

He shook his head. "No, she didn't. That was one of the first things we looked into when she went missing. Good thought, though," he said more to Joanna than to me.

I felt a slight twinge of jealousy that she received the praise and then scolded myself. This man was the enemy. Lack of sleep must have my brain and feelings jumbled up.

"There has to be a reason someone sent this to me."

The detective wiped his hand over his mouth as he stared harder at the map. "Could be someone playing a prank? It was all over the news. Most of the locals who come to your café know you live here. It would be easy to do."

"But why? Everyone who comes into my shop is friendly. Why would someone go through the effort to upset me?" I pointed at the map to emphasize my next point. "Not to mention, this was sent to me *before* we found the body. It could be someone who actually knows something. Maybe he or she was a witness but is too afraid to come forward for some reason," I countered.

"If that were the case, then why not bring it to the police instead of you? It makes no sense."

"Nothing about this makes sense."

He looked down again to assess me for a moment before speaking. "We'll get to the bottom of this. I'll see if forensics can pull DNA and fingerprints. They may be able to identify the handwriting, too. We'll figure out if this secret admirer of yours is credible or not." He paused for a moment. "Unless it was you."

I threw my hands up in frustration. "Enough already," I warned. "You should be thanking me for bringing this to you. Right now, your guys have nothing. This could actually be something."

He glared at me as he mulled it over. "We'll see. In the meantime, stay put and don't get involved. Give me a call if anything else turns up," he directed before leaving.

It wasn't that I didn't trust authority figures. I just didn't particularly care for the one I was having regular encounters with lately. This clue could be the key to finding out what really happened and get the blame off of me. With a new sense of hope and purpose, I mentally devised a plan for today.

Don't get involved? I'd be damned if I didn't investigate.

CHAPTER 6

Later that afternoon, I stood outside 50 Morning Street, a well-kept Cape Cod-style house typical of this area. Gray clapboard was offset by brilliant white moldings. Four stairs led up to a small porch with a wicker loveseat, making the house seem homey. A mature tree provided partial shade to the porch. As I looked around, I was certain the trees lining the road would create a quintessential New England scene during the autumn, with vibrant orange and yellow leaves.

A house like this was absolutely perfect for someone as flawless as Melissa Maher. My stomach turned in knots as I thought about Trevor living here with her. Now that he was successful, it only seemed right that he had the things to match his new lifestyle. He got the car, the girl, and apparently a house straight out of *Better Homes and Gardens*. It was hard to compete with that. I wondered if he still stayed here even though Melissa was gone.

A soft wind laced with the scent of sweet, salty air from the Fore River blew hair away from my face. I took a deep breath to calm my nerves. I shouldn't be jealous of a dead woman, but it was hard not to compare. I didn't stack up and Trevor had decided to trade up.

A newspaper sat on the red-stoned sidewalk outside of her home as if she'd be there later in the day to pick it up, like she probably always did. Everything seemed so ordinary, so peaceful. It felt surreal to know she wouldn't come back home again.

I saw a flash of movement in the enclosed porch of the green house next door. Someone peeked out of the sheers hanging along the window. A nosy neighbor? Maybe they'd be the key to finding out what happened the day Melissa went missing.

I walked to the neighbor's house and stood outside on the porch. My fist hovered just in front of the door, ready to knock, but I couldn't bring myself to do it. What was I looking to accomplish here? Was this even a good idea? Before I could let the doubt infiltrate my mind, the door opened, and a small older woman stuck her blue-rinsed head outside.

"Yoohoo," she said in greeting. "Are you here about Melissa?" Her voice was strong despite the fact that she looked to be pushing ninety.

"Um, yes." I guess I was committed to this now.

"Are you the police?" she questioned suspiciously, her gray eyebrows furrowed.

"No."

Her face relaxed. "The newspapers?"

"No, ma'am. I'm just a colleague looking for some answers," I lied.

That seemed to satisfy her. She nodded and opened the door to invite me in. "I'm Gertrude Trembly, but everyone calls me Gertie."

I followed her through the front dining area to a small living room in the back. It was a slow process. Her little legs and slightly hunched back made walking more difficult.

I craned my head around to take in my surroundings. Her house looked like it hadn't been redecorated since the seventies. The rug, a strange pea-green color, had seen better days. The mustard-yellow walls were an eyesore. But what was even worse than all the colors was the smell. The aroma of mothballs and litter box assaulted me. I breathed through my mouth as I took a seat on a plastic-covered sofa.

She took a seat in a tattered brown recliner and clicked off the ancient TV. "Was just watching my stories," she mumbled as she fumbled with the remote. "How can I help you?"

I cut right to the chase. "Are you familiar with Melissa's morning routine? Specifically, her running route?"

She slid her glasses up and nodded. "Oh, yes. She usually runs a few times a week around five in the morning. My bladder wakes me up early these days and I can't seem to get back to sleep. I wake up just before she takes off."

"And her route?" I passed her a map I had printed out and marked off from memory. "Is this it?"

She held the map close to her face as if the glasses she wore did nothing for her eyesight. "Hard to say," she replied as she squinted and adjusted her glasses again. "I never asked her where she went. We're friendly neighbors, but not very close, you see. Neighbors aren't like they used to be. Everyone keeps to themselves. They're too busy with their faces in their damned phones. There's no sense of community anymore.

"I remember when my husband—God rest his soul— and I first moved here as newlyweds. We were very close with everyone on the street. We had dinners together, let our kids play with one another. It was a different time.

Now all these people move in and don't say a word to one another. A simple hello would be enough. But no, they'd rather keep their heads down and pretend other people in the world don't exist." She tsked.

I nodded encouragingly throughout her mini-rant. "I hear you. Anyway, is there anything else you can tell me about her runs?" I tried to keep her on track.

She shifted in her recliner and straightened her powder-pink cardigan. "She would be gone for about half an hour, give or take. I'd see her take off toward the promenade and come back up from Fore Street. I suppose this map could be accurate based on that." She handed it back to me and clasped her hands over her belly as she settled back into the chair.

"Do you remember seeing her the morning she disappeared?"

"Yes. I was up a little earlier than normal. Damn bladder. I think it was around four in the morning if I'm not mistaken. Seemed like things were a little different though."

I leaned in. "How so?"

"Well, for starters, she didn't run. She got into someone's car."

My breath caught and my mind raced. "Do you know who?"

"No idea. Looked like it could have been a man driving. It was one of them, uh, one of those, um…" She waved her hand around in frustration while she tried to think back. "It was a BMW. Looked like a dark gray or navy. Then again, my eyesight is terrible. So I could be wrong about the color, but I know it was definitely a BMW."

My stomach dropped. Trevor drove a car that matched her description but he said he had been sleeping when she left. "Have you ever met Melissa's boyfriend?"

Her face lit up. "Oh yes! Nice gentleman. He helped

me hang my Christmas lights. That's how I knew it was a BMW. It looked like his car."

I stiffened in my chair. That bastard was cheating on me for that long? I cleared my throat, trying to remember the purpose of this meeting. "Could it have been his car?" I asked.

She scratched her chin as she thought. "It did look a lot like his but I'm not sure. I can't remember if he parked in his normal spot in front of the house." She gave a small shrug. "Maybe it was him driving?" she offered with uncertainty.

"Is there anything else you can share, Gertie?"

She took a moment to think. "Well, from what I remember, neither Melissa nor the car came back. Then again, I could have been in the kitchen making my oatmeal. That room faces the back of the house, so I could've missed it. Either way, I know she wasn't home that day. I would have seen her leave for work or puttering around the house if she was home." She squinted at me. "Come to think of it, I did see her boyfriend leave the house later that morning but that was it."

"Did he seem out of sorts?"

She shook her head. "Not that I could tell. He seemed like he was late for work or somethin' and rushed out to the car and drove off." Gertie let out a sad sigh. "I didn't even know she was gone until I saw on the news that her body had been found."

"Did you tell the police all of this?"

She snorted. "Those good-for-nothin's? I'll tell ya, the quality of police has really gone downhill since my son retired fifteen years ago. I wouldn't trust 'em if my life depended on it."

I had to nip this in the bud before Gertie went on another long-winded tangent. The plastic covers creaked as I got off the couch and followed her to the front door. "Thanks for answering my questions. It was helpful," I said as I stepped down from the porch stairs.

"I don't think I got your name, dear."

Shit. I had hoped she missed that. "Emma," I said quickly. "I was a work friend of Melissa's." It was a lie but if the police circled back with her and Gertie finally opened up, I couldn't have her telling Detective Hunter I was poking around after he specifically warned me not to.

The meeting with Gertie had left me with more questions than answers. I walked down to the Eastern Promenade to East End Beach, trying to get a feel for Melissa's typical routine. The sound of seabirds and rolling waves was peaceful, and I could see why she would have chosen to start her day here. But why did she deviate from her normal plan on that particular morning? Who was Melissa meeting with and why?

I debated whether or not I should call the detective. If I did, I would be admitting I had gone against his warning. At the same time, Gertie's insight could help the police look for whoever was driving that morning. Then again, the woman wasn't sure of the color and didn't catch a plate number so I wasn't sure how helpful it would actually be.

That debate was put to rest when I pulled up to my apartment an hour later and saw Detective Hunter waiting by my door. Brooding, as usual.

"Go anywhere special today?" he gruffly asked when I approached him.

I looked at him without giving an answer.

"Melissa Maher's neighbor mentioned a visit from a former colleague named Emma. My guys must have just missed her when they stopped by Mrs. Trembly's," he finally supplied with a hint of dry sarcasm. "Melissa had never worked with an Emma. Know anything about that?"

I glanced at him under my eyelashes. "I'm not sure what the right answer is here."

He ran a hand through his hair. "Damnit, Emily. I told you to stay away from this investigation!" His voice was deep, sending shivers down my spine.

I crossed my arms over my chest. "Before you get mad, did your team tell you about the car?"

He let out a pent-up breath. "No, the woman wasn't very forthcoming with us. Something about not trusting the police."

I tried to hide my smile as I unlocked the outer door to my apartment. "Maybe you should come inside," I suggested.

"Fine. I have something I want to share with you anyway," he conceded.

Hm. Share with me? That was a new one.

We made our way up the stairs and into my apartment. I strolled over to the kitchen and stretched to reach the top shelf for a couple of mugs. Detective Hunter came up behind me silently and grabbed the mugs for me with ease. I tried not to let the feel of his hard body against me make me lose my senses. Was that a gun or was he happy to see me? I peered down.

A gun. Definitely a gun.

I scurried over to the refrigerator and poured us some cold-brew coffee. It wasn't as good as the stuff we made at my store, but it was close enough. A pang of sadness hit me as I realized how much I missed Crafty.

I took a seat on the bar stool next to him and reluctantly shared what Gertie had told me, including the details about the car that had picked up Melissa the day she went missing. As much as my defenses were up when it came to Detective Hunter, Joanna was right. I needed to be forthcoming with him. Working together might be the only way

I could clear my name from this mess.

He took a long sip of his coffee as he absorbed it. "I don't know what it is about you that makes people over-share, but much to my displeasure, it's working in our favor. This is a good piece of intel."

His face, usually directed at me with anger or suspicion, softened a bit before he spoke again. "Speaking of that, I have some updates for you about the map."

I placed the coffee mug onto the breakfast bar with a thud and turned to him. "And?"

He sucked in a big breath as if he was preparing himself to admit he was wrong. "And we can definitely say it wasn't your handwriting."

"No shit."

He cocked an eyebrow. "So far what we know is that the person who wrote it disguised their handwriting by using varying strokes. It would take some time to perfect that. I don't suppose you put in the effort."

"Sure. With all my free time," I replied dryly, going back to the kitchen to refill our cups. "If I was that skilled in penmanship, my outdoor blackboard for the café would look a lot better than it does." I turned to face him and leaned against the counter. "Anything else? DNA maybe when the person licked the envelope?"

"I highly doubt someone would spend the time going through that writing exercise just to drop the ball by licking an envelope. But we're testing it anyway. Otherwise, no fingerprints or DNA were present in our initial research."

I crossed my arms. "What's with the face? You look like you sucked on a lemon."

He sighed and rolled his eyes. "Well, since you don't appear to be a prime suspect currently—"

"I shouldn't be at all," I cut him off.

He closed his eyes and looked like he was counting to ten. "Anyway," he said through gritted teeth, "it would seem to make sense to partner in some sort of way. As in, if someone tries to contact you again like they did with the map, you'll work with me on it."

"The running route was right, wasn't it?"

"The running route was right," he agreed. "But we also got the tests back from Melissa's body. The dirt under her nails wasn't from around here. We're still looking into it, but chances are, you wouldn't have had enough time to close the café, get her, drive her far away, kill her, bring her back before your next shift, and also clear out any evidence." He rubbed a hand on the back of his neck. "Plus, if you help me, I can also give you some information about the case." He stopped before I could speak. "Need to know only. You're not completely in the clear. I don't think I need to tell you that withholding information is a felony," he warned.

"Joanna already mentioned that," I muttered. I let out a breath and held out a hand. "Okay. Fine. Deal."

He shook his head as if to say I was ridiculous but gave my hand a firm shake. "Don't make me regret this," he said as he stood to leave.

"Wouldn't dream of it."

He stopped before the front door and eyed a box on the ground. "What's that?"

"Some of Trevor's stuff that his goons missed when they grabbed his things a couple of weeks back. I was debating on giving it to him but the last time he saw me he pretty much threatened to take me down for Melissa's death."

"If what you say is true about the car the day she disappeared, Trevor has other things to worry about than you."

CHAPTER 7

"So what are you going to do about it?" Joanna asked. "You've been staring at it for two hours now."

Detective Hunter's departing words about Trevor's possible involvement weighed on me. I was with Trevor for four years and couldn't picture him being caught up in a horrible crime like this. But his infidelity had gone on much longer than I initially realized. Now I was left wondering if I knew him at all. If he was capable of hiding those lies, what else could he have kept from me?

"I think I need some distance," I finally said. I grabbed packing tape from the junk drawer in the kitchen and sealed up the cardboard box of his things. "Holding onto his crap after a breakup isn't healthy to begin with, let alone with a murder case in the middle of it all. I'm going to take this down to his office now and be done with it."

"What about what the detective said?"

"I'll leave it with Lois or something."

"Need some moral support?" I could tell Joanna was also going stir-crazy without the café. She was on edge with the idle time, and the need to bake was causing her to fidget.

"I appreciate it, but I need to do this on my own. Want to grab an early dinner so we can get out of this apartment?"

She beamed. "Yes!"

"Great. You pick the place. I'll text you when I'm done at Trevor's and see where to meet up. Wish me luck."

"You've got this," she said encouragingly.

I grabbed the box from the floor and balanced it on my hip while I hoisted my purse onto my shoulder and left the apartment. As I uncomfortably shifted the box while walking down the stairs, I decided lugging it a few blocks to the office wasn't the best choice. I walked to the parking lot across the way for patrons and residents and placed the box in the back seat of my car before driving off in the direction of his office. With any luck, he'd be in a client meeting and I could avoid talking to him. I needed the closure and it would be easier if I didn't have to face him again.

"Hello, Miss Ayers," Lois said as I entered the lobby a few minutes later. Her normally spiked pixie cut was deflated, as if she had been running her hands incessantly through it. "Mr. Miller is tied up at the moment. Can I leave him a message on your behalf?"

She seemed agitated, as if she was trying her hardest to keep her composure. Her indifferent attitude toward me also raised some flags. She was all but chasing me through the offices the last time I was here. Why was she so quick to write me off today?

I shifted the box from my left hip and placed it on the reception desk. "I just came to drop off some of his things."

"Of course," she replied quickly, rising to her feet and grabbing the box. Nervous energy radiated off her. "I'll see that he gets it. Have a nice day!" She practically shoved me out of the lobby.

As I turned to go, a loud commotion sounded from behind the glass door separating the offices to the lobby, stopping me in my tracks. First, a set of officers carrying a computer and hard drive came walking through the door. This was followed by a disheveled Trevor, who was being escorted out by another set of officers. His suit was rumpled and his hair wild. His hands were cuffed.

"I never sent those!" he yelled as he was being pushed along to the elevator.

Fred Kaminsky, majority owner of the firm, was hot on their heels. "Trevor, boy, keep your mouth closed," he demanded, patting sweat from his forehead with a handkerchief. "I'll be right down there to represent you. Don't speak a word until I'm there."

A frazzled Lois hurried out behind them, her colorful skirt swishing about. "I'll make arrangements and get this sorted," she promised as the officers, Trevor, and Fred left the lobby.

I looked back to the doorway leading to the offices and saw Andy, the IT intern, peek out. "What's going on?" I loudly whispered to him.

He shifted from foot to foot, a tic no doubt. "It all happened fast. They came in with a warrant to search his computer and apparently found some emails he sent to Melissa."

"What's so weird about that? They worked together. I'm sure they sent emails about cases all the time." And probably emails about dinner plans and secret plans to rendezvous in between.

"Yeah but this was different." He looked around to make sure no one was listening and leaned in closer. "He sent her an email the afternoon before she disappeared, talking about some surprise vacation they were going on."

"Vacation?"

He nodded tightly and peered over his shoulder again to make sure no one snuck up on him. "He apparently booked a trip for them and sent a last-minute email to both their assistants to let them know they'd be out. The strange part is, neither of the assistants recalled getting an email about it but the emails were in both their inboxes marked as read," he added conspiratorially.

I chewed my lip as I processed the information. "So, where was Trevor taking her?"

"There was a plane ticket booked out of Boston heading to Paris. The thing is, it was only for one person. Trevor."

• • •

My head was still spinning when I met Joanna at Duckfat for dinner half an hour later. She had already ordered our favorite Belgian fries with garlic aioli to munch on as an appetizer. By the time I caught her up on what happened with Trevor, our paninis showed up.

Joanna sat there in shock for a moment. "So, what do you think really happened? Do you think Trevor could have been involved?" she asked as she took another bite of her sandwich.

As usual, my stress levels were causing me to inhale everything edible in sight. I grabbed Joanna's pickle from her plate and took a big, crunchy bite out of it. "I don't know, Jo. He seemed so distraught the day we found her. Something doesn't add up."

"Maybe he was distraught that she was found, not because she was dead."

I stuffed a handful of fries into my mouth before responding. "I'm still not sure. Paris? Trevor said he was never interested in visiting Paris. Said it was a tourist trap. He only wanted to go to places that are a little wilder. Like hiking through the Amazon or walking through some ancient Mayan grounds."

Joanna gave a laugh. "Trevor? Roughing it? But how would he survive without dry cleaning and a mirror?" she said sarcastically. "Although, Melissa seemed like the type who would like Paris. Maybe he was doing it for her."

"Then where was her plane ticket?"

Joanna shrugged as she waved a waiter down for a to-go box. I wasn't sure how she had the willpower to stop eating in times like these. "If they weren't going on a trip, then where were they driving to the morning she disappeared?"

"We still don't know if that was Trevor driving," I reminded her.

"Just seems like the evidence is stacking up against Trevor now."

"As long as it's not against me."

"And what's the deal with Detective Hottie? You're working with him now?"

"Hottie?" I cocked an eyebrow.

"Oh, c'mon. Are you blind? How can you not notice him? He's so sexy with his piercing hazel eyes, deep voice, and smile. Did you not notice that one dimple hiding under his stubble? Swoon-worthy." She gave a lustful sigh.

"He's usually frowning at me, so no. I haven't noticed his smile or hidden dimples."

She held up a finger. "Just one dimple. Makes him more interesting and dreamier." She had a faraway look. "Too bad you two are all wrapped up in this case. He would have been great for you after your split with Trevor."

Called it. Joanna was notorious for meddling in my love life when we were growing up. I guessed she was secretly thrilled I was on the market again for that reason alone.

"Yeah, well, things are how they are. Anyway," I said, getting back on subject, "he thinks someone knows something but we don't understand why they want to involve me. He wants to keep me in the loop if any other clues come in."

Just then, my phone buzzed, indicating I had a new email.

"Oh! This might be that local farm I was telling you about the other week. They had some great options for fruit so we can make more summery baked goods and really elevate the menu."

I opened up my email and saw the sender information was blank. The hairs on the back of my neck stood on their ends. Perplexed, I wondered if it was spam but felt compelled to open it anyway.

The email body said, "Could Trevor have known?" Followed by a forwarded email chain from Melissa Maher to an indecipherable email address. Judging by the context, it seemed like Melissa may have had another man on the side.

"Holy shit."

"What?" Joanna grabbed the phone from me. "What is this?" she asked when she scrolled through. "Was she also having an affair with someone other than Trevor?" She skimmed the emails again. "'I had a great night with you last night,'" she read. "'I did too but we shouldn't be doing this.'" She looked up at me. "Seems scandalous. Did you see some of the back and forth? It sounds like a forbidden romance."

"It appears that way."

She handed me my phone. "Seems like that could be motive."

"To kill her? Trevor cheated on me and we had a much longer, more serious relationship. I didn't kill him when I found out he had an affair."

"Yeah, because you're always the rational one. Trevor is self-centered and egotistical. Maybe it was enough to send him over the edge."

"I'm not buying it." I threw a piece of uneaten crust onto my plate. "What I'm more concerned with is the fact that this is the second lead I've received. Why me?" I picked at the crust, feeling unnerved.

Joanna grabbed my hand to stop my nervous tendency.

"Who do you think is sending you these messages and why?" she asked seriously.

"I have no idea but I need to call the detective."

• • •

As usual, Detective Hunter was waiting for us at the apartment by the time we got back. We all made our way upstairs and congregated around the breakfast bar. I handed over my phone and gave him time to read and reread the email before I interrupted.

"Well?" I prodded impatiently. The disconcerting feeling bubbled up again, causing a tightening in my chest.

"Some things aren't adding up," he finally said and handed back my phone. "We looked into the emails that Trevor allegedly sent to Melissa about the trip. They were sent at 1:32 p.m., but we have witnesses who placed him in court at that time. He was questioning someone on the stand and was nowhere near his computer or phone to send it."

I paced back and forth to relieve some of the tension. "Maybe he did one of those delayed message things," I suggested.

The detective grabbed me with strong hands and held me in place. I tried not to like the feel of him touching me and failed. "You're making me nervous with your pacing. Well, more nervous than usual." He let me go once I stopped fidgeting and considered my question. "We thought it could be a possibility, but no. It was sent immediately, which leads us to believe he never sent those emails."

"Who else would have access to his inbox?" Joanna spoke up.

"His assistant manages it, but we already knew she was out of the office for a dentist appointment at the time."

"She could have easily sent it from her phone."

"True, but she was tied up getting a root canal, so that theory is out, too." He sat there, deep in thought. "So what do we have so far? A running route, a BMW, a trip, and now these emails. Nothing seems connected other than Trevor. He knew where she ran, he owns a BMW, he supposedly booked a trip, and he would have motive if Melissa was having an affair. All possibilities but nothing concrete. This case is becoming more complex than I initially thought."

"How so?" I asked.

"Our research team is having trouble digging into Melissa's life to find any relevant clues as to who would have a motive to kill her. Other than what we found on her throughout the last five years or so, she remains a mystery to us."

My eyebrows knitted as I recalled the same issue when I was Google-stalking her a few weeks back. "Is that normal?"

"It's not unheard of but it's not common, especially for lawyers. She would have needed to pass a background check for the bar association. She couldn't have practiced law without it."

"Why would someone have a missing past?" Joanna asked. "Witness protection?"

He shook his head. "No. Already checked with my contact at WITSEC. There's no record for her. More dead ends."

"How could she have gotten a background check for the bar without any information?" I asked.

"My team is looking into it. We're waiting to hear back from the bar association, but all of these missing pieces and delays are making our jobs a hell of a lot harder. Without that insight, it limits leads. Time is everything when it comes to these murder investigations. It's already bad enough she'd been dead for days before you found her."

"What about the plane ticket? Did you find out anything about that?" I started pacing again. Detective Hunter grabbed me by the elbow softly and placed me on the bar stool next to him like he was taming an unruly toddler who was high on sweets.

His gaze captured my eyes, trying to keep me focused. "The ticket was purchased around the same time but with his credit card. So if it wasn't him who bought it, it was someone who had access to his accounts."

"What about this?" I said, gesturing to the phone.

He eyed it carefully. "I don't know but we're going to have to look into it. I'll see if my team can find out who sent it to you. Chances are it's the same person who sent you the running route."

I felt vulnerable and exposed. "Should I be worried?"

He looked down on me, concern etched on his on his face. When he wasn't tormenting me, he wasn't half bad to look at. Okay. He was really, really good to look at. I felt myself melt a little at the look on his face. Maybe he did have a softer side to him after all.

"I don't know," he replied slowly. "This person doesn't seem to be malicious, but we don't know what the end game is yet. Just be vigilant and call me if you need me." He got up and left Joanna and me alone with our swirling thoughts.

She scooted up next to me, sensing my internal anxiety attack. "We'll get this figured out, Em," she said softly while giving me a little squeeze.

Who was this person and why did they choose me?

CHAPTER 8

Memorial Day weekend had come and gone, and Joanna and I were feeling out of sorts without Crafty Café. To get us out of our funk, we took some "us" time and spent a beautiful June afternoon pursuing the splendors of downtown Portland.

It was in the mid-70s and sunny, providing the perfect weather for leisurely shopping. The warm air enveloped me like a friendly hug, and I suddenly couldn't remember when I had last taken time to do things for myself. Managing a business was more than a full-time job. Even when the store was closed or when I had a day off, it was spent thinking about the café. Wandering around the city and checking out new shops made me feel better. I made a mental note to make an effort to do this more often.

I was surprised Joanna had lasted this long without baking something but today she finally cracked. She had woken up early this morning to make fresh sourdough bread, banana nut muffins, and lemon blueberry scones. We packed those up, went to the deli to grab makings for sandwiches, and strolled down to the promenade for a picnic. The sun warmed my cheeks as I enjoyed the peaceful sounds of seagulls squawking and water lapping against the shore. It was soothing and, for a moment, life felt normal. We stayed for as long as we could but eventually the air cooled, and it was time to go.

"Are you sure you're going to be okay without me tonight?" Jo asked as we walked back to the apartment. "You can always come with me."

Even though she planned on staying with me for the next few days, she had already promised a friend she would take care of her dogs while she went away for a business trip. This meant a drive down to Portsmouth, New Hampshire, and my first night alone since everything happened.

"I can't. Remember? I'm not supposed to leave town." Although I wasn't a prime suspect anymore, I wasn't completely off the hook. What I wouldn't give to be anywhere but here right now. I squeezed her shoulder. "I'll survive for the night. Plus, I want to be available in case the police tell us the shop can open."

Crafty Café had been closed for four days. If the police finally gave us the all clear, I didn't want to waste another second. We were taking a hard hit every minute our doors remained locked during the summer rush.

We made it back to the parking lot across from my apartment right as the sun was setting. The brilliant oranges and pinks lit up the sky, promising more warm weather ahead. "So what are you going to do tonight?" she asked while getting into her car.

"Probably have a glass of wine and look over paperwork for Crafty." Detective Hunter had given us a loose schedule of when we could open again, which was potentially in two days. I hoped sooner. "I also have ideas for a social media campaign to announce we're open again and drum up business. Meg and Charlie said they'd help." I was hopeful that getting back on a routine would provide some sense of normalcy that I desperately needed.

Jo, who typically told me to stop being a workaholic and live a little, didn't argue with me about my plans. She gave a small smile. "Okay, but don't work too hard. Some of that administrative stuff is mine to do, too."

"Don't worry. I'll leave you plenty of tedious order forms to sort through when you get back." I laughed and closed the driver's door. We waved goodbye and she was off.

The sun had officially set, and a cool breeze gave me goose bumps. I zipped up my light fleece and made my way to the apartment, lost in my thoughts of marketing plans as I walked up the stairs.

I unlocked the front door and froze immediately as I sensed someone in the apartment. A faint shuffling came from my bedroom and confirmed my suspicions. I weighed my options: retreat or defend what was mine.

Maybe I had gone crazy. Maybe the stress of the last few weeks caused me to snap.

Rather than running for help like a sane person, I quietly tiptoed to the kitchen and grabbed a large knife. I crept silently down the hall toward my room, pausing every few moments to listen for my intruder. I steadied my breath. The shuffling stopped suddenly, and I feared the trespasser would spring out and attack me.

Heavy footsteps sounded again on the hardwood floors, followed by drawers slamming in my bedroom. I slid against the wall, noting that the bedroom door was open just enough for me to see the reflection in the rustic floor-length mirror leaning catty-corner against the far wall. The image of a large man passed by the mirror quickly, causing my heart to pound in my ears. I gripped the knife tighter in my hand. Looking back at the mirror, I saw my room was a total mess. Clothes were strewn everywhere. Drawers were opened haphazardly, their contents dumped on the ground. I saw more things being tossed from a corner hidden from my sight, adding to the disarray of my personal space. I felt violated.

It wasn't until I heard a string of curses from the person destroying my room that I recognized the voice.

Trevor.

"What the hell do you think you're doing?" I exclaimed as I threw open the door.

He yelled from surprise and whipped around, eyeing the knife I was still clutching. "Jesus Christ, Em. Drop the knife."

I dropped the knife to my side but still held it firmly. It was my safety net since I still had no idea what his role was in this whole thing. Or why he was in my apartment. Or why he felt the need to wreak havoc on my room.

"What are you doing here, Trevor?" I seethed. I was furious that he felt he had a right to not only enter MY apartment but to create such a mess.

Trevor looked worse for wear. Even worse than the time he got the flu during finals and resembled someone who had contracted the bubonic plague. His tie was undone, his hair hung limply over his forehead, the circles under his eyes were a dark shade of purple, his shirt was wrinkled, and he was sweating like a pig. He looked like he had been through the wringer.

"I'm looking for something," he replied as he started feeling around the dresser.

"All your stuff is gone. Either you had it moved out or I dropped off the last of it at the office."

He turned his back to me. "This is something else. You wouldn't have known where to look." He stuck his hand through the drawer opening and rubbed it along the inner wood on top. "Melissa left it here," he added quietly.

I was fuming. "What do you mean Melissa left it here? Were you two fucking in *our* apartment?"

Even though he was turned away from me, I saw his neck and ears turn crimson. As if he remembered the knife in my hand, he spun quickly around. He held his hands up in surrender. "This is not the time, Emily. I need to find this. It's important."

"I don't give a shit! Get the hell out of my apartment, Trevor, before I call the cops. I'm sure breaking and entering won't look so good after you were just released."

"It's not B&E if you still have a key," he argued. I raised the knife automatically. He eyed it nervously. "Whoa. Whoa. Easy there."

"How dare you! Leave the key here. You aren't welcome."

"You don't understand. I need to find—" he started to say in a condescending tone.

"I have Detective Hunter on speed dial. I'd be happy to give him a call." I pulled out my phone. His shoulder sagged as he realized this was one argument he wasn't going to win. "Get. Out."

He stared at me for a moment before retreating. He dropped the key on the breakfast bar and left without another word.

I stared at the mess in my bedroom and felt betrayed. And angry. And sorry for myself. I wanted to throw up, knowing that the woman he cheated on me with had been in my home, my safe haven. In my sheets. I couldn't fathom when he would have had her over. I work right downstairs. I could have easily taken a break and caught them in the act. Did his infidelity have no bounds?

How could I have been so blind and stupid? Four years with him and I didn't even know this man. How could I have meant so little to him to be treated this way?

I marched back to the kitchen and slammed the knife onto the counter. The metal clattered on the granite top. Screw the paperwork. I'd had about all I could take right now. First item on my agenda tomorrow would be calling a locksmith.

Two-bottle kind of nights were becoming a habit, I thought as I opened a bottle of Montepulciano. I knew drinking my problems away wasn't the healthiest decision and with all that had happened lately, keeping a level head would be smart. But I was tired of being smart and rational. I just wanted to forget. I needed a release from the pain and stress. I felt trapped in this endless cycle of post-breakup blues, and seeing Trevor constantly was hindering my ability to get the closure I deserved. I knew I'd have to cope with the new things I was discovering about Melissa and Trevor's relationship, but I wasn't ready to tackle it head-on just yet.

Two hours had passed, and I was halfway through my second bottle of wine. If I didn't get sick tonight, it would be a miracle. My mind felt fuzzy yet liberated. It was the freedom I had been seeking for the last three weeks. Despite feeling like a newborn calf on wobbly legs, I blasted my favorite Spotify playlist from an app on the TV and wildly danced around my living room alone.

A knock sounded at the door.

"Who the hell is it now?" I slightly slurred as I opened the door. Of course Detective Hunter was standing on the other side. Who else would it be? Joanna was out of town, Delores would have called beforehand, and Trevor no longer had a key.

God. Were those the only people I knew? I really needed to get out more.

Detective Hunter's presence filled the doorway, and I loved how his largeness seemed so manly to me. A look of concern flashed across his handsome face. Joanna was right—he was stunning. I wanted to rub my hands along his stubble and see what his full lips tasted like. I wanted to see the dimple he hid from me. I wanted to know what his strong arms felt wrapped around my body.

"Are you drunk?" he asked, pulling me out of my sexual fantasy.

"Yeah, so?" So eloquent. I gestured for him to come in and saw him appraise the empty wine bottles. "Don't judge me," I slurred again. My mouth felt lazy from the wine. Speaking was becoming an effort.

"I'm not." He looked around the room. "Where's Joanna?"

"Gone for the night." I plopped on the loveseat, about to take a sip of the remainder of the bottle of wine. He snatched it away from me. "Hey!"

"I said 'be vigilant,'" he nearly growled. "Not only are you by yourself but you're practically incoherent. Did you even check the peephole before you opened the door for me? Anyone could take advantage of you."

"Oh yeah. Like Trevor? He already did." I hiccupped and sprawled more on the couch.

"He did what!" Anger filled his face and his voice took on a protective tone. He crouched down in front of me, forcing me to make eye contact.

I waved my hands around. "No, not like that. He just invaded my apartment."

"What do you mean?" His voice was low. Dangerous.

"Go take a look at my bedroom." I pointed to the back of the apartment and eyed him suspiciously. "Don't be stealing my panties or anything."

He rolled his eyes and took off in the direction of the bedroom, stomping back into the living room a moment later.

"How did he get in?" He was furious. At least it wasn't at me for once.

"His key."

"Jesus, Emily. You need to call me about things like this." His large hands grabbed my shoulders lightly. "He's still a suspect in the case. He could be dangerous. Why can't you understand this?"

I shook his hands off and glared at him. "I'm sorry I'm just a mere human with feelings and was dealing with said feelings. My first reaction to seeing my ex tear apart my personal space wasn't to call someone who's practically a stranger. I needed a minute. Couldn't I just have a minute?" I pleaded, feeling heaviness in my chest. I was coming undone.

"Emily," he said softly. "All someone needs to hurt you is a minute. I'm here to protect you." He looked over at the door. "You need to change the locks first thing. Why was he here?" The edge of his voice had left, making me want to open up to him.

I gave him the condensed version before I started blubbering. "How could I've been so stupid?" I cried out while wiping my eyes with the sleeve of my fleece. I hugged it tighter around me. "I sensed there was some distance growing between us but figured it was just a rough patch. He was busy with work and so was I. I didn't realize it was because he was in love with someone else." I looked up at him. "I feel like an idiot sharing this with you. This is embarrassing." I hid my face in the throw blanket draped across my lap.

His features softened as he sat on the loveseat next to me. The small space caused him to press up against me and I wondered if he was as aware of me as I was of him. I sensed some hesitation. He probably wondered what was appropriate. After all, I was still a potential suspect in his case. As another loud sob came from me, he seemed to let go of his rules and pulled me into his arms. He wiped away a stray tear with the pad of his thumb. The rough texture—hands of a working man—brushed it away with a delicate swipe.

"Breakups are hard, and your situation is that much harder. Most people don't have to deal with cheating and murder," he said, trying to console me.

"How do you know what's hard? You've got such a tough demeanor. I bet nothing hurts you."

"My job makes me that way. I can't let emotion get in the way or someone could get hurt. Underneath it all, I'm still a human with a heart. We all have our baggage." He looked away for a moment.

I let out a sigh. "I'm sorry for crying on you." I tried to pat the wet spot on the shoulder of his t-shirt with the blanket. It was useless.

"We're going to figure this out. It will be okay," he tried to reassure me.

I looked over at him with a new sense of appreciation. "You know, you're not so bad." For a moment, I was seeing the man behind the stoic exterior. He was turning out to be much more than I initially thought.

"Yeah, which is why I'm not allowing you to stay alone tonight. You're vulnerable, intoxicated, have door locks that are compromised, and have a crazy ex and stalker keeping tabs on you." He looked at his watch. "I normally would have called an officer to watch over your apartment but it's after midnight and they've been working hard. I'm already here. Do you mind if I sleep on the couch?"

"Are you sure?"

He gave me a grin, finally revealing that sexy dimple Joanna was going on about. She was right. It was swoon-worthy. "I'm sure."

"Would it be too much to ask for you to stay in my

bedroom with me… until I fall asleep?" I added quickly.

He took a second before answering, as if debating. "I can do that."

He helped me up from the couch, and I began to stumble on my jelly legs. Before I could protest, he scooped me up bridal-style into his arms and carried me down the hall. I wrapped my arms around his broad shoulders and laid my head in the crook of his neck, inhaling that relaxing woodsy scent of his. Safe and comforting.

He still held onto me while he moved some things out of the way on the bed and then laid me down gently before tucking me in. He disappeared for a moment and came back with aspirin and water. "Take this," he ordered. "Do you mind?" he asked while waving the TV remote around.

"Go for it." I nestled into my bed as he sat on the opposite side. Still trying to remain professional, he sat on the bed with one leg hanging off the side, as if to keep some level of distance between us.

I shifted on the bed, trying to get comfortable despite the slight spinning of the room. Surprisingly, I felt myself getting sleepy even with a man I barely knew sitting in bed with me. Before I knew it, I drifted off to sleep with the faint murmur of the TV in the background.

• • •

The buzzing from my phone on the nightstand stirred me awake. With one eye open, I saw the clock read just after four a.m. I shifted in the bed, feeling a heavy weight on my hip. I turned my head to see the detective had also fallen asleep, one leg on the bed and one leg still dangling off. His arm was lying across me like dead weight. I had no idea how that position was even possible, but to me, it was comforting.

I inwardly sighed as I felt the heat from his body warming up my back. His face was relaxed, and I had the urge to run my hand along it. He looked unburdened and it was endearing.

My phone buzzed again. Who the hell would be texting me at this hour? I picked it up but before I could click it on, a deafening sound pierced through the quiet apartment. Detective Hunter sprang up and pulled a gun out of his holster in one fluid motion. I was impressed that he could react so quickly from a dead sleep.

The sound stopped and we stared at each other in the dark room, the blue light from the TV flickering across us.

"Are you okay?" he asked through labored breaths.

"Yeah. What was that?"

As soon as I asked the question, the sound went off again, along with other noises. Our cell phones shrieked, the emergency alert noise beeped on the TV, the alarm clock rang, and other undecipherable noises came from the kitchen and living room. My heart raced as I was assaulted with sounds.

"Stay here!" he yelled. At least that's what I thought he said. It was hard to hear with my hands covering my ears.

The sound stopped again, and the sudden silence caused my ear to ring. He moved out of the room like a cheetah stalking its prey. His gun was still drawn, and I could hear him making his way through the apartment, checking door locks, and looking in the closets.

Even though the blaring noise had stopped, the glow of the TV still lit up the room. Nothing was on the screen but static at first, and then suddenly a large hooded figure walked across the screen and sat down. Although I couldn't see its face, it looked like it was staring at me directly.

"Bennnn..." I called out, never letting my eyes leave the screen. He raced back into the room and looked at the

TV.

Hundreds of whispers sounded all around us, hissing my name over and over again. I turned my head and realized the whispers were coming from every device in the apartment. They were muted but it was enough to evoke a sense of eeriness. We looked at each other again, not sure what to say or do. I went to speak but was interrupted by the abrupt quiet again. Then, the figure on the TV spoke.

"Emily. You are failing." The voice was distorted, as if using a device to disguise the person's true voice.

"How?" I managed to say even though I figured it was a recording. My surprise was palpable when the person turned their head in my direction and answered.

"I've given you information and you've disregarded it. You need to learn the truth," the voice seethed.

"I don't know what you want me to do with it!" I tried to steady my breathing.

"We need backup," the detective said as he pulled out his cell phone. He let out a yell and threw it onto the bed, shaking his hand. "The fucking thing shocked me," he hissed. He looked at it in disbelief. "It's fried."

The figure turned to address him. "Enough!" the voice boomed. Then, the person looked back at me. "Follow the clues." The order was quiet but menacing.

"Why me? Why not give this to the police?"

"IT HAS TO BE YOU," the voice roared louder.

"Wh-who are you?" My voice shook.

"You may call me Overwatch." The voice gave a pregnant pause. "More will come soon. Do not disappoint me, Emily." And with that, the TV turned off and the apartment was left in darkness and quiet.

I spun around to Detective Hunter. "Still think I did it now?"

CHAPTER 9

"So what do we know so far?" Detective Hunter asked me for the umpteenth time.

I sat perched on the stool at my usual spot at the breakfast bar. He stood across from me, hands firmly placed on the granite as his eyes bore into mine. Sleep was out of the question after the events of last night, and we both were feeling on edge. I pinched the bridge of my nose, willing the hangover away. My head pounded and I was almost certain I was still slightly drunk from the night before.

"I told you and showed you everything I know."

He rubbed his eyes. "And nothing leading up to her disappearance is any help. We got the rundown of her schedule the day before she went missing, and there was nothing out of the ordinary. No leads there."

"Did she have a will?"

He nodded. "She updated it recently. The funds go to a charity. Some obscure one. We're looking into the legitimacy of it."

He looked down at the sheet of paper resting on the counter in front of him. It housed all the information we knew about the case, including the few clues this "Overwatch" person had given me. I didn't know if I should be thankful for the clues or frustrated that no one could figure out how this person was infiltrating all of our devices.

"A running route, a BMW, a plane ticket, dirt under Melissa's nails from places unknown, emails to a mystery person, something of hers hidden in your apartment, and someone named Overwatch," he said more to himself than to me. He picked up a pen and scribbled a couple notes at the bottom, drawing a line from one name to another. He stared at the sheet, deep in concentration.

"Detective Hunter," I said softly, trying to pull him from his thoughts.

He faced me, a crease in his forehead as he processed the information. "You can call me Ben. I think we're past formalities."

My cheeks warmed as I thought of his arm resting on me earlier this morning. I guess once you dropped the title of prime suspect, he loosened up a bit. "Ben," I started, getting used to the feel of his name. "I think the things we need to consider now are the emails I received about Melissa's alleged affair and whatever Trevor was looking for. He said Melissa left something here, but I've come up empty-handed."

He nodded. "Already called my team to see if they uncovered any new details from her hard drive and phone records. Like I mentioned, she's been a ghost most of her life. We're missing a lot without that information." His phone dinged with a text and he read it. "They said we should know something in a few hours."

I twisted on the bar stool and looked up at him. His thick hair was mussed and his eyes looked bloodshot. For a moment, he looked more human than the detective with a hard exterior I first met weeks ago. I felt an urge to comfort him. To tell him to take care of himself and take a power nap.

His eyes met mine and the hard lines of his face seemed to ease. Something unspoken passed between us and I had to make a conscious effort not to reach out to him. I broke the tension by offering him another cup of coffee. That was the extent I could take care of him.

Keep your distance.

He graciously accepted it, took a healthy sip, and ran his hand through his hair. I took an appreciative glance at him over my mug. "Look but don't touch" would have to be my motto with Ben, which was hard. I really liked this casual look on him. He seemed more approachable.

"Those emails you got could be anything," he concluded, bringing me back to the case. "It could have been a doctor's appointment, a meeting with a client, a hair appointment."

"An affair. Some shady business," I supplied. "I don't think this menace who's force-feeding me information would feel the need to forward me an appointment for a manicure."

"We don't know this guy's MO yet."

I frowned and rested my cup on the counter. "How do you know it's a man? Women can be just as capable." *As if a fight for feminism was really needed right now.* I mentally rolled my eyes at myself.

He let out a sigh and looked up to the ceiling. "It was a figure of speech. I wasn't trying to be demeaning to women."

"I'm home!" Joanna sang-yelled as she burst through the front door, carrying a bag of bagels from my favorite shop in Portsmouth. Her cheery disposition was a stark contrast from ours. She paused, and her smile faltered as she saw the two of us. "What's going on?"

I patted the stool next to me. "Where to start?" For the next thirty minutes, Ben and I filled her in on last night's event and where we were with our research.

Her brown eyes went wide with worry. "Can that 'Overwatch' person hear us right now?" she whispered.

I shrugged. "Probably."

"Do you know how creepy that is? What's to stop him from reading our private texts or prevent him from turning on the camera on our phones or computers? What if he sees me naked?" she screeched.

"We'll comb the apartment," Ben assured.

I shrugged again. "That's not our biggest concern right now, Jo. We need to figure out what this person wants us to uncover."

Joanna shook her head, clearly disturbed, and got up to busy herself with the bagels. She shoved them into the toaster and cranked it to medium. A moment later, the toaster popped, and she slathered on cream cheese before distributing them to us. "So now what?"

"We investigate whatever this person wants us to."

Ben rubbed a hand along his defined jaw, his stubble more pronounced. "I don't like putting all my faith in this. We're going in blind. Overwatch is very capable of hacking and God knows what else. For all we know, he—or they—could put us in a dangerous situation. We don't know his role in all of this. Melissa could have just been one target of many. Who's to say this person isn't leading you into a trap?"

"You're right. This person is very capable. Which means if I ignore it, he could destroy my life. He could steal my identity, ruin my business, put me on the streets." I paused for a moment. "Kill me," I added quietly.

"My point exactly. The question is, why you?"

I chewed on my bagel before answering. "Could be because I knew both Trevor and Melissa."

"Could be that you know who the killer is," Ben suggested.

I turned to Jo. "Joanna, are you the killer?" I asked sarcastically. She shook her head. "Ok, that's the extent of the people I know aside from Delores, Trevor, and Melissa."

He pursed his full lips, not amused. "I'm sure you know more than those four people."

"Everyone I know is back home in Rhode Island. I went to college in Boston but didn't keep touch with many people from there. I started dating Trevor a year before moving up here with him. We were kinda in our own little love bubble as we both grew our careers." I tried not to gag at the term *love bubble*. "Aside from Jo, he was all that I had here for the first few years. Joanna and I became closer to Dolores over the last year or so, but she barely knows how technology works."

I waited to see if some sort of pitying look would appear on Ben's face, but it never did. "Bad at technology? Could be a great cover," he replied suspiciously.

I scowled at him. "Yeah, right."

"What about the other people at the firm? Trevor has worked there for years. I'm sure you've met his colleagues at the office or at events."

"I've met most of them, but there are some new people too." I tapped my chin. "What about that Andy guy? He's a techie. Could he be our hacker?" I had a hard time believing it. The kid seemed sweet and shy from the few times I'd met him, but he fit the description: tech-savvy, and knew Melissa, Trevor, and me.

Ben pulled out his notebook and flipped a few pages. "Good thought but we already confirmed it wasn't him. We looked through his apartment complex's camera footage. He was home all night. Never left. Plus, he was more than willing to allow our team to check his devices. Not only does he not have the tech or computing power to pull this off, but there was no evidence that showed he'd been messing with Melissa or you. He's in the clear."

His hazel eyes fixated on me as he dropped his notebook onto the breakfast bar. "Honestly, I'm surprised the firm hired him at all. We ran a check on him and he's a super senior. Seven years in school with no graduation in sight. Also, his grades don't instill a lot of confidence in his abilities."

My eyebrows rose in surprise. "Really? Trevor said something about Fred doing a favor for a family friend, so maybe his skills don't matter. Then again, Trevor and Fred aren't exactly technically-inclined, so Andy probably seems like a genius to them."

Ben gave a sarcastic snort. "With the firm's many prestigious awards, you'd think they'd only want the *crème de la crème*." He shook his head. "What about customers? Any regulars? Are you close with neighbors or other business owners?"

"I mean, sure. All of the above. I make small talk for the most part. I know when people's kids are getting married, where people went on vacation, their pets' names. Stuff like that. I don't know any deep dark secrets they harbor. We're acquaintances, nothing more."

"It has to be Trevor," Jo spoke up.

"He hasn't been ruled out but the evidence we gathered isn't strong enough," Ben answered.

A buzz came from my cell phone that was charging on the counter next to me. The email icon lit up with a new message. I stared at it, my stomach dropping. Could I handle another email from this Overwatch person?

"Do you want me to get it?" Jo asked, rubbing her hand

on my back to comfort me. I nodded.

She grabbed the phone and clicked a few buttons to pull up the email. "It's a video," she said. Ben and I leaned over her shoulder as she pressed play.

Trevor and Melissa were in an unidentified parking lot. The video was in black and white and grainy, as if it was pulled from a security camera. The time stamp on the corner showed it was filmed a couple months ago.

"What are you getting into, Melissa?" Trevor ground out through gritted teeth. He had her pinned against her car with his arms caging her in.

"Leave it alone," she argued, pushing him forcefully away. "We might be together but I'm still my own person. Until you get rid of Emily, you'll just have to deal with me having my own life, too. My life. My decisions. This is none of your business."

"This is ridiculous! Of course this is my business. This is all of our business!"

She pointed a finger in his face. "Don't fucking use that tone with me. I could easily tell your beloved fiancée what you've been up to," she threatened.

He stepped back, his anger fading slightly. "I told you. I'm going to tell her."

She placed her hands on her hips. "You've said that for six months now, Trevor," she snapped as she turned to get into her car.

He grabbed her wrist roughly and spun her toward him, bringing her mere inches from his face. "I'm serious. If this gets out, we'll all take the fall for it."

"I've got it taken care of," she said as she whipped her wrist out of his hand and stared at him pointedly. "After this, I'm done. Just let me take care of it." She got into her car and drove off.

Trevor stood there for a moment, watching her drive

away before he slammed his hand on the hood of his car. "God damn it!" he screamed. He loosened his tie and rubbed his hand over his mouth while he paced back and forth. Finally, he got into his car and drove off. The video ended.

A text message from an unknown number lit up my phone.

What was she involved in? - Overwatch

We all looked at each other. Ben took out his cell phone and dialed a number. "I need everything you have on Melissa Maher and Trevor Miller. Emails, phone records, video footage, anything. Now!" he barked.

This was getting more complicated.

CHAPTER 10

Later that morning, Ben left the apartment to meet with his team about the case. Somehow, I managed to get myself into the shower to wash off the ickiness from my hangover. I had stood in my tiny bathroom for nearly forty-five minutes before I could bring myself to get in. I shuddered with each attempt, knowing someone could be watching me. After three tries, my disgust from my own BO finally convinced me to get into the bathtub and get it over with. Having a stranger see me nude was the least of my worries at this point.

Feeling a little more human, I threw on yoga pants, a sports bra, and a hoodie and flipped my wet hair over my head to wrap it firmly in a towel. I left the humid bathroom and found Joanna puttering around the house when I emerged.

"Whatcha doing?" I asked her as she flittered here and there.

"Straightening up. Did Overwatch also break into the apartment?" she asked as she arranged a few knick-knacks on my bookshelf and folded the throw blanket on the couch.

I looked around and realized how disheveled the place had been. I'm a semi-neat freak and seeing things out of their places normally bothered me. I guess getting wrapped up in the events from last night had made me blind to the mess. I grabbed the empty wine bottles from the counter and threw them into the recycling bin.

My cheeks warmed. "Nope. I guess that was all me and my dancing." I bit my lip. "And the fact that Trevor broke in."

"*What?*"

I filled her in on the encounter with Trevor, assuring her that I'd change my locks today. Working side by side, Joanna and I had the place looking nearly pristine a short time later.

"Only one day until we go back to work," Jo said with a happy sigh as she handed me the last clean dish to dry. She must have been as stir-crazy as I was. "This time off has given me an opportunity to think about our summer menu. I feel inspired."

I raised an eyebrow. "Inspired by murder?"

She shook her head and rolled her eyes. "No. You and I are constantly running the shop and don't take breaks long enough to decompress. That can really affect creativity," she went on. "Having the last few days off afforded me some time to actually follow through with the self-care I wanted to do for a while. A little yoga and meditation really go a long way. You should try it sometime." She turned off the faucet. "Anyway, I was able to clear my mind enough to think of new things to offer."

"Such as?"

"An artistic spin on some of our best sellers. You know, everyone uses social media these days. Why not get free advertising from our customers by creating unique or pretty food and coffees? Of course, the flavors need to be out of this world, too," she added. "But it's all about presentation. We need to create the 'wow factor' and give people an experience they want to share. We need to tap into their FOMO."

"FOMO?"

"Fear of missing out. I swear, you live under a rock sometimes."

I thought about it for a moment. "Do we even have the bandwidth to do it? We're already stretched thin as it is." Jo and I pretty much ran the shop aside from Charlie and Meg, who worked part time during our busy hours. On top of working a six a.m. to three p.m. shift seven days a week—aside from the occasional day off—Joanna came in early every morning to prepare our baked goods. I usually stayed late to manage our books and place orders. Even with our part-timers, the struggle of running a shop was real. And exhausting.

She waved a hand to dismiss me. "It will be fine. I know some easy tricks that can make our food look gorgeous with the same amount of effort I currently put into decorating."

"And the coffee? We'll have to teach the girls how to do it."

"Don't worry. They're smart." She grabbed me by the shoulders and gave me a lighthearted shake, causing my towel to come undone. I pulled it off and threw it on the bar stool. "You really need to stop being a control freak. Have a little faith in Charlie and Meg. What's the worst that can happen? They mess up a design in the froth? It's not the end of the world, and practice makes perfect."

I hesitated for a moment, fighting with my unrealistic expectations to control everything. "Fine. I'll loosen up a bit if you think it will do Crafty some good. We really need the boost after being closed for a week."

Joanna beamed and clapped her hands in excitement. "Great! Check out some of these sketches I did last night." She grabbed her purse that was still sitting by the front door and pulled out a sketchbook, flipping through a few pages before setting it down in front of me.

I inspected the drafts, moving through several pages. "Wow, Jo. These are amazing." I stopped on one design, unsure of what it was. The cupcakes, pastries, donuts, and breakfast bowls were easy to decipher. But this one was hard to make out. "What's this?"

She smiled. "It's experimental. I'm still figuring it out, but I think this could be our 'wow factor.' Every coffee shop can have pretty cakes and flaky croissants but we need something no one else has." She tapped her finger on the picture. "This could be it. We'll make a limited amount a few days a week to get that sense of urgency."

"Thus tapping into the 'FOMO.' I see," I responded, finally understanding the appeal.

She looked hopeful. "Maybe if I do well enough, we could have lines out the door like Magnolia's in New York."

"All right, let's not get ahead of ourselves. We might not get to that point, but I think this is a step in the right direction."

She shook her head and smiled. "You sure know how to kill an optimist's spirit."

"It's called being a realist."

"You'll be eating crow once you see how it works out. Just wait."

A knock sounded at my door and I sighed. "I swear, I've never had as many visitors in the entire time I lived here as I've had these last few weeks." I reluctantly made my way to the door, Ben's words from the night before resounding in my head. "Please don't be a murderer. Please don't be a murderer," I whispered under my breath as I stealthily checked the peephole and saw the detective standing on the other side. I relaxed and swung the door open. "Back so soon?" I noticed a duffle bag hanging from his hand. "What's that?"

He made his way past me and dropped it on the island with a monumental thud. "I'm moving in," he announced.

"What!" I sputtered.

"You clearly need police protection after what we saw last night. The person who's sending you messages has advanced skills. We don't know what we're dealing with." His voice was stern, warning me not to argue.

"Police protection? Don't they usually assign someone to sit outside the house?"

"Typically. But if you don't recall, whatever happened last night came from INSIDE your house." He picked up his bag and looked down the hall opposite my bedroom. "Should I set up in the guest bedroom?"

I rushed to his side and yanked the bag out of his hand. "Whoa. Hold up. I never agreed to this. Besides, Joanna is staying in the guest bedroom."

We both turned to her. She looked back and forth between us as if watching a tennis match. "Emmmm," she said softly, the voice she used when she was about to say something I wouldn't like. "I'm worried about you." She fidgeted with her hands. "I think it would be best if Detective Hunter stayed with you. He's going to be much better in a dangerous situation than I would be."

I gave her the angriest look I could. "Traitor."

Ben cocked his head and gave me a smug grin, flashing his dimple. "If I recall, you asked me to stay with you last night." He walked closer to me and leaned down. "And you were very insistent about it."

My mouth dropped open, but I recovered. "I was having a... trying night. And anyway, staying for a few hours one night is not the same thing as temporarily moving in. What about boundaries?" I couldn't help but recognize that our relationship seemed to have changed because of last night. Our dynamic was shifting into a gray area. For the sake of my sanity, I needed to draw some form of a line.

He shrugged a shoulder. "This is my case and it appears Overwatch has taken a liking to you. You receive key information at odd times. I want to be there the next time you hear something." He placed his bag back on the breakfast bar and unzipped it, pulling out a strange black wand.

I squinted as I inspected it. "What's that? A secret fetish? Am I going to be bunking with a sexual deviant?" I asked sarcastically.

He narrowed his eyes at me. "For your information, this device is going to help us sweep for bugs. The person on your TV was able to respond to you in real time, which means he or she could hear you. They likely tapped into the mic on your cell phone, but I want to check just in case."

"Check where?" I questioned while following him around the small common area.

"Everywhere. Bugs can be small. They can be hidden in even the most secluded and smallest places."

Like my underwear drawer.

He gave me a look that bordered on seductive, but I couldn't be sure.

So much for boundaries.

"Any chance I'll be left with a bit of dignity after all of this?"

He glanced at me over his broad shoulder as he waved the wand around the bookshelf in the living room. "We'll see." He placed the wand on the coffee table. "Can I speak with you outside for a second? Leave your cell phone inside," he instructed.

I looked to Joanna. She just gave me a shrug. A lot of help she had been today.

I threw my hands up. "Sure. Fine. Whatever." I sighed while following him to the hall. "What?"

He slipped a black flip phone from his back pocket and stuffed it in my hand. Leaning in closer to me, he whispered into my ear. I tried not to notice his presence invading my personal space, but it was no use. I liked it, much as I hated to admit it. "Seeing that your 'admirer' has access to your cell phone, I wanted to give you a burner. A number to my burner phone is programmed in there. Use it when you have something sensitive to tell me if I'm not around."

"Why couldn't you tell me that in the apartment?"

"Potential bugs, remember?" He looked at me like I was an idiot. "Speaking of which, you need to be careful about what you say while you're in your apartment. That also goes for your café." He scratched his chin. "And around your personal cell phone, too," he added.

"Should I just become mute?"

"One could wish," he smirked. I socked him in the arm. Maybe assaulting someone in his line of work was frowned upon but he deserved it. He rubbed his arm, pretending to be wounded.

We walked back into the apartment to find Joanna zipping up her own bag. "Jesus, I walked outside for two seconds and you managed to get packed up already?"

"I didn't unpack from Portsmouth yet," she explained while throwing the bag over her shoulder.

I leaned against the door. "I can't believe you're abandoning me," I whined, laying on the guilt.

"This is for the best until we get things figured out. I'll

just be down the street and we'll be back at work tomorrow." She gripped her sketchbook against her chest. "Plus, I'm eager to test out these new things before we get back to the café." Her dark-brown eyes seemed to sparkle at the thought.

"Yeah, yeah." I gave up, wrapped her in a quick hug, and waved her out the front door.

I turned back to Ben, who managed to dominate the room with his broad body. Just us. I didn't know why it felt so awkward today. It wasn't like I had a one-night stand with the guy. Maybe it was weird having another man staying in my apartment after living with Trevor for so many years.

"So," I started to break the silence. "Any new developments on the case?"

"Need to know," he replied gruffly as he lifted the couch and waved the wand underneath.

"Well, apparently this Overwatch person thinks I need to know. You wouldn't even have these leads if it weren't for me," I argued lightly. He paused from lifting up the couch cushions to look at me but said nothing. "You better put everything back when you're done tearing up the place. Joanna and I just cleaned this."

"Yes, ma'am." He went back to terrorizing my couch before he paused. "All right. I suppose you're right."

"Well? Spill it."

"Those emails Melissa was sending to someone...well, Melissa was meeting someone regularly on Tuesday evenings for a month before she went missing. Her assistant said she left early on those days to go to a new pop-up yoga class over on Commercial Street. We checked into it and not only has she never even been to that studio, but it actually took place across town."

"How do you know she's been meeting someone?"

"A few additional cryptic email exchanges." He opened up the kitchen cabinets and stuck the wand in.

"So you don't think it was an affair like we were assuming?"

"I'm starting to think not. The emails didn't give us much to go on, but the little bit that was in there didn't seem romantic in any way. The team is working to figure out who was sending the emails and where their meeting spot was. A few of the messages were written in some kind of code. Might take some time to crack it."

"If it was an affair, do you think Trevor could have killed her out of jealousy? Or maybe the other guy she was seeing had a wife who lost it and killed Melissa when she found out?"

"Your guess is as good as mine at this point. Normally, I'd say you're romanticizing this into something you'd see on TV but this case is anything but cut and dried. I honestly don't know what to expect anymore. Even the outlandish suggestions you're making might not be far off."

"Any word about the video?"

"Not yet. We'll be bringing Trevor in later today to discuss the contents. Hopefully, he'll be forthcoming and shed some light on it." He shot me a disapproving look. "But you know lawyers. They are good at ensuring they don't implicate themselves." He opened the fridge to check for bugs and paused. "You hungry?" he asked.

"The answer will always be yes."

He pulled out a dozen eggs, mushrooms, peppers, and shredded cheddar cheese. "I'm starving. I didn't get a chance to eat yet today. I'll whip something up."

"Such a thoughtful guest," I teased.

He threw the peppers and mushrooms into a pan to start sautéing. "You'll definitely think so if I stop you from getting killed next."

That sobered my vicious mood right up. With no retorts from my end, I watched Ben in comfortable silence as he cracked eggs into a bowl, whisked them up, and threw them into the pan. He moved gracefully, the task of cooking almost putting him at ease. It made me wonder what kind of person he was when he wasn't busy being a hardass at work. Was he quiet and thoughtful like he was right now? Was he a fitness freak like his body seemed to indicate? Did he read books or was he more likely to grab a pint with the guys and watch a game? Who was Ben Hunter?

He pulled me from my thoughts when he slid a warm plate of cheesy eggs in front of me. "Better eat up. We've got a full day." He leaned against the opposite counter, devouring his plate.

"What do you mean *we* have a full day?" I asked between mouthfuls.

"We're going to find out what was *actually* on Commercial Street that had Melissa going back for weeks."

"Is bringing a potential civilian and suspect part of normal police protocol?"

"Nothing about this case is normal. As much as I would like you a safe distance from any of this, our cyber friend seems to want you involved. I worry the trail would run cold if I kept you in the dark."

"Aren't I just the luckiest girl," I said, defeated. I scooped up the last of the eggs and relished the extra-cheesy bite. Nothing like taking something healthy and making it artery-clogging. That was how I liked it, and I couldn't deny it was nice to have someone else cook for me. It had been a while. "So what's the plan?"

"We're making a pit stop off West Commercial Street to Cassidy Point Drive." He took our plates, rinsed them, and placed them in the dishwasher.

He grabbed his keys off the counter. "Ready to go?"

I pulled my damp hair up into a messy bun. "Sure, just let me slip on some real clothes," I said grudgingly as I made my way back to the bedroom. I pulled on a pair of jeans, a casual sweater, and my Toms, and grabbed my cell phone from the nightstand. "Ready," I called when I made my way back to the living room.

We headed outside, and I stopped short when Ben walked off in the opposite direction of the parking lot. "Where are you going?"

"I need to get my truck from the station. It's not even a half-mile walk."

I speed-walked to catch up with him. "Do you sleep there or something?"

"Sometimes," he answered honestly.

We walked briskly to the police department and although I was typically a fast walker, I found it challenging to keep up with his long strides. He walked with purpose, each confident step making him seem more masculine. We made a right on Middle Street and waited for the crosswalk on Pearl.

The sign gave us the go-ahead to start crossing. I took a step off the curb when my phone dinged with a text message. I pulled it up and noticed it had no sender information.

It's only a matter of time before I figure out how to access your burner phones. - Overwatch

My breath hitched, and I suddenly felt myself being flung back from the curb by a pair of strong hands. I slammed hard against Ben's chest. A car zoomed by barely a second later.

"Jesus Christ, Emily," he breathed heavily, still clinging to me tightly. "A car almost hit you. You were so caught up in your phone you didn't even notice," he scolded.

We stood there for another moment, catching our breath. At least I was trying to. It was hard to keep my breathing steady when Ben held me like that. His body felt solid against me. His heart was beating at a quick, yet harmonious pace with mine. The warmth of his breath on top of my head felt comforting. Being in his arms felt safe and stable.

I pulled myself away from him. Those feelings were only happening because I was vulnerable. Not only was this the most terrifying and invasive situation I'd ever been in, but I was in it alone. I had been part of a pair for so long, it was hard to go through this without my rock. Sure, Jo was there but it just wasn't the same as when you were intimate with someone. And now Ben had firmly planted himself in my life physically, but I still barely knew him.

This feeling wasn't new. Not really. Trevor wasn't around much at the end of our relationship, but I had managed to conveniently ignore that. Now I was paying for it. The sense of being utterly alone washed over me. It was starting to kick in that I was going to face a lot of things—both good and bad—on my own. I would simply drift through life with no one to claim me. My insides twisted at the thought.

Ben dipped down to look me in the eyes. "Hey, you okay?" he asked while searching my face. "I didn't mean to yell at you."

I nodded. "Yeah. I think the shock of what happened just threw me off."

"Maybe. But there's something else, too." How could this man see so deeply to my core?

I didn't want to admit what was really going through

my head, so I pulled up the text message from Overwatch instead. "You're right. This is what distracted me."

"Shit," he muttered. "We'll have to figure that out later. Come on." He handed the phone back and led the way to the station. He stuck close to me, as if protecting me from another car bound to barrel through the intersections we crossed. We made our way to the enclosed parking lot and hopped into his truck.

"Nice," I commented while buckling in. The pickup truck seemed large and dominating, much like Ben himself. It was meticulously clean, yet I could tell it had seen some labor in its days. "Yours or an undercover?"

He scoffed. "Mine," he said with pride, rubbing a hand along the dashboard. "I only use that junk of an undercover car when I actually have to go undercover."

"So what's the plan?" I asked while he pulled out of the lot and headed in the direction of West End.

"We got a few pings from Melissa's phone in the same general location. We're just going to poke around. See what's there and if anyone has seen anything. The closest address our ping came from has been vacant for three years but there are businesses close by. Maybe someone was around when she was."

We pulled up on Cassidy Point Drive ten minutes later. The truck tires crunched on loose gravel as we drove slowly over the nondescript roads that attached several parking lots for commercial warehouses. A rusted chain link fence hung haphazardly on its metal poles. The buildings were a mix of decaying and fully functioning. However, even the buildings in use seemed like they'd had better days.

I instinctively wrapped my arms around me as we pulled up to the most dilapidated building of them all. Ben turned off the truck and I jumped out of the passenger seat. Although it was a sunny day, this part of town reminded me of a bad gangster movie. I was half expecting to walk into one of these abandoned warehouses and find Al Capone leading a mafia meeting. It made me feel uneasy.

"This is where we saw the steadiest pings. Records show she would be in this area for about thirty minutes each time," he called out as he walked ahead, scanning the windows and doors for movement.

I trudged along, keeping up with him despite my apprehension. "What was a woman like Melissa doing in a place like this? She was all high-end, luxury brands and this place is an amusement park of disease." I wondered if I needed a tetanus shot just from being in the vicinity.

I followed him through a rusty door with broken windows. The threshold of the building was open with concrete floors and rickety metal lights hanging from the ceilings. Our footsteps echoed through the open space, and I had the uncanny sensation we were being watched. Ben flicked a switch, but nothing turned on, as expected with a building that had been abandoned for this long.

Daylight fought to stream in from the grimy, small windows at the top of the tall walls. The dirt blocked out most of the light but left just enough to make out the area. I almost wished it hadn't.

"Doesn't seem much like a place someone would go for an affair, does it?" He kicked around some dirty rags on the floor.

I pointed to a catwalk that bordered the whole space. "Look up there. It looks like that catwalk leads into an office space. We should check it out."

Ben held up his hands. "Whoa. This place is dangerous. We don't know how sturdy these catwalks are. I can't have a civilian breaking her neck if the walkway gives out."

I glared at him. "This is my life we're talking about, too. I may still be alive but, somehow, I'm tied up in this mess. Not to mention you felt the need to bring me along. Now you're just going to make me sit on the sidelines?" Alone. In the dark. Where ghosts of workers past could spook me.

He crossed his arms, which made his biceps bulge slightly under his shirt. I eyed them as discreetly as I could. "Has anyone told you that you're an impossible woman?"

I cocked my head and tried not to drool over his muscles. "Not really. I'm usually the responsible one. But desperate times call for desperate measures. I want to make all this madness stop so I can get on with my life. I want to move on."

He stared me down for a moment and then gave in. "Understood."

"You're not going to argue with me on this one?"

"I know what it feels like to want to move on," he said seriously. "Plus, I know your type. You're determined. I have a feeling you'd take matters into your own hands if I didn't let you. You're safer with me."

I forced a grin. "For once a man has a smart idea."

"We have our moments. Come on," he said. I followed him to the base of the stairs. "Wait here while I test this out. I'm not letting you up here if there's even a remote chance this thing could give way."

"Deal." I waited as patiently as I could while Ben tested the catwalk. There were a few metallic groans, but he deemed it safe enough for me to join him. We walked slowly along the walkway, taking our time to ensure there were no weak spots. Within a few minutes, we made it to the office.

Ben twisted the handle. "It's a little stuck but it's unlocked."

He put his shoulder into it, forcing the door open. Our eyes took a moment to adjust to the dark room. I walked over to the far wall of windows and pulled up the flimsy blinds to let in more light. Ben moved slowly around the room, doing a sweeping look of the contents. He clicked his phone flashlight on and stopped at the desk. "Look at this."

I looked at the area he was pointing at but saw nothing. "What am I looking at?"

"There's practically no dust on this desk, but look at the filing cabinets and bookshelf. There's a thick layer there." He turned to the wooden chairs on the opposite side of the desk. "These are clear, too."

I looked up at him. "What's this mean?"

"It means someone's been here recently."

"Do you think this is where Melissa was going?"

"Could be. Let's get outside so I can get my team over here and see if they can find fingerprints or hair."

My mind was reeling as we carefully made our way outside and Ben placed a call. He informed me his crew would be there soon, so we decided to wait outside in the interim to see if anyone nearby had seen anything.

A heavyset man with dusty jeans and well-used work boots exited from a building directly across from us. Ben called out to get his attention, showing his badge.

"I'm Detective Ben Hunter," he announced when the man finally made his way to us. "We're hoping to ask a few questions."

The man took off his hard hat and wiped sweat from his forehead. He seemed overexerted from his walk over to us, and I wondered how he worked in a heavy-labor job. He was practically on the verge of heart failure from walking a few yards.

"Hi. I'm Chip Matthews." He let out a puff of air. "I'm the project manager for Rainear Construction. What can I do for you, Officer?"

"Detective," Ben corrected. I rolled my eyes. "We're investigating a homicide that happened a few miles from here and have reason to believe the victim frequented this building on Tuesday evenings. Have you seen anything?"

Chip scratched his balding head. "Nah. To be honest, my crew starts early in the morning, so they're gone by five p.m. Myself included." He paused to think. "Wait, now. Come to think of it, I was here late about a month ago doing payroll and I remember seeing some people enter the building that night."

"Can you describe them?"

"I saw a woman show up first. Tall. Red hair done real pretty and some fancy clothes. A little bit later two men showed up. It was getting dark, so I didn't get a good look at 'em. I just assumed the woman was a realtor showing them the building. There's been talks about developers coming in here to do something with it. Lofts or some hipster crap."

"Anything else you can tell us?"

He thought again. "I saw the woman leave about twenty minutes later. She looked like she was in a rush. I left a few minutes after her."

"What about the men?"

Chip shrugged. "I didn't pay much mind. Sorry."

Ben handed him a card. "If anything else comes to mind, please call me directly. Any detail can be helpful."

Chip took the card and stuffed it into his wallet. Saying his good-byes, he slowly walked back to the building and disappeared through the door.

"This is getting weird," I finally said once Chip was out of earshot.

Ben made a noise of agreement. "We have to find out who she was meeting with and why. If that video you received was any indication, Trevor knows more than he's telling us."

CHAPTER 11

I quickly learned Ben was not only efficient, but also passionate about his job. He believed in justice. He believed in finding his man. And he worked tirelessly to do it. Now that his determination was pointed away from me, I appreciated his integrity.

I sat at his desk at the Portland PD station an hour after we left the warehouse. I spun a pencil around on his otherwise empty desk. It was a sturdy wood and metal desk that housed a computer, keyboard, and mouse. Other than his name card sitting on the left-hand corner, nothing about it gave me a glimpse into his life. There were no personal effects that I could see, making it seem sterile and forgotten. As we spent more time together, I couldn't help my curiosity. Who was Ben Hunter?

If I had two flaws, one was impatience. The other was the tendency to go a little nutty when I didn't know the answer to something. Both of these flaws were in high gear as I sat at Ben's plain desk. At this point, I would have gladly read the human resources handbook to squelch the boredom.

Trevor had been brought in for questioning regarding the video but since I wasn't technically supposed to be involved in this investigation and I had a history with Trevor, Ben thought it'd be best if I waited at his desk. As much as I wanted to know what was going on, I was glad I didn't have to spend any more time in Trevor's presence. It was overwhelming.

I chewed on overly salted almonds from the vending machine as I processed everything. I wanted to know who Melissa was meeting with. Were they related to the person who picked her up the night she went missing? What was she involved in that made Trevor react that way? And why, damnit, did someone feel the need to seek me out and give me clues to this whole thing? Why not just come out and tell me who the murderer was so we could get this over with? What was Overwatch's role in all of this?

I looked up when I heard movement down the hall. Trevor made his way swiftly out of the main door, followed by Ben. Ben stopped at the open arch leading to the area with the desks and curled a finger, gesturing for me to follow him.

I popped out of my seat—because I was eager to know what Trevor said, not because a sexy man was giving me the "come hither" motion—and rushed to meet him. He grabbed me lightly by the elbow and pulled me into a private room, closing the door behind us.

"Well?" I urged.

"We got something," he whispered.

I met his whisper and leaned closer to him. "Why are you whispering?"

"Because I shouldn't be telling you as much as I am. And who knows who's listening." He scanned my body, making goose bumps rise on my skin. "Where's your cell?"

"Left it on your desk."

"Good." He raised his voice to nearly normal.

"Long story short. Trevor was at Melissa's house one day when she was running errands and heard some sort of notification ringer going off in the house. He thought it was her phone, but she had it with her. Apparently, he followed the noise and found a laptop hidden under loose floorboards in a guest room she never really used. The noise was an email alert."

I sucked in a breath. "And?"

"He pulled it up and saw a number of emails back and forth about some sort of deal. Most of it was in code but he got the impression Melissa was making a deal for one of her clients to ensure they didn't end up in jail. But as he thought about it more, something seemed off."

"Like what?"

"For starters, the name Anthony Giuseppe came up."

I frowned. "Am I supposed to know who this is?"

"No, but our friends at the FBI do. It's a known alias for a man by the name of Carlos Chakalos. He's a big-time drug dealer they've been after for over a decade. He's stayed under the radar and there have been no leads on his whereabouts until now."

I shook my head, confused. "Why did Trevor seem suspicious about that?"

"He thought it was curious that she'd go through the trouble of hiding the laptop, so he looked into it. He's got some connections high up in the FBI and found out about Chakalos. That's what he was arguing about with her in the video.

"He confronted her and learned Chakalos owns the warehouse you and I went to earlier today. However, he owns it under another unknown alias. Melissa was selling it for him secretly and was supposed to transfer the funds from the sale to an offshore account."

I scrunched my face in confusion. "Why would Melissa be involved with a high-profile drug dealer like Chakalos?"

Ben looked at me intensely, the muscle in his jaw ticking. "Your guess is as good as mine, but chances are this might tie into her missing history. Could something she had done before 'Melissa Maher' emerged have been related to this?"

I let out a low whistle and sat on a chair nearby. "No wonder Trevor was pissed. If it got out that Melissa was working with a drug lord, their whole practice could go under. Not to mention, she was withholding important information from the FBI."

"Yeah, well, we remedied that today. Seems like Trevor might be more forthcoming now that we got that squared away. Also, I had an update regarding the warehouse."

"And?" I eagerly asked.

"They found a strand of hair that matched Melissa's. That at least confirms the legitimacy of Trevor's story about her going there." He gave a smile, causing the dimple to deepen. "And it looks like you're free to open up shop again tomorrow."

"Thank God. I need one normal thing in my life." I sighed wistfully. "I never thought I'd miss the smell of fresh coffee and baked goods this much."

He gave me an uneasy look. "Don't get too excited. It's not going to be exactly how you imagined."

"What do you mean?" I nearly pounced on him for destroying my happy moment.

"You're still a key piece of this very confusing puzzle. Either I or another officer will be sticking around to keep an eye on things, and I may need you to accompany me while we tackle some leads." He gave a pitying look. "I know this isn't what you wanted."

"No, it's not," I said flatly. "You realize this is asking a lot of me, right? The times you need me to 'accompany' you, I need to get coverage from an already lean crew. That's not ideal."

"I'm sorry" was all he could say.

I rubbed my temples. "It is what it is. I'll give Jo a call and let her know so she can plan a menu. In the meantime, now what?"

"I have to make some calls about this warehouse and find out more about it. Although Chakalos owned the building, he leased the land it was on. I'm hoping the property manager will be able to shed some light on the murky areas of this story."

• • •

Twenty minutes later, my eyes burned holes into Ben as I sat at his desk, impatiently waiting for him to wrap up his call. "Well?" I demanded when he hung up the phone.

"I got in touch with the property manager and learned Melissa was acting as a power of attorney for the owner named Greg Lafray. I'll have the FBI look into this new alias we discovered. Now the question is, why was she doing this?"

Before we could ponder the possibilities of why Melissa was involved with Chakalos, the woman who sat at the front desk popped by. "Miss Ayers?"

"Yes?"

"This was dropped off for you." She handed me a thick envelope with my name scrawled across it in those familiar black, bold letters.

I took it from her with shaky hands. "Did you see who brought it?"

The young woman blushed. "No. I went to the ladies' room and when I came back, there it was."

I turned to Ben and held his gaze. He looked as alarmed as me. "Is there a security camera?"

He straightened. "Karen, can you see if there was any footage from that time?" His voice was all business.

"I'll get on it, Detective Hunter." She gave a curt nod and left the room.

I stared at the envelope in my hands. "What do you think it is this time? Feels thick." I moved it up and down to get a feel for the heaviness.

"Only one way to find out."

He gingerly took the envelope from me, ripped it open, and pulled out the contents. A stack of black and white photos slid out along with a handwritten note that simply read, "My, what webs we weave. Overwatch."

He put the note to the side, and we looked at the photos. There were a least a dozen of them, taken from afar with a telescopic lens. Melissa was present in all of them. Throughout the series of photos, you could see her meeting with the same man. His face was obscured, making it hard to identify who it was.

She met him on various occasions. At a restaurant. In her car. In an alley. It wasn't until I reached the second to last photo that I finally saw who the mystery man was.

"Holy shit. It's Fred Kaminsky," I stated as I picked up the photo for closer inspection.

Ben looked over my shoulder. "That's Kaminsky, all right," he confirmed. "Those photos look innocent enough. She works at his firm. I'm sure they're meeting about something case-related."

I flipped to the last photo. "Or something else." The photo showed Fred embracing Melissa tightly and kissing her passionately in a secluded alley. "I guess an affair isn't off the table then."

"That means the focus might be back on Trevor."

"Or Kaminsky's wife," I added. "She might be part of the 'ladies who lunch' group who look the other way from their husbands' infidelities in return for the well-off lifestyle, but Sarah Kaminsky didn't strike me as someone who would be okay with that. I've met her a few times over the years. She's bright and has one hell of a backbone. I don't think she'd let someone walk all over her like that."

"Enough backbone to kill?"

I shook my head. "She might have the smarts to pull it off, but I don't think she'd be stupid enough to actually do it. Then again, I've only met her a few times. Even people you think you know best could hide secrets." That seemed to be the theme of this murder mystery.

Ben rubbed his eyes as he processed the information. "Looks like the date stamped on these photos are from three weeks before Melissa went missing." He shook his head and let out a frustrated breath. "Fred didn't mention this sort of relationship when we questioned him about Melissa. He said they were strictly professional."

I waved the photo in Ben's face. "Seems he's also been withholding information."

"We can't rule out Fred Kaminsky either. For all we know, Melissa could have threatened to tell his wife like she threatened Trevor in the video. There have been plenty of men who have killed their mistresses to keep their secret safe."

"How could one person have so many secrets?" I said quietly, more to myself.

A nervous Karen appeared again. "Detective Hunter, we looked up the video footage from the lobby."

"And?" His voice was on edge.

"And," she started, "the cameras were down." She rattled out the sentence as if she were pulling off a bandage.

"What do you mean down?" he practically growled.

She shrunk back. "I don't know. It's never happened before. They went down for five minutes."

I couldn't help but feel impressed by whoever was giving me these hints. Yeah, it was scary as hell knowing they could do so much, but it also gave me some sliver of hope that maybe they'd lead us to the real killer. I just hoped this person was on our side.

Ben addressed me. "I want you around when we bring in Fred."

• • •

"What's the meaning of all this? I've already given you my statement, Detective." Fred Kaminsky took a seat at the interrogation table. His expression was guarded, and I worried that he'd keep his lips locked. I sat behind the double-sided mirror and watched Ben take a seat across from him, sliding the photo of him and Melissa kissing across the table.

"Can you explain this?"

A panicked look crossed his face. "Where did you get this?"

"An anonymous source. How long were you having an affair with Miss Maher?" Ben questioned Fred directly.

Even with the glass between us, I could see a bead of sweat drip from Fred's head down into his shirt collar. I inspected the man for a moment and wondered why Melissa would choose to step out on Trevor for him. Sure, he was decent-enough looking for a man who was pushing his late fifties. But his age and the stress of running the law firm were starting to show. He was tired, gray, and had defined crow's feet around his eyes.

He may have been suave, but Melissa was barely in her thirties. She was stunning, with long legs, bouncy hair, flawless skin, and impeccable style. She took care of herself, and she was cunning. She could choose anyone she wanted, so why Fred? Was it a power thing? A money thing?

No, that couldn't be right. As a lawyer, Melissa was well-off on her own. So what would possess her to be with him?

"Mr. Kaminsky, I'm going to ask you again. How long were you and Miss Maher seeing each other?" Ben repeated.

Fred pulled at his collar, his face turning red. "About two months. It was nothing, really. I was mentoring her through a tough case, and I guess we bonded over those sessions. There was attraction, sure. You'd have to be blind not to notice Melissa's beauty, but I kept my attraction at bay until she started getting a little flirtatious. Before I knew it, we were meeting for other reasons. But I swear it never went beyond kissing. It was harmless."

"Why would you withhold this information when we questioned you the first time?" Ben pressed.

Fred let out a nervous cough. "I didn't see how it was relevant. I had an alibi for the night she went missing and her time of death. And I have a wife, you know? We only were intimate—if you would even call it that—three times. I didn't want to lose my wife over some meaningless kissing."

Ben leaned back and assessed Fred for a moment before speaking again. "You seem to be pretty concerned about your wife finding out. Concerned enough to tie up loose ends?"

Fred looked at him with disgusted shock. "What are

you implying, Detective?"

"Did you have a hand in Melissa's disappearance or death?"

"Ab-absolutely not!" Fred sputtered in outrage. "Melissa was a colleague and a friend. Despite the brief...*flirtation*, she still meant a lot to me as a person. I could never and *would* never hurt her." He stood abruptly. "We're done here, Detective Hunter. Get in touch with my lawyer if you plan to continue to spout this utter bullshit at me. Unbelievable."

Ben stood as well, unfazed by Fred's fury. "One last question. Despite how discreet you and Melissa thought you were, it's clear from these photos that at least one person saw you. Do you think your wife has any clue about this?"

Fred took a step back as if he had been slapped. "Sarah would never do what you're insinuating. She's on the board of several charities, Detective! She wants to help those around her, not hurt them."

"Love makes people do crazy things. Violence stemming from an act of passion isn't unheard of."

Fred stuck a finger in Ben's face. "You leave her out of this!"

"I'm afraid I can't, Mr. Kaminsky. She's now part of our suspect list, which means she needs to be questioned, too. I'll do everything in my power not to reveal details about your indiscretions but I can't make any promises." Ben looked at him pointedly, staring him down. "Sarah is a smart woman, so I've heard. She might figure it out on her own. Don't you think?"

"How dare you!" Fred screamed before exiting the room and slamming the door behind him.

Ben turned to the two-way mirror and gave me a shrug. I pressed a button on an intercom that connected to a speaker in the interrogation room. "We've been at this for four hours. If I don't get something to eat, I might die." He nodded and gestured for me to meet him in the hall.

"This day is frustrating," I said, stomping out of the station like an angry toddler. The late-afternoon sun shone down on us, warming me after sitting in the chilly station all day. "We keep getting these clues, but nothing is panning out. We're not any closer to finding Melissa's killer."

"Something is bound to work out. Don't worry," he replied reassuringly. "Everything we're doing has a purpose."

He looked around. "Where are we going?" he asked while following me down the street.

"I need something with saturated fats. We're going to Flatbread Company. Their pepperoni flatbread is my favorite and I think it would really hit the spot right now."

He looked at me and shook his head. "How does a woman who eats the way you do stay as fit as you are?"

I tried not to smile at the backhanded compliment. "A somewhat fast metabolism and working on my feet all day. I try to squeeze in a run here or there."

He was right. I'm a huge foodie, which was part of the reason I loved Portland to begin with. There were a ton of amazing restaurants within walking distance. This town was foodie heaven, and right now I wanted to self-medicate with something fattening and loaded with carbs.

Making our way into the building, the smell of roasted garlic raised my spirits. We sat at the corner section of the bar, away from the rest of the patrons. A younger man, probably in college, took our order and slid a couple of waters in front of us. I took a hardy sip, willing the last remnants of my hangover away. It was only three in the afternoon, but this already felt like the longest day in history.

"Okay, so what do we know?" I finally asked after taking a moment to process the day's events.

Ben adjusted in his seat, a contemplative look etched on his face. "We know there's a lot more to this story than what's on the surface. Melissa was involved with a drug lord and we still don't know why. Now there's this whole thing with Fred Kaminsky."

I leaned back in my chair. My stomach gave an inhuman growl, making Ben laugh. I ignored him. "How did she have time to fit all these extracurriculars into her schedule? I knew the hours Trevor kept and she was right there with him." I thought for a minute. "Literally." I frowned. "So what's next?"

"I can't interview Sarah until tomorrow. She's out of town until later this evening."

The skinny bartender appeared again, holding the divine smelling pizza. My mouth salivated as I looked at the greasy, saucy goodness in front of me. The bartender barely put the pie down before I grabbed a slice and took a bite, burning my tongue in the process.

Ben looked at me, amused. "Was that worth it?" he asked with humor in his voice.

"Every bit of it," I responded through my mouthful of pizza. Puffs of steam left my mouth as I spoke. I chewed, swallowed, and took another sip of cool water to ease the pain in my mouth. I hoped my irritated taste buds wouldn't dull the flavor of my meal. "Any news on Overwatch?"

Ben's shoulders sagged a little. "Nothing. Whoever this is covers their tracks well. We're short-handed on the tech side of things, too. Our one-man team quit on us."

"So what's that mean?"

"So it means it might take longer to get answers. We're trying to get help from our neighboring precinct but they're also running lean. The right talent seems to be hard to come by up here." He made a wary face. "We might have to enlist Andy's help in the meantime. He knows enough about the firm's servers—or so he says—to give us a head start until we get someone more skilled. Let's just hope he's better with real world experience than he is in school." Ben shook his head. "Knowing our luck, the kid will wipe the whole thing clean with no recovery options."

"Hey, don't knock him. He's nice."

"Nice doesn't mean he can pull it off, but we're in a bind. Unfortunately, he's all we've got."

"Maybe he'll surprise you." Ben snorted at that. "Anyway, how is this going to work? I'm back at the café tomorrow. You mentioned things would be different."

"I've got you covered. We'll have two officers keeping an eye on you while I do my investigation. One will be outside the door leading to the alley and one will be parked in your café."

"After the rumors about Melissa's death, I feel like having a cop sitting in my shop is going to kill business. No pun intended. My café is supposed to be relaxing. Having the police there isn't going to put people at ease," I protested.

He grabbed my shoulders as a way to calm me before I got all worked up. "I know that," he said gently. "Which is why the person watching you in the shop will be in plainclothes and will work on a laptop. He'll be posing as a regular person who likes good coffee and free Wi-Fi. Don't worry."

I gave him a small smile, enjoying the feel of his large hands on me. "Okay," I conceded.

He smiled back before releasing me and grabbing himself a slice. His full lips blew on the pizza before he took his first bite. "You're right. This is amazing."

"How have you never been here yet?" I had to admit I was curious about Ben. The man was basically attached to my hip these last couple of days, not to mention my new temporary roommate, and I knew nothing about him.

"I haven't been in Portland long." He shifted uncomfortably in his chair and didn't make eye contact.

"Oh?" Interesting.

"I was transferred from North Carolina two months ago," he explained. "It was time for a change, and this was a great opportunity to build my career in the direction I was ready for."

I swallowed my bite as I considered this. North Carolina would explain his faint accent that I couldn't quite place. Although he was broody, he definitely didn't carry the personality traits of someone who grew up in the Northeast. He was persistent bordering on pushy, yes, but he was also chivalrous in a way. Caring at times. Then again, I'd never been wrapped up in a situation like this so I couldn't determine if his actions were standard practice or something else.

"What part?" I asked.

"Wilmington. It's a small coastal town. Reminds me a bit of Portland except more humid and you can actually swim in the water without freezing your ass off."

"Wilmington? As in the town those Nicholas Sparks books are based on?"

"The very one." He grabbed a second slice. "It was a great town to grow up in. But sometimes you grow out of a place and need to move on."

I thought about my old hometown in Rhode Island. The tiny little seaside town was a wonderful place to have a childhood. But I understood Ben's sentiment. Sometimes you were ready for bigger things. "Have you always been in the force?"

"Since I was old enough to apply to the academy. My father was a sergeant. His father was a sheriff. I guess it runs in the blood."

I looked at him and something in me warmed. The small-town feel that radiated off him from his simple story was comforting. After living in the hustle and bustle of Boston during college, then leaving there to forge my own future in Portland, there was something special about the thought of a Mayberry kind of life. For whatever reason, I could imagine Ben visiting home to find his parents sitting in rocking chairs on the porch of a historic house, sipping on sweet tea.

I liked to believe I had decent intuition, the Trevor situation aside. But I trusted Ben was good at his job and that he really believed in justice. In my gut, I felt he was a decent man and I could trust him.

He caught my eye and my breathing slowed. An unspoken connection passed through us, and I somehow felt closer to him. "I'm glad you're here," I said honestly.

An earnest smile played on his lips. "I promise I will do everything I can to keep you safe."

I looked at the depths of his hazel eyes, full of energy and knowledge. "I know you will." And I meant it.

CHAPTER 12

I took in a deep breath and almost fainted with joy when the smell of fresh-ground coffee hit me. Crafty Café was back in business! I had a spring in my step as I walked across the glazed concrete floors to the front counter. A warm, orange glow from the early-morning sun entered through the large storefront windows and filled the small sitting area. I was hopeful for the first time in the last few weeks as I scanned the empty space prior to opening.

This was my favorite part of the day. Things were quiet, allowing Jo and me to get into the zone and prepare for the day ahead.

As I looked around the cheery dining area, my eyes rested on the officer sitting at a two-top, making it all come rushing back. There was still a murderer out there and I was being babysat by the Portland police.

Although Ben technically was babysitting me too, his company was much more desirable than the plainclothes cop who sat uncomfortably on a bench. He looked out of place and stiff, not at all like the patrons that frequented the café. At least with Ben, we'd fallen into a comfortable routine living together. It was only a day in, and he somehow felt like a permanent fixture in my life and my home. After the pizzeria, we had spent a few hours going over the details of the day before taking a break. All that talking left me ravenous, so Ben had whipped up chicken piccata and a fresh salad for a late-night dinner. I learned that he loved to cook and found he was exceptional at it.

That worked in my favor since I'd become insatiable from the anxiety. Poor Ben was going to feel like a run-down personal chef by the end of all this.

We had enjoyed the dinner with a couple of glasses of citrusy white wine at my tiny dining room table. Conversation with him was easy and natural. As I went to bed that evening, I wondered if the sensation of belonging was an effect of the stress from the last few weeks or if he and I really had fallen into sync that effortlessly.

I waved good-bye to Ben this morning as he handed me off to the daytime officer assigned to watch over me while Ben went to work. Our new habits almost felt like they'd been in place forever. My stomach dropped when I realized once this was over, he would be out of my life. My apartment would be empty again and a piece of me would be, too. I'm not sure how the irritating detective had wormed his way into my life so quickly but it wasn't something I could ignore.

Not anymore.

Joanna pushed through the swing door leading from the kitchen. She balanced a tray of freshly baked croissants and scones and placed them in the display case next to fresh quiches and muffins. She wiped a strand a hair from her face, smearing a bit of flour on her forehead.

"I can't tell you how much I missed being in that kitchen," she admitted as she closed the case and walked to the front to unlock the door and turn on the open sign.

"Tell me about it," I agreed as I made my way to the back office to grab the till out of the safe. I came back to the front counter and put it into the register. "I need this just to feel sane."

Joanna disappeared into the kitchen to bring out another tray of baked goods. "Check these out. I was able to try two of my ideas." She rested the tray on the counter and pointed to a miniature cake. "This cake is a three-fer. The bottom layer is more fudgy, the middle is custard, and the top is like an angel cake." She pointed to another pastry. "This is mille-feuille. I learned how to make this when I was interning at that Parisian restaurant while in school. It took forever to get the thin layers of pastry just right but it's so worth it. I added a twist, too. Some have fruit, Nutella, or dark chocolate mixed in."

"These look and sound amazing, Joanna. You've outdone yourself."

She waved me off modestly. "Please, these were the easy ones. I have more ideas up my sleeve." She placed the new creations front and center of the display case and wrote up the specials on the chalkboard near the register.

"So what's Ben going to tackle today?" she asked.

"He's going to question Sarah Kaminsky and plans on talking to Trevor. Again."

"Trevor?"

"He wants to feel out whether Trevor knew Melissa was messing around with Fred, because that would once again give him a motive for murder."

Joanna blew out a breath and placed a delicate hand to her chest. "My goodness. This could be a Lifetime movie. So many plot twists."

"If only I could fast-forward to the end when this is all over." I shook my head with dismay.

"So, how's cohabitating with the detective?" She waggled her eyebrows and gave me a coy smile. I whipped a dish towel at her, which she narrowly dodged.

"He's just doing his job, Jo."

"You've got some amazing willpower."

"Things are already messy enough. I don't need more complications. Not that he would even be interested."

Joanna let out a squeal. "So you ARE interested in him."

"Shh. Keep your voice down." I nodded my head toward the cop sitting in the café, who was now eyeing us with curiosity. "I don't need the whole world to know my business. Anyway, I'd have to be blind not to notice him. But it's not even about that. As I get to know him more, he's actually a decent person. We just got off on the wrong foot."

"Interesting," she said as she tapped her chin in thought, something she did when she was plotting.

"Don't you meddle! I have enough to deal with right now."

"Fine. Suit yourself." The sparkle didn't leave her eye, though.

The door's overhead bell dinged, indicating our first customer and the start of the morning rush. The morning went quickly, with plenty of our regulars coming in to tell us how lost they had been without the shop being open. Delores also popped in briefly to see how I was holding up and to try one of Joanna's new creations, which she gushed over. An hour in, Charlie, one of our part-timers, came to offer a hand.

Charlotte aka "Charlie" Browne was a spitfire. She was quirky, cute, a bit naive but totally reliable. At only nineteen, she had taken the year off from college to "find herself." Thankfully, that free time meant she made herself available no matter how late the notice. I wasn't expecting the need for an extra person today, but she was all too happy to accept an extra shift when I called her in desperation.

I wasn't sure what kind of turnout we'd have after being closed for a week and being tied to the murder, but all three of us found ourselves bustling nonstop until things died down after the lunch rush. We were cleaning up the tables and restocking the case when the bell chimed over the door. I looked up to see Ben walking in. My heart did a flip.

"Hey you," I greeted as he walked up to the counter.

"Hey. Thought I'd check in and see how you were doing." He gave a nod to the officer in greeting.

"Everything's fine here. Felt good to be back and busy." "Glad to hear it. I also wanted to share some details from my day. Mind if we go somewhere private?"

"No problem." I motioned for Charlie to cover the front and led Ben into the kitchen. "What's up?"

Ben looked down at me, reaching out to run his fingers through loose locks of hair framing my face. His knuckles traced my cheek. It was slow and electric, and I thought I stopped breathing.

"Sorry. Looked like you had a bit of icing in your hair," he said hoarsely.

"It happens," I responded in a shaky voice. My reaction to his slight touch surprised me. I felt spellbound by it and I had half a mind to put more frosting in my hair if it meant being touched like that again. I straightened to regain my composure and tried to change the subject. "So, what happened?"

The moment was over as fast as it came. Ben was back to business.

"I looked into Sarah Kaminsky and learned she had an alibi for the time Melissa was killed. She was visiting her sister in New York for the weekend."

"Did she know Fred was stepping out on her? Did you tell her?"

"No and no." He rubbed a hand over his mouth. "If I can avoid telling a stranger their significant other is cheating on them, I try to take that road. It's not my business. Hopefully, Fred will come to his senses."

"That's noble of you to give him a chance to set things right and give his side of the story," I said with appreciation. "But how are you sure she didn't know about him and Melissa?"

"Sarah also visited a travel agent while she was in New York. She was planning a surprise all-inclusive trip to Aruba for her and Fred to renew their wedding vows. It's their 20th anniversary in July."

I leaned in, intrigued. "Could it be a cover?" I asked skeptically.

"I thought so too but it all checks out. She was in contact with the agent months before Fred and Melissa were meeting and set the appointment a week after they started becoming intimate."

"So where does this leave us?"

He shot me a look before answering. "Trevor still doesn't have an alibi."

"Neither do I, but it doesn't mean I'm a killer."

"You're right. It doesn't. But just because you aren't a killer doesn't mean someone else is as innocent. Someone murdered Melissa in cold blood and it's clear it was someone she knew."

I heard the distant sound of the bell ringing. Charlie popped her head in. "Jo's on break. Can I get a hand? There's a large group that just came in."

"Be right out." I looked at my feet, not ready to leave the cozy space I shared with Ben. It felt like a safe place from this crazy reality. "I better help Charlie," I said reluctantly.

"That's fine," he said, oblivious to my internal conflict. "I need to dig into some other leads anyway. I'll see you back at your place later."

It was strange how comfortable that sounded. And I liked it a little too much.

It was a little after five p.m. when I heard a knock on the office door. Ben poked his head in. "Hey. I went to find you at the apartment, but Officer Shapiro said you were still here. I told him he could head home now. How'd it go?"

I spun in my chair to face him. "It went a lot better than I expected. You were right. Officer Shapiro blended right in after he loosened up a few hours in." I pointed to the computer behind me. "I'm about finished up. Just need to submit this inventory order and I'm good to go." I turned back to the computer screen, selected a few buttons, and hit submit. I grabbed the paperwork on my desk and filed it in the metal cabinet in the corner. "All done."

I got up, flicked off the office lights, and locked the door behind me. We made our way through the kitchen, confirming the back door was secure and all appliances and lights were off. Walking through the dining area, we exited the front door, locking it and shaking it firmly it to make sure it was good.

"I hope you like seafood," Ben said as we walked up the stairs to my apartment. "I picked something up from the grocery store before coming to the café. I'm planning to make scallops with a mushroom risotto."

I let out a small moan. "You're too good to me."

He laughed at my reaction. "I would love to take that credit but truthfully I'm sick of eating out all the time. I lived in a hotel for my first month here so most of my meals were some form of takeout. I hadn't even found a place to call my own before this case went down."

"Well, I guess I'm benefiting from your nomadic life." I dropped my purse in the entranceway and hung my keys on the key rack by the door. Ben followed me in and went straight to the kitchen, pulling out ingredients from the refrigerator. "I know how hectic it can be to move, especially to a new city. Is this your first big move?"

He put a pot of water on the stove and fussed with the scallops while the water boiled. "More or less. I've done some undercover work in other cities but those were only for a few weeks. Sometimes a couple of months. I've never actually changed my residence from Wilmington until now."

I sat on the bar stool and leaned on my hand, fascinated by the life Ben lived. "Interesting. I always wondered what it was like to go undercover and have to assume a whole different identity. Isn't it scary to know that if you mess up your story even slightly it could blow the whole thing?"

I saw him stiffen slightly. He took a beat before speaking. "Yeah. A lot can happen when you're undercover," he said seriously.

The air in the room shifted slightly and I wondered if I had struck a nerve. Judging by his posture and the fact that he kept his back to me as he worked on dinner, he wasn't willing to talk about it. I decided to bring the conversation back to something neutral.

"I bet. Maybe *as* exciting as moving to a new city," I added lightheartedly. His posture relaxed a tiny bit. "It can be overwhelming trying to figure out where all your 'spots' are, ya know? Like where's your favorite grocery store? Who's going to be your dentist? What's your go-to place for pizza and a pint? Things like that really make somewhere feel like home. Until you discover that, it can feel like you're out of place."

He looked over his shoulder and gave me a quick smile before tending to the risotto. "You hit the nail on the head. Sounds like you've done it a lot."

"Only a couple of times and never as big of a change as you're probably experiencing. I grew up in a small beach town in Rhode Island. About 5,000 residents. Really small. Then I went to school in Boston, which was a huge shock. I had visited a couple times growing up since we were so close but it's different visiting somewhere and actually living there. Thankfully, I had Jo to help me navigate the big city. She's been my best friend since growing up and even though we went to different colleges in the city, we made sure we saw each other nearly every day.

"After college and a few years of the hustle and bustle working in the city, Trevor got the job opportunity up here. I fell in love with Portland instantly. It was quiet enough without being as sleepy as my hometown and still had amenities and things to do. And as you can tell, things get a lot livelier here in the summer. It had the right balance for me."

He nodded, still with his back to me. "Well, the Northeast is definitely different than the South. There's no doubt about that. However, Portland isn't too far off from Wilmington in terms of size and proximity to the ocean, so it isn't a big shock. Even the brick streets and buildings remind me of areas in downtown Wilmington." Ben took a second to contemplate. "Although it will be interesting braving the winters here. Wilmington only gets a dusting of snow here or there and even then, the whole city shuts down."

I laughed at the thought. "Haven't you ever had an assignment in a place that snowed a lot? You're going to be in for a rude awakening once it's time to shovel out your car. If you're lucky, you'll actually be shoveling out the *right* car. It piles up so high that it's not uncommon for someone to dig and dig, only to discover they cleaned off the wrong car."

Ben let out a hearty laugh while he stirred the risotto. He checked the scallops cooking on the pan next to it. When he confirmed everything was okay, he turned to me and leaned on the counter, periodically glancing at the stove.

"I've been to places that were known for snow, but I was never there during winter, strangely enough. I used to snowboard in Boone but like you said, visiting is different than actually living in it."

"Don't worry. We've got plenty of time to get you winter gear. You'll look like a local in no time." My smile faded as soon as I said it. After this case was closed, Ben would go on to live his own life. We weren't friends. He was simply keeping me safe until we found a killer.

I was glad he chose that moment to tend to the stove and plate our food. I wasn't ready to answer any questions about my sudden change in mood. Knowing I was the type of person who wore my emotions clearly on my face, I was frantic to keep him from seeing. I was worried what he'd read into it if he turned around at that precise moment.

"Dinner is served, milady," he said while carrying the plates to the table.

I scurried over to the wine rack resting on the kitchen counter, determined to use that moment to compose myself. "Wine?" I asked as I opened a bottle.

"I'll take a beer, please. I put a six-pack in the fridge."

I pulled out a bottle of unfiltered wheat beer and popped the top. "I would have taken you for more of a stout man." I walked back to the table with my wineglass in one hand and his beer in the other.

He took his. "There's a season for everything. With summer approaching, I was in the mood for something a little lighter. Besides, it goes better with the meal."

"Touché." We clinked our drinks and fell into comfortable silence while we dug into our meals. That is, until I let out an uncontrollable groan. I couldn't even be embarrassed by it. "God, Ben. This is amazing. You missed your calling as a chef. I bet you and Jo could open a restaurant together and make a killing."

He gave a boyish grin, making his dimple stand out, and took a swig of his beer. "It's never too late to make a career change," he joked.

Ben's cell phone rang loudly, breaking our moment. He pulled it from his pocket and frowned. "You can take it if you need to," I offered.

He stared at the phone. A deep crease formed in his forehead and for a second I thought he winced. His face was hard to read but if I could describe it, it was as if he had seen a ghost. Eventually, the phone stopped ringing but soon as it stopped, it started up again.

"Ben, are you going to answer that?" The shrill was piercing, putting me on edge.

He flicked the sound off and shook his head slowly, then let out a breath and nodded. "Hello?" he said as he got up from the table and walked into the guest room, closing the door behind him.

I took a sip of my wine and wondered who could cause a reaction like that. If it was work, he would have stayed at the table and answered right away. It had to be something personal. I'd seen Ben angry, concerned, determined, thoughtful, and playful. But this was something entirely different. He looked vulnerable and seeing him like that made me feel uneasy.

The voice coming from the guest room was muffled at first but after a few moments, it increased just enough to make out what he was saying. I felt dirty for listening, but

I couldn't help it.

"I'm sorry to hear that but it won't change things," he said. There was a pause as he listened to the person on the line. "No. I'm here to stay." Another pause. "Damnit, Callie. Don't come here. I don't want you here. And stop calling me," he growled.

His voice stopped and I assumed he had hung up on the caller. Even if he ended the call, he stayed in the room for a few moments longer before emerging again. His face looked pale as if in pain and his shoulders hung in defeat. He took his seat at the table and picked up his fork but didn't take a bite.

I touched his hand, pulling him from whatever deep thoughts were taking place in that gorgeous head of his. Seeing Ben like this was unnerving. "Do you want to talk about it?"

His jaw tightened, causing a muscle in it to twitch as he stared at our hands together. "I shouldn't bother you with these things. It's unprofessional."

"I don't care if it's unprofessional. We're human and I care," I responded quickly before he could put up the wall he was trying hard to build between us. I squeezed his hand. "Talk to me."

He looked up at me, his hazel eyes turning a shade greener. "It was my wife…my ex-wife," he corrected. I examined our hands and for the first time I noticed the fading tan line on his ring finger.

For some reason, it surprised me to hear Ben had been married. It shouldn't be so unfathomable, realistically. He was probably in his early thirties, after all. However, I just couldn't picture it. Not that he wouldn't be a good husband, but his detached demeanor made me think he didn't get close to anyone easily. It was as if he purposely kept people at a distance.

My stomach dropped.

Maybe the distance he kept with people only applied to me.

"What did she want?" I asked softly, trying not to let emotion fill my voice.

He took a healthy chug of beer but still allowed me to hold onto his hand. "She wanted to work things out."

"Can you tell me what happened? I don't mean to pry but it looks like you need to let it out."

He gave a long sigh and peered out the window before looking back at me. His face showed the struggle raging inside of him, as if he wanted to unburden himself and tell someone but wasn't sure if that someone should be me. After a few moments of prolonged silence, he finally answered. "She cheated on me with my best friend."

I let out a little gasp. Although Trevor didn't cheat on me with a friend, the pain of being betrayed was all too real. "How did you find out?"

"When I came back from being undercover for three months and found she was six weeks pregnant." He gave a harsh, humorless laugh. "You were right. You can blow the whole thing going undercover. Except it wasn't my alias that I messed up; it was my real life."

My hand flew up to my mouth. I couldn't imagine how heartbreaking that would have been. I couldn't find the right words, but the floodgates had opened and Ben continued.

"She was my high school sweetheart. I loved her so damn much. We got married when we were twenty-three. I thought she was happy. She seemed happy." His voice cracked just a bit.

"How long had you known your friend?"

"Grayson grew up next door. I knew him almost all my life. He was like a brother to me. We did everything together. We got in trouble, played sports, hung out with the same friends, chased girls together. He was by my side through it all." He gave a sad smile. "He's known Callie as long as I have. He was the best man at my fucking wedding." He ran a hand through his thick hair.

I gave him an empathetic smile and he pressed on. "I found out five months before taking the promotion up here. She told me my undercover assignments were the issue. During those times she wasn't able to have contact with me, so she worried as the days went on. Was I hurt? Had I been made? Eventually, it all weighed on her so much that she turned to the only person who knew what she was going through—Grayson. He was there for her when I wasn't. They swore up and down they never meant for something to happen but it *just did*." He shook his head. "That's why I took the job here. I needed a career change. Something that would have me coming home each night so I wouldn't run into the same destruction that being undercover caused."

My eyebrows shot up. "Makes it sound like you have hope for a future with someone eventually, if that's how you're looking at it."

He gave a shrug. "That's the furthest thing from my mind right now. It's going to take a while for me to trust someone again after that."

"So why is Callie contacting you now?"

"She called me to tell me she lost the baby."

I bit my lip, at a loss for words. "That's horrible. But why would she call to tell you that?"

"She said she made a mistake and wanted to work things out. Said she'd even move up here to be with me." He looked down at his beer as he twisted it back and forth in his hand. "There are just some things a couple can't bounce back from. Maybe a stronger man would have done everything to make it work but I can't bring myself to do it. I can't get past the betrayal."

I nodded. "I understand."

He shook his head and straightened in his chair. "No. I need to apologize," he said quickly.

"For what?" I asked, confused by the sudden change in conversation.

"For how harsh I was toward you when I first took on this case," he explained. "It was all still fresh, and hearing that infidelity may have been the motive clouded my judgment. I never let personal feelings get in the way of my job. I was unfair to you." He let out a dry laugh. "Which is ridiculous because you weren't even the one being unfaithful. Just goes to show you how fucked up I am over this."

"Hey." I grabbed his strong chin and made him look at me. "You have every right to feel the way you do. I was torn up about a four-year relationship. Your wife and your friend were both big parts of your life. Betrayal or not, that's a huge loss."

His features softened and I was suddenly taken aback by his look of gratitude. The color came back to his cheeks and I wondered if telling his story helped him quiet his demons, even if only for a moment.

He put his free hand over mine, engulfing it completely, and gave it a soft squeeze. "Thank you," he whispered. The tension in his body seemed to release its hold on him and in that moment, I saw deeper into the man he was.

It had only been a few short weeks since he first blew into my caféé about Melissa's disappearance, yet we'd grown closer in the time that I've known him. Without a doubt, I believed he was the type of man that would leave a void in my life once he was gone.

And, as much as I hated it to think of it, he'd be gone soon.

CHAPTER 13

"Slide it a little to the right. Perfect," Charlie said the following morning as she inspected the lighting. She held up her phone and snapped photos of Joanna's newest creation, a twist to the standard coffee cake. I placed a cup of steaming coffee next to it. "Oh, that's amazing. The steam makes it much more inviting. Really makes it pop," she cooed.

Meg sat at a nearby table, plugging away at her laptop. "It took me a second, but I figured out the ad stuff on Facebook and Twitter." She pulled her gaze from the computer and looked up at me. "How much budget do you want to throw at it?"

I shrugged. "I don't know. We're not rolling in the dough here."

Meg rolled her eyes. "Great pun," she said dryly. "I think a little can go a long way. I just need to set up the audience targeting correctly. Five hundred dollars for each?" she suggested.

"Sure."

Charlie sat down next to her, tapping away on her phone. "And sent." She regarded Meg. "I just emailed you a few photos I took yesterday and today for the social media campaigns."

Meg's laptop dinged with a new notification. She pulled up the email.

"Wow, these are awesome, Charlie. Even my mouth is watering, and I don't eat sugar."

Meg had a crazy sweet tooth growing up, causing childhood obesity. She managed to change her diet and lose the weight by cutting out sweets completely. Aside from a special occasion a couple of times a year, she never indulged.

Charlie shot her a look. "Yeah, you're crazy. Who surrounds themselves with sugar if they won't touch it?"

Meg gave a little shrug. "I like to test my willpower, I guess." She turned back to the computer, clicking and typing away. Twenty minutes later she declared the ads were launched.

"Wow, I feel like a big deal. We're in *advertising* now," Joanna joked. "If the fact that we ran out of my new delectables within a few hours yesterday is any indication we're on the right path, I wonder what this marketing is going to do for us. We might need to hire a part-time baker to help keep up with the demand."

I gave her a grin. "Wouldn't be the worst problem to have."

The morning went in a blur as regulars and new customers came in to grab their old favorites and try Joanna's new daily treats. Charlie stood outside with samples, which only increased the flow of people in and out. It was rare to have all four of us on during one shift but today I was glad. It was a madhouse. And during all the craziness, I almost forgot how badly my life was derailed.

Almost.

Ben was off working leads, trying to find a way to crack Melissa's secret laptop. Without tech support, things moved slower than normal. It felt like we were on a wild goose chase, with viable options for suspects falling through one by one.

However, it wasn't looking great for Trevor as we vetted out the leads. The BMW that picked up Melissa did match the description of his and he seemed to have motive, but I couldn't wrap my head around him truly being the murderer. I was with this man for more than four years. Even if he lied and broke my trust, my gut told me he wasn't who was behind this. He cared too much about his reputation and career to be so careless.

Unfortunately, I'd been wrong before.

I just finished pouring Officer DeAngelis—my designated babysitter for the day—another cup of coffee when my cell buzzed in my pocket.

My heart sank when I realized who it was from. I clicked on the message, stealing a quick look at the officer before I read further. I chewed on my lip as I processed the instructions: a loud commotion would take place across the street in approximately five minutes. I was to slip out while Officer DeAngelis would undoubtedly investigate and make my way to Chandlers Wharf, to the area where they housed cargo containers, and find a crate numbered N308. From there, I would receive further instructions.

A second message vibrated my phone. "No police. Do exactly as I say," it simply stated with an underlying threat.

I wiped my sweaty palms on my light-blue striped apron as I considered the message. I would be defying Ben's trust if I slipped out from the police's watch. And I clearly couldn't tell him what I was doing, which would make him furious. But taking this risk might mean Overwatch trusted me enough to reveal who they were and put an end to this once and for all.

My stomach flipped as both worry and excitement coursed through me. Would I finally learn who killed Melissa and why? Or was I walking into a fatal trap?

Who was I kidding? I had no choice. Whoever sent me this message was calling the shots. If I didn't obey, I worried what the consequences would be. And if I didn't go, I feared I'd lose the only shot at finding a connection to Melissa's murder. I had made a promise to myself to investigate and do everything I could to uncover the truth. The sooner I did that, the sooner I could get on with my life.

As I dealt with my internal struggle, the sound of shattering glass from the storefront across the way rumbled through the café, causing a few patrons to freeze in their tracks as they took in the chaos emerging from the women's boutique. The owner, Carmella, came rushing out of the front door, screaming bloody murder as she stared at the fire engulfing the expensive clothing in her window display.

Three women came scrambling out behind her, and people walking by stopped and stared in horror.

"Someone call the police!" I heard a voice yell from somewhere.

"Is anyone else in the store?" a man asked as he raced up to a frantic Carmella, her livelihood burning before her eyes.

Officer DeAngelis was on his feet immediately, calling for backup. "Stay put," he instructed as he ran out the front door to aid two more people who emerged from the store, coughing from the smoke.

As soon as a distraught Carmella latched onto him, I made my escape. "I'm running to the apartment real quick," I called out to Meg who barely acknowledged me as she watched the scene unfold.

I cautiously made my way out the front of the store, hiding from the officer's view, and slinked down the side roads to the wharf. I made my way down Market Street and cut up Wharf Street. The narrow, stoned street was the perfect path for me to remain unseen by the masses. I hurried through the overfilled parking lot by the wharf and scanned the area for the shipping containers.

The bright sun reflected off of the water, causing me to squint from the harshness of the light. Far off, I saw what looked like the tops of the large square containers. I tentatively took a step, nervous about what I would find once I got there.

When I reached them, I searched the crates, ducking in between rows and rows of overwhelming metal. Toward the back, I located a navy blue one with N308 spray-painted in white. I walked in that direction, taking in my surroundings. Would Overwatch be waiting for me in the shadows? Why here? Why this crate? Was there something they needed to show me?

A chill ran up my spine as the sensation of being watched washed over me. I suddenly regretted coming.

My heart thumped and I took a shallow breath as I approached the container. I noticed this one didn't have a chained lock wrapped around its handles like the others. I reached out to grab the handle when a large hand clutched my wrist roughly and pulled me into a small space between two containers. I let out a scream, but it was muffled under my captor's other hand. The person wrapped an arm around my waist and pulled my body against theirs. I was conscious of a man's broad chest pressed against my back, and his muscular arms felt like an anaconda squeezing the life out of me. He loomed over me and held tighter to stop my squirming. Panic bubbled inside me as I realized I was no match for him. He could kidnap me or kill me right now. I had no chance.

Overwatch had tricked me. I was going to die.

"Goddamnit, Emily. Stop struggling. Be quiet," the familiar voice growl-whispered, his warm breath leaving goose bumps along my neck and down my spine. He slowly removed his hand from my mouth.

I spun to face him. "What are you doing here?" I demanded in a low voice.

He bent down so we could be eye-level and scowled. "I should be asking you the same thing!" Even though he kept his voice quiet, it still felt like a yell. Ben had scolding down pat. He held up his burner phone. "After I got a call about the shop on fire, I went to call you. GPS alerted me you were somewhere unusual."

"You put a tracker on my phone!" I shouted.

He shushed me and looked around. "Need I remind you there's a murderer on the loose and somehow you're in the middle of it all? Of course I put a tracker on your phone! I knew it was only a matter of time before you went AWOL to investigate and you'd eventually find a way to get around the officers dedicated to your safety. You stubborn, stubborn woman. Why are you here?"

I pulled up the messages and showed him. "You think he's still here?"

"Are you out of your damn mind, Emily? You came here on your own to meet God only knows who without telling anyone where you were going." He grabbed my shoulders and gave me a light shake before leaning in closer. I tried to turn my face away like an obstinate animal, but he grabbed my chin and forced me to look at him. "You could be the next person who ends up dead in a dumpster. Don't you get that?"

It was a sobering thought and one I had chosen to bury deep in the recesses of my mind. Of course I knew it was dangerous to be here. Stupid even. But my need for answers made me take the risk. Unfortunately, Ben's voice of reason made me realize how ridiculous that was. I should be grateful he showed up when he did.

"I just want this all to be over," I replied in a steely voice, trying not to let the sense of defeat come through when I spoke.

His shoulders slumped for a second, taking in my statement. "I know. I know." He ran a hand down my face tenderly and my body reacted. I was about to lean into his stroke, but he grabbed my shoulders again before I had a chance. "And we're going to get there. The right way," he said with conviction.

I looked over my shoulder. "Do you think Overwatch is still here?"

Before he could answer, my phone dinged again with a text message.

"I specified no police. This was a test and you failed. You'll pay," it warned.

"Shit," I said, showing Ben the message.

"Fuck," he hissed through his teeth. "Emily, we still haven't gotten a pulse on who this person is or what they're capable of. We don't even know if the information this person is sharing is legitimate."

"They started the fire at Carmella's," I admitted. "They wanted to create a distraction so I could get away."

Ben's body shook and he looked like he was doing everything in his power to stop himself from punching something.

I sucked in a deep breath. "Should I be worried?"

"Based on what we've seen so far, yes. Very worried."

CHAPTER 14

The thing they didn't show you in movies was all the waiting in murder investigations. It wasn't all packed with action, with clues and leads found around every corner. Warrants take forever. Scheduling people to talk, getting calls back, and research make the process move at a snail's pace. And with no new leads coming in, we were at a standstill.

Ben's team was able to locate the whereabouts for Fred Kaminsky the night Melissa went missing. After scouring hours of traffic footage, they were able to confirm he was passing through a toll booth on the Mass Pike at the time Melissa had gotten into the BMW and disappeared.

In other words, the lead was a bust.

It had been three days since my adventure to the wharf. Ben had been furious with me, as I expected. But rather than yelling, he stewed in silent anger. To me, this was more unsettling. Thankfully, after a solid twelve hours, he came around.

Since that day, Overwatch had gone radio silent. I

didn't know whether to cry for joy that he was leaving me be or worry that he had something malicious up his sleeve. The lack of communication made me anxious, especially with the way things were left.

Ben could sense my unease and tried to find ways to help me unwind. He knew not to outright coddle me or force me to talk about my apprehensions. Instead, he focused on giving us a normal routine. That included home-cooked meals, light conversation, and watching reruns of *The Office* before calling it a night and heading to our separate rooms.

I tried not to look too deeply into our newly found rituals or how easily we blended into each other's lives. I was happy to see him puttering around the kitchen each morning and felt a sense of relief when he returned home to me each evening. Being around him felt right. Living with Ben was companionable, maybe even more comfortable than I had been with Trevor.

Well, as comfortable as you could be with a thick layer of sexual tension hanging in the air.

Ben's presence could be all-consuming. He was safe, and frustrating, and sexy, and caring, and tough, and so much more all rolled into one. He kept me on my toes but still managed to make me feel like we were on the same level.

After Trevor started to make a name for himself, he found subtle ways to put me down while elevating his own status and ego. I never realized how hurtful and harmful those snide remarks and selfish actions really were until I had some distance from him and saw how Ben was treating me.

Ben made me feel seen and heard. His compassion for me was more than I could ever hope for in this situation. Even when I went behind his back and tested his trust, he didn't let his anger push aside the fact that he cared for my well-being. He promised to keep me safe and he would be damned if he broke his word. He was a man of honor.

The fact that Ben and I were a step up from mere acquaintances and he still showed me more respect than my former fiancé spoke volumes about my relationship with Trevor. Finally, I felt my heart starting to mend. Of course, I knew I'd never fully recover from losing a dream and life I had envisioned for myself for so many years, but at least I was turning a corner, ready to consider a new dream. A different dream.

It was another quiet night in the apartment and Ben and I were binging on Netflix as usual. He sat close to me on the couch, causing my hormones to go into overdrive and making me feel restless. His masculine scent awakened my senses. I wondered if he was as affected by me as I was by him. As I snuck a glance, I saw his demeanor was relaxed and mindlessly focused on the TV and Michael Scott's antics. He definitely didn't seem interested, I realized with disappointment.

Suddenly, a loud banging sounded at the door.

"Emily! Open up!" Joanna yelled from the other side. I jumped off the couch and hurried to open the door, finding a panic-stricken Jo before me.

I let her in. "What's going on?" I asked, concern filling my voice.

"The money. It's gone. It's all gone!" She tugged at her long hair, wringing her hands as she paced back and forth in the living room.

Ben was on his feet, reaching out to Joanna to stop her in her tracks. "Deep breath," he instructed. She obliged. After her breathing slowed, he spoke again. "What's going on, Jo?"

She perched on the edge of the couch like she was ready to bolt. Her face was distressed, causing my stomach to drop. Joanna didn't frazzle easily. Not like this. "I was doing the books tonight after closing and logged into our bank account. All the money was gone."

My knees felt weak. I steadied myself onto the couch. "What do you mean gone?"

She stared at the floor and bounced her foot. "I-I thought maybe it was a computer glitch so I called our banker." Tears welled in her eyes as she looked up at me. "It wasn't a glitch, Em. Someone transferred money from our account to an untraceable source. We've been robbed." The tears spilled down her cheeks and I grabbed her into my arms, trying to soothe her.

My chest tightened. We'd put everything into Crafty Café and in the blink of an eye, it was gone. Just like that. No warning. No time to prepare. If we didn't sort this out, we'd be screwed.

Before I could speak, an alert from my bank pinged on my phone. "Fuck!" I yelled while reading the alert. "My personal accounts were drained, too." I looked up at Ben. "Do you think it's you-know-who doing this?" Fear laced my voice. How could this happen? How could someone toy with my life so easily? I had no way of stopping it.

Before he could answer, the sound of paper sliding under my front door made us all jump. We rose to our feet. Ben unholstered the gun on his hip and raced to the door, flung it open, and ran down the stairs. A moment later, he was back in the living room with an envelope in hand.

"This person is a ninja. There's no way they would have made it down the stairs before I opened the door. Do any of your neighbors have access to this hallway?"

"No. We all have private entrances to our walkups. There's no access to other apartments from here except from the street, and you'd need a key for each of the individual doors." I took the envelope from his hand. "What is it?"

"Judging by the writing on the front, I would say it's from Overwatch."

I started at the blocky black letters written with precision on the envelope. With trembling hands, I tore it open and pulled out a piece of paper. "Follow these instructions and your funds will be returned," I read out loud. Scanning the rest of the page, I discovered the next lead he wanted us to follow up on. "Dark-silver BMW 5 Series. Maine plates with a partial plate of NYZ 4." I looked up at Ben and Joanna's expectant faces. "He wants us to look into who picked up Melissa the night she disappeared."

"Hm. Partial plate. We haven't had that before." Ben stood, hands on his hips, a determined look on his face.

"That's if it's even legit," Jo replied skeptically. "How long is this person going to hold our funds hostage?" She flopped down on the loveseat again and rubbed her temples. "We already lost a week of business during the crime scene investigation. We can't afford many more hiccups like this, especially after the winter we had. We had a lot more weather-related closures than normal. I'm worried, Em."

"We'll get this figured out," I said hopefully, trying to convince myself as well. Then I sucked in a breath when I realized something.

"What?" Ben asked.

"Trevor bought a gray 5 series a few months before we broke things off. He was so proud of it when he brought it home."

"He's still a suspect but that doesn't mean the partial plate would match." I was surprised that for once Ben wasn't quick to consider Trevor as the killer. "This lead is more than what we've got for the night Melissa disappeared. Our team looked at traffic cam footage, but nothing stood out. This could be the key to figuring this thing out."

"I guess we'll find out."

"I'll put a call in and see if they can get a list of plates from the DMV that would match." Ben pulled out his cell and made the call while I wrapped Joanna in a tighter hug.

"I didn't want you to get dragged into my mess," I said guiltily against her soft hair.

She squeezed me back. "This isn't your mess. None of this is your fault."

"Maybe not, but someone feels I have a responsibility to see this through." I let her go, leaned the back of my head against the couch cushion, and stared at the ceiling. "It's one thing for me to deal with it. I don't want our business to suffer, too."

"Like you said, we'll figure it out. Right? We're in this together," she said encouragingly.

I gave her a small smile. "Right."

"We should have some details within the next couple of hours," Ben told us as he ended his call. "If this pans out, it could be the strongest lead we have yet."

"What I want to know is why didn't Overwatch provide this to begin with instead of making us go on a wild goose chase?" It was as if he was forcing us deep into Melissa's secret life, but I had yet to see how all her shadiness connected.

He shrugged. "No idea. There must be a method to this madness. Maybe everything we learned so far links up but we can't see it just yet."

"Hopefully you guys figure it out before our business goes bankrupt," Joanna said miserably while getting up. "I'm heading home and curling up with a romance novel to get my mind off this. Keep me posted when you hear anything. Bills are due next week," she reminded me.

"You'll be the first to know."

Alone again. I turned to Ben and found him watching me intently.

"Hey," Ben said softly. "You look beat."

"I would like to say I can handle a high level of pressure, but I think I've met my threshold for stress lately. I'm spent."

He took a seat next to me, his large frame making the couch sink slightly and causing my body to roll up against his. He was warm, solid, and smelled good. I had the sudden urge to lay my head on his shoulder but resisted at the last minute. Although we'd had a few private moments with one another, we never crossed that line.

As much as I wanted to.

"I know this is hard," he replied while wrapping an arm around my shoulder and tucking me against him. Butterflies filled my stomach as I realized he was the one to take that next step. Maybe the gesture meant nothing but kindness to him, but having him wrapped around me stirred up emotions I didn't think I'd have again for a long time.

I closed my eyes, relishing the feeling of strength and security enveloping me. He'd never know how the simple act calmed me… and poked at the burning embers lit within me.

I wasn't sure how long we stayed like that. The comfort of Ben had lulled me into a deep sleep. And if Ben wasn't turning out to be a decent-enough guy as it was, he stayed like that the duration of my nap, not moving an inch so I wouldn't be disturbed. It couldn't have been comfortable.

My cell phone rang, startling me awake. I rubbed my eyes and grabbed it from the coffee table. Trevor's name appeared on my screen. Ben gave me a look.

"Hello?" I was curious as to why Trevor was calling when he all but threatened me the last few times we had seen each other. If I had been more awake, I may have had some witty response when answering the phone, but my brain felt sluggish after the short nap.

"Emily," he breathed into the phone, his voice sounding hushed and worried.

I sat up, alert. "Trevor, are you okay?"

Ben's phone rang next. He picked it up on the first ring and walked off to the guest bedroom.

"Emily, I need you to meet me at my office first thing in the morning." The background noise made it seem like Trevor was somewhere outside by water. I looked at the clock on the DVR and saw it was just after midnight. I wondered where he was and why the tone of his voice was making my hair stand on edge.

"What's going on?" I urged.

"I just need you to be there at eight a.m. sharp. Okay?" he pleaded. He sounded vulnerable, something I'd never heard from him in all the years I'd known him.

"Uh...yeah. I'll be there."

"Come alone."

I looked down the hall to the guest room. "I can't come alone, Trevor. I'm under police protection. Where I go, they go."

He cursed. "Fine. Just have them wait outside in the lobby while you and I talk in my office."

"Trevor, what is going on?" I asked again.

He sighed. "I'll explain everything tomorrow."

"Okay."

He hung up.

Ben walked back from the bedroom, stuffing his phone into his back pocket. "That was the precinct. We got some potential matches for that plate and car."

I looked at him expectantly.

"Trevor's car was one of the ones that matched up. They're working on getting traffic cam footage to confirm this lead is legit." He gave me a serious look. "It doesn't look good for him. None of this has."

CHAPTER 15

I felt ill. The sleepless nights, constant anxiety, and irregular routine had caught up to me. It was almost impossible to get out of bed the next morning. My body ached. My eyes were puffy. The unrelenting need to sleep for a solid week was overwhelming and I almost gave into it when the memory of Trevor's voice the night before popped into my mind. He sounded anxious. Scared. I wondered if he knew the police were onto him. Was Overwatch sending him threatening messages too?

I made it to his office ten minutes before eight. I was surprised I even made it that early after all the grief Ben had given me about going.

"He's a prime suspect, Emily," he said as I drank my coffee earlier that morning. "You shouldn't get involved." His voice had the stern edge to it, the one he used when he didn't want to be argued with.

I wasn't having it.

"He called me for a reason," I retorted. "What if he has useful information for us?"

NO PLACE TO HIDE | 147

"Like a confession?"

I placed my cup in the sink and unwrapped the towel from my wet hair. I eyed the clock and saw I was running behind. Air-dried hair would have to do today.

"Like anything, Ben." I pinched the bridge of my nose, a tension headache starting to form. I shuddered when I thought of the dark-purple circles I had discovered under my eyes when I showered this morning. I was run down. I didn't know how much more of this I could take. "He wouldn't be asking me to see him unless it was important," I added.

He shook his head and came around to my side of the counter. He stood close to me, forcing me to instinctively take a step back, and wedged me between the counter and his body. He meant to be dominating but all it did was make me want to rip his clothes off. Being this close to him while sleep-deprived was dangerous. I couldn't be held accountable for my actions.

"I don't like this," he said in a low voice. "If he's the killer, I don't want you near him. He could hurt you."

"Well, good thing you'll be in the lobby in case things head south." I pushed past him to grab my purse and keys, ushering Ben out the door.

"You'll tell me everything that goes on, right?"

I nodded. That would have to be good enough for him.

• • •

We stood in the lobby as Lois made her way to the front desk from the back offices, flowy skirt and colorful earrings in tow. "Oh! Miss Ayers. Mr. Miller said to send you back as soon as you got in." Funny how Lois's tone had changed since the last time I saw her. She picked up the phone, punched a couple of buttons, and spoke into the receiver. "Miss Ayers is here." She hung up the phone. "Right this way."

"I'll be right here," Ben said. I gave him a tight smile.

I followed Lois through the office to the section where the partners' offices were. She stopped in front of Trevor's large solid-wood door and knocked.

"Come in," Trevor called. She opened the door and allowed me in. "Water? Coffee? Tea?"

"I'm fine. Thanks." I tried not to roll my eyes as she talked in her overly solicitous tone. I knew it was all an act.

"Lois, please close the door on your way out," he instructed.

"Yes, Mr. Miller." She exited the room, leaving Trevor and me alone.

"Well, I'm here." I took a seat across from him. "What do you want to talk about?" I tried to seem clueless about the license plate and wondered if he'd be forthcoming about it. Ben already told me the police had contacted him for further questioning.

His shoulders sagged as if he were deflating. His skin looked pale and greasy, and his hair had grown longer, losing its perfect shape. It was as if he was reverting back to the disheveled law student who was just trying to get by. It was hard to see him like this.

"I know I haven't been great to you during all this madness, Emily—"

"And before this madness. You know, with the cheating?"

His lips formed a thin line. "I'm sorry about that. I truly am. I should have handled things better with you."

"That seems to be the least of our worries now."

He gave a quick nod. "Despite the last month, you've

known me for more than four years. You know the kind of person I was…I am. I'm not a killer. A cheater? A liar? Yes. But I wouldn't kill Melissa."

"Why are you telling me this?" I felt my blood start to boil. I didn't want to reopen fairly fresh wounds right now. I wanted to get in and out.

"Things aren't looking great for me in this investigation. If it comes down to it and they ask you questions or if they need a character witness, I want to know you'll be truthful about who I am. I made mistakes with us and I apologize for that. But don't let those few bad experiences paint the picture of who I actually am. I need someone on my side if it comes down to it. You were the closest person to me for a long time. They're going to turn to you."

I let out a breath. "Trevor, I—"

"Please, Emily," he pleaded. "You know me. Why would I do this to someone I love?"

My body tensed, and I let out a shuddering breath. He picked up on it and quickly sputtered. "I'm sorry, Em. I didn't mean for it to happen or to share that with you. I'm falling apart here."

"I'll do what I can," I said roughly while standing. "I can't promise anything. Even if I tell them what I know, it might not be enough to save you if it comes to it." I stared him down. "Truthfully, I don't know what kind of person you are anymore. As I learn more about your lies and everything you've kept from me, I'm not sure what I believe. If I'm put on the stand, the jury is going to see right through me. They're going to see my shaky confidence. That won't work in your favor."

"I understand," he responded soberly.

"We're done here. Bye, Trevor." I was harsh and short, but I couldn't get out of there fast enough.

I opened the door quickly and nearly ran right into

Andy. He jumped out of the way and steadied the wobbling laptop in his hand. "Whoa!" he exclaimed, clearly startled. Poor kid.

I grabbed him and steadied him too for good measure. "I'm so sorry. I didn't see you there."

He placed the laptop on an empty desk next to him, slid his glasses up the bridge of his nose, and tucked a strand of loose hair behind his ear. "No harm, no foul." He glanced into Trevor's office, where he sat at his desk with his face in his hands. "Everything okay?

"This case is taking a toll on him. On all of us, actually," I admitted. "I just wish we had answers so we could finally get closure and move on with our lives."

He gave me a reassuring grin. "I'm sure something useful will pop up before you know it. We're all working hard on it."

"I hope you're right." I closed Trevor's door to give him some privacy and ensure he was out of earshot. "By the way, have you discovered anything new from Melissa's personal computer yet?"

He frowned. "I only just started on it the other day. Normally, the Portland PD would have a tech guy on it, but since they're down a person, they enlisted me since I knew the ins and outs of the firm's network. I had to go through a background check and some training before they'd even let me near the thing. I also have an officer who's basically breathing down my back to make sure I'm not tampering with any evidence." He shuddered.

"Wow."

"Yeah, it's not been ideal." He shifted weight from foot to foot as if he was about to disappoint me. "She had a lot of safety measures in place. Password protection, two-way authentication, a contingency plan to wipe her drive if there are too many failed attempts to log in. I have to be very careful, but I think I can find a way to get around it eventually." He gave a wary look. "Hopefully. I just want to make sure I have a backup plan to recover the drive's data if I'm wrong." He sighed. "I'm just so nervous of messing up. I only have a couple of years' experience. Her security measures are a little out of my league. It's exciting to get my hands on it, but there's a lot at stake if I mess up. I don't have the right skills for this yet, so there's a good chance I could do the wrong thing and lose any chance we have to find out what happened."

I gave his shoulder a reassuring squeeze. "You're quite brilliant for someone so young."

He looked down at his feet shyly, causing his glasses to slide down his nose again. "Thanks, but I haven't gotten in yet." He frowned. "Detective Hunter *really, really* emphasized what would happen if I screwed up. It's clear he doesn't have much faith in me. He told me point blank he'd rather have someone else."

I shook my head. "Don't let him get to you. He was intimidating when I first met him too. You're more help than you realize. You'll reach out as soon as you find something, right?"

"Of course."

"Just call me or the station and ask for Detective Hunter once you're able to crack the laptop."

He shrugged, his lack of confidence apparent. "*If* I can do it."

"You'll do it. I promise."

Two police officers walked through the threshold, followed closely by Ben. They pushed past us and made their way into Trevor's office, closing the door behind them.

Ben paused outside the door to address me. "They're taking him in," he answered my questioning look.

"Why?"

"We found the traffic cam footage. The driver is hard to identify but Melissa was definitely in the car. It doesn't look good, Emily."

Seconds later, the officers exited the room with a cuffed Trevor in tow. He looked absolutely miserable. He stopped in front of me and whispered "Remember what I said" in my ear before he was led out of the office. He didn't even put up a fight.

CHAPTER 16

left the law firm feeling out of sorts. How could Trevor have been the one that was seen in the car with Melissa the night she disappeared? His shock and fear were palpable. I knew he could lie, but could he fake it that well? Were the police jumping to conclusions because it was his car on the cam? It was just too easy.

Ben dropped me at the café and made his way to the station to question Trevor, which meant I was once again being surveilled by an officer from the Portland PD. When I entered Crafty Café later that morning, I was surprised to see both Officer Shapiro and Officer DeAngelis sitting in the dining area.

I pointed back and forth between the two of them, confused. "Isn't there only supposed to be one of you?"

"New protocol," Shapiro said gruffly and looked back down at his newspaper.

Apparently after my stunt at the wharf the other day, Ben had decided to beef up security. I sighed, accepting the fate I had forced upon myself. It was going to be a long day.

As I headed through the swinging kitchen door to grab an apron, Joanna popped out of the office, thrilled to see me. She clapped her hands together in delight.

"Ah, great. You're here! I have wonderful news," she said as I tied the apron around my hips. "All the money has been returned!"

"Really?" I guess our mysterious partner wanted us to play by his rules.

I had a sinking feeling in my stomach. If that was the case, we would have to follow his rules more closely. I didn't like to be at the mercy of anyone, let alone this one. What if we didn't follow through? What if we messed up? I saw how easy it was for him to hack our accounts or cause destruction to Carmella's store. How far would this person go?

I thought back to Ben's argument after the wharf fiasco. Overwatch was no longer a potential informant, but a felon. After what I witnessed, I couldn't deny the fact.

"Yeah, you should check your personal accounts too to see if your money's been returned." She let out an appreciative squeal. "I'm so thankful this didn't go on longer. I don't think we could have survived if we had to close down the shop again so soon."

I gave a tired smile. "Me too." I ran a hand through my hair to untangle a knot and threw it up in a ponytail. "By the way, Trevor was arrested." I gave her the rundown on what happened.

"My goodness. Do you think he could have done it?"

"All signs seem to be pointing to yes, but my gut says no." And I truly meant it.

"You're not letting your relationship with him cloud your judgment, are you? You let him get away with a lot when you were together," Jo chided.

"This is different. Whether I loved him or not, that wouldn't make me overlook homicide. Things just don't add up."

"Nothing about this case does," she agreed. "Listen, I've gotta run. See you tomorrow morning?" She pulled her apron off and hung it on a peg by the office door.

"Bright and early."

As she made her way to the front to leave for the day, she poked her head back into the kitchen. "Oh, I almost forgot."

"Hm?"

"A woman was asking for you. I've seen her here a couple times and figured she was a new customer from those social media campaigns you were running."

I was on high alert. "Did she say what she wanted?"

"No. Just said she wanted to speak to you." She thought for a moment. "Come to think of it, I didn't even get her name. Once I told her you weren't in yet, she said she'd be back another time and hastily left."

I bit my bottom lip. Could this woman be tied to Overwatch?

I shook my head. I couldn't be suspicious of everyone or it would drive me insane. Joanna was right. It could very well have been a new customer from our campaigns. Maybe she was a food blogger looking to get a quote. Maybe it was a marketing agency wanting our business. This woman could be anyone. It didn't mean she was working with Overwatch and coming for a kill shot.

I needed to get a grip.

• • •

After another busy day at Crafty, I trudged upstairs, flanked by the two officers. One entered my apartment and did a sweep before giving us the all clear. I walked into the foyer and closed the door behind me, leaving the officers to stand guard outside. Ben would have preferred one of them in the apartment with me but it just felt weird. I needed some space, even if only for a couple of hours.

I hung my keys on the rack, dropped my purse on the bar stool, and flopped down on my loveseat. Ben had called me a few moments earlier, letting me know that things with Trevor took a turn. His team located additional footage from other cameras outside of the city and cleaned it up so they could get a better look at the driver. Although they couldn't make out the person's face, there was one distinct feature they could identify.

The man had long, shaggy hair. Something Trevor clearly did not have.

From the few seconds of footage, it looked like Melissa and the man were arguing. She didn't seem scared or nervous. If anything, she acted as she knew the driver.

Now the question was why did they take Trevor's car and return it that night? Was this person specifically trying to set Trevor up or was there something else at play?

Ben said they were doing a sweep of the car for prints or hair but doubted they'd find anything with the way things were going with this case. It had been too long since that night, and rain and sun most likely would have removed any oils left by someone's hand. And with Trevor's obsession with detailing the car, Ben knew it had been cleaned since that night.

As for the long-haired man, no one at the firm or who was close in Melissa's circle matched the description. Ben's team had scanned photos and camera footage to see if anyone had long hair at that time and may have cut it since then but came up empty-handed. The leads were just getting more confusing.

When we ended the call, he told me not to bother waiting up.

A night without Ben? Without his presence, the apartment felt quiet. Less homey. Our habits had become my new routine, one that provided reassurance and a sense of steadiness in my out-of-control life. It bothered me that one single night without him had made me feel disoriented in the same way as when Trevor left.

However, tonight afforded me valuable time that could be spent doing orders, sourcing new vendors, and maybe adding more posts to our social media account. I could even clean the apartment or do laundry for the first time in forever. Or if I was looking to treat myself, I could binge on that new show I had been dying to see on Hulu or read that book that had been collecting dust on my nightstand.

But none of that seemed appealing to me. I wanted to stare at the wall and shut off my brain for once. I couldn't muster up the motivation to do anything else. The lack of motivation made me worry I was falling into a state of depression. Then again, who could blame me?

I must have dozed off as I stared at the living room wall because before I knew it, the afternoon sun had transformed into the golden light of early evening. I checked my phone and saw it was six p.m. I had been out for nearly three hours. I wished I had slept longer but at this point, I was happy to get what I could.

I rubbed my eyes, still feeling drained, and tried to muster up the energy to get off the couch. I shuffled over to the fridge and took a peek inside. There were plenty of groceries available but nothing I had the mental capacity to make. I was getting spoiled by my regular meals with Ben. He always created dishes I would never dream up. Breakfast, I could do. That was why Crafty had become as successful as it had been. Well, that and Joanna's amazing baking skills. As for dinner, my cooking left much to be desired.

I closed the fridge and checked my phone again. No calls or texts from Ben. I thought of giving him a call to see if he wanted me to order him something for takeout but decided against it. Radio silence from him might mean he was getting somewhere with the case. We needed to catch a break, and I didn't want to interrupt his interrogation to ask him if he wanted chicken fried rice from Zen.

I decided to place an order for Chinese delivery and ordered a few extra options for the officers outside and in case Ben was hungry whenever he got back home.

Funny how I thought of my apartment as home for Ben.

The person who took my order said the restaurant was slammed and it would be about an hour wait. With time to kill, I decided to take a shower. A warm soak from my rain showerhead would hopefully relieve the tension from my muscles.

I ran the water, letting the bathroom steam up before I stepped in. Trevor always wondered how I could take such hot showers but I loved it. There was something soothing about hot water and steamy air. It was cleansing and relaxing and Lord knew I needed to relax. These types of showers always helped me clear my head.

I finished lathering and shaving and was now simply enjoying the feel of the water falling over me when a loud, piercing noise rang out throughout my apartment, snapping me out of whatever tranquil scene had been playing in my head.

I put my hands over my ears, my body on high alert. It was a noise I'd never heard before and one that could wake the dead.

I ripped open my shower curtain and looked around the bathroom. I had nothing available that could be used as a weapon. I made a note to carry a kitchen knife with me the next time. I threw a towel around my wet body and considered my options. Should I go out there and find out what was happening or wait in the bathroom until the officers watching over me could take care of it?

As the sound blared on, my heart raced. It had to have been at least a couple of minutes now. Why hadn't I heard any movement outside the door? Why hadn't either of the officers come to check on me?

Fear took over. This had Overwatch written all over it. What if whoever or whatever was causing the noise took out the officers? I was a sitting duck all alone. I pressed my ear against the bathroom door but couldn't hear anything other than the deafening sound ripping through the apartment. I took a step back and made the decision. I was going out there.

I slowly pulled open the door and went in the direction of the living room when I ran headfirst into a large figure lurking outside the bathroom. I screamed and threw up my hands, causing my towel to fall to the ground. My wet, exposed body was there for the taking. What an embarrassing way to die.

I felt substantial hands grip my shoulders and could vaguely hear what sounded like my name through the noise. I opened my eyes and saw Ben holding me. His face was flushed as he tried to keep his eyes on mine rather than looking at my naked body.

But he slipped.

His eyes took me in from top to bottom. His breathing quickened and his fingers dug slightly into my skin. I could see his heartbeat pumping in his neck and wondered if it was adrenaline from the situation or if I caused that reaction.

"Emily," he said hoarsely above the noise. The muscle in his defined jaw moved.

I looked up at him, his eyes reflecting the same want I was feeling for him. And for a minute, I thought maybe he would scoop me up and take me into my bedroom.

But the loud noise ringing throughout the apartment put a halt to that. I quickly scooped up my towel and wrapped it around me.

"What is that?" I yelled.

"It's—" he started to yell back but the noise stopped, causing him to pause. The sudden silence made my ears to ring and his voice to sound muffled, like the sensation you feel after leaving a loud concert.

Ben walked back to the living room, exchanged a few words with someone and then came back to the hall where I was standing. He held up a device in his hand. "It's this. I was doing another bug scan of the apartment while you were showering and found this hidden behind the DVDs in your media center. When I touched it, some sort of alarm went off."

"How'd you get it to stop?"

"Officer DeAngelis is pretty good with this stuff. He's a robotics hobbyist."

"Any idea what it is?"

"From what we could tell, it's a pretty advanced bug. Not only can it record and hear anything you're saying or doing in your apartment, but it can also intercept anything you're doing on your computer or cell phone. I'm assuming it's the person who's been contacting you with leads. Probably explains how they've been able to easily hack your devices, banking accounts, and so on."

"Are there any others here?"

"Not that we discovered." He ran a hand through his thick hair. "But that means this person had to physically be in your apartment to place it. I'm going to call a locksmith to change your locks again, but I don't feel like it's much use. This person is good. I think our best strategy is to have someone watch over your apartment and the café even if you're not there."

"Was there a bug in the café too?"

He nodded. "In your office."

I let out a breath. "I feel...violated. To know some stranger has been in my apartment, can see everything I do or say, to be able to dictate my life. It's...it's disturbing." I thought for a moment. "Disturbing isn't even a strong enough word." I started to shake as my chest constricted. A panic attack was threatening to unleash its fury.

Ben wrapped me in his strong arms. My head rested snugly against his broad chest as he rubbed his hands along my damp, chilled skin, the warmth from the friction making my goose bumps go away. "I promise I will take care of you, Emily," he whispered into my wet hair.

As we stood there, me practically naked in his arms, I couldn't help but hear the subtle meaning laced in his words.

CHAPTER 17

I was reluctant to go to work the next morning. After the discovery of the bug, the sensation of being watched and listened to weaved its way into my psyche, making me feel like a helpless organism under a microscope. I was trapped.

With Ben back at the apartment that night, I had my safe little bubble. Being near him made me believe things would be okay. That I was untouchable. It was almost addicting in a way, which is why leaving the secure confines of the apartment this morning was difficult to say the least. In our bubble, I could pretend nothing was wrong.

My emotions were frayed as I managed the steady flow of customers at Crafty. Joanna worked hard in the kitchen, periodically bringing out freshly baked goods to the display case. To try to keep business growing, Joanna kicked it up a notch when it came to presentation. Today she used iridescent dyes, shimmering sugars, carefully crafted fondants, and edible paints to create beautiful masterpieces that barely hit the display case before they were sold out again. Charlie was all too happy to snap photos and post them online. These one-day-only offerings sparked urgency, making people desperate to be one of the lucky few to snatch up Joanna's creations.

She was a genius. If things kept going at their current rate, we'd make enough money to compensate for the hit we took during the week we were closed. I was ecstatic as I busted my ass to help the unusual number of customers circulating through the door. Seeing the success of the new menu made me feel positive, giving me a break from the stress I was under.

By late afternoon, there was a lull in the crowd, so I shooed off Charlie and Jo to take a break. I was grabbing change from the safe in the office when the bell chimed, announcing a new patron.

"I'll be just a minute," I hollered from the back. I quickly swapped the larger bills for smaller ones and closed the safe. When I reappeared, I found a woman scanning the display case. Aside from the officers, she was the only one in the café.

"I apologize for the wait. What can I get you?"

The woman turned to me and I was taken aback by her delicate beauty. She wore a beautiful blush-pink summer dress with a white cardigan. A pearl necklace hung around her long neck. Radiant blond hair hung in loose curls to her shoulders, and her bright blue eyes were fixed on me.

"Hi there," she greeted with a Southern drawl. "Are you Miss Emily Ayers?"

My muscles tensed. Was this the woman Joanna was telling me about? I eyed the officers in the dining room. They were unfazed by the woman but something didn't sit right with me. I put a hand in my apron pocket and gripped the burner phone Ben had given me.

"I am. Yes. How can I help you?" I tried to play it cool. Like I considered yesterday, she could simply be a fan of our café. Not everything had to be sinister.

"I have a message," she started. I looked back to the officers, who were still unaware of the interaction. Did I want to cause a scene and look like a fool if it was nothing?

I fiddled with the phone still hidden in my apron, finding a way to alert Ben. I clicked a button and hoped it was the right one.

"Um, what kind of message?"

"A message for my husband. I need you to pass it along to him."

"What?" I asked, confused.

She looked at me like I was an idiot. "You *are* the woman he's shacking up with, are you not?" she questioned in a disdainful tone.

Realization dawned on me. "You mean Ben?"

"Yes. *My* Ben." Straightening herself, she stared at me down the graceful swoop of her nose. I wondered if she picked the intimidation stance up from Ben or if it was a tactic taught in Southern schools. "My name is Callie Hunter. Surely he's mentioned me?"

Although her voice was sweet as pie, the possessiveness that laced it was not to be missed. "He said something in passing."

She eyed me up and down, sizing me up. "Yes, well. I'm sure a man wouldn't want to talk too much about his wife when he's in the bed of another woman."

"Whoa, whoa, whoa. It's not like that," I shot back defensively. My hackles were up, and I was tempted to put her in her place. She was the one who went off and got pregnant with her husband's best friend. What right did she have to judge Ben's situation with me?

She glared at me, waiting for an explanation. "I wouldn't get too attached, sweetie. We're getting back together," she added vehemently when I refused to respond.

I wanted to tell her what I really thought of her. It was on the tip of my tongue but before I could say anything I regretted, Ben stormed through the door.

"Damnit, Callie. What are you doing here?" The look he gave her was deadly.

She turned to him and gave him a demure smile. "I came to find you, of course." She went to wrap him in a hug, but he held her away, stopping her in her tracks. I wanted to laugh in her face. That would show her.

"I told you not to come here," he said severely.

She rubbed a hand daintily down his chest. "I know, honey. But you were just angry. I thought it would be easier to talk in person. We'll get this all sorted out. We made vows and I know we're going through a rough patch, but I still believe in the 'till death do us part.'"

Ben flicked a quick look to me before returning his steely gaze to Callie. I had to give it to her. She didn't flinch.

"There's nothing to sort out. You have the divorce papers. You sign them and that's that."

She gave him a pout. "You don't mean that, Benjamin."

He noticed all our eyes on them and growled. He grabbed her lightly by the elbow. "Let's talk outside," he asserted in a low voice.

I watched them leave the café and disappear out of view. Was Callie telling the truth? Did Ben cave in a moment of weakness and make her believe they had a chance? If so, then why did he seem so adamant about making the divorce final?

I tried not to let the interaction with Callie rattle me. Yes, my feelings for Ben were growing stronger each day, despite how foolish it was to have them. We were both getting over long-term relationships. It was hard to fathom a relationship between the two of us based on that alone.

All this logic still couldn't stop me from wanting him.

Callie's declaration of their reconciliation instilled doubt. A future with Ben was even less likely now. Jealousy and disappointment consumed me. It was nice to consider the possibility of being with him and these last few weeks of living together made the idea easier to picture. But Callie's visit had shattered those perfect visions for me, causing a quiet ache deep in the recesses of my heart.

I was falling for him. All it took was his soon-to-be-ex-wife waltzing into my café to make me come to terms with it. Funny how that worked.

I spent the rest of the afternoon stealing glances through the front windows. It had been an hour since Ben walked off with Callie. Still no sign and no word. Not even the late-afternoon rush could stop it from gnawing at me. What could they possibly be doing? Ben had served her the papers for divorce. One could assume they already had a lengthy discussion prior to that, right? Would there be a need to hash out the details again for this long?

Or had she convinced him to give her another chance?

I had no right to feel territorial over him. He was a grown man, and there were years of history between them. He had seemed torn up when she called him only a few days ago. Maybe her showing up had opened the floodgates and he finally had an opportunity to say what he needed to say.

Or maybe he was second-guessing his decision.

Still, I couldn't help but feel like an outsider suddenly. I was so used to being a duo with Ben, knowing he would protect me and be there when I needed him. When he walked out that door, I felt cast aside. The real world was putting a wedge between the bond I had built with him and I hated it.

I sighed. I was being childish. And selfish.

He lived a whole life before he knew me and just because I had grown feelings for him didn't mean they were mutual. Whether Ben decided to go back with her or not was none of my business.

It was closing time, and all was quiet. Joanna and Charlie had gone home for the day and I was left alone to mull it over. I made my way to the front and flipped the sign to closed when Ben appeared at the door, startling me. I had been so lost in my thoughts I didn't see him approach. I did, however, notice he was alone this time. I unlocked the door and let him in.

He acknowledged the two officers before looking at me. Or, I assumed he was looking at me. I immediately turned back to the register to tidy up and avoid his penetrating stare. He saw right through it.

"Emily," he said to get me to turn around.

I looked at him sheepishly, giving him just enough eye contact to suffice but still found excuses to busy myself. I couldn't handle his gaze. He'd know what I was thinking, and it wouldn't be fair to put that on him. He clearly had unresolved issues and I didn't want to add to it.

"Emily," he insisted again as he approached me, grabbing my hand lightly to stop me from wiping down the already immaculate counters.

I peered up at him under my eyelashes. "Yes."

"Are you almost done here? I'd like to have a word. In private." The seriousness of his tone made my anxiety spike. Would this be where he told me he was going back with Callie and that it would be best if he moved out?

Would he be gone just like that?

I looked into his hazel eyes and searched for a hint of anything. But he had his detective face on, making it completely unreadable. "Give me one minute."

I walked into the back to take off my apron and put the till in the safe. I noticed the paperwork piling up on my desk but decided to leave it. It could wait until tomorrow. Right now, I needed some answers before I lost it.

We said our good-byes to the officers as we all walked out and I locked up. Ben followed me wordlessly to the apartment, making me feel even worse. By the time we settled in, I damn near exploded.

"So, how did it go with Callie?" I finally asked, trying not to seem defensive.

He winced and grabbed a beer from the fridge. He offered me one and I gladly accepted. It seemed like the kind of discussion that required it.

"Good. Bad. I don't really know," he answered honestly. He sank into a chair at the dining table across from me. His features were tense, and he looked worn down.

"We don't have to talk about this," I offered.

"No," he replied with resolve. "I think it's time we did." He took a gulp of beer while he considered where to begin. "First off, I want to apologize for her showing up like that. Callie can be…"

"Abrasive? Manipulative?"

The side of his mouth twitched in a hint of smile. "Protective was what I was going for, although I can understand your sentiment. She's known me almost all our lives and we were friends before anything. She can be a bulldog when it comes to people she cares about. It didn't give her a right, though."

"How did she even know who I was or where to find you?"

"Her father is on the force. He worked with mine for a

number of years. That's why we knew each other so young. I have a feeling she convinced him to look into it. As you can tell, she's a bit persistent."

I gave a snort.

"I don't know what she said to you prior to me showing up but I did catch the tail end of it, obviously. What she said about us getting back together isn't true. I need you to know that."

I looked away. "It's none of my business."

He reached over and gently grasped my chin with his rough fingers. He turned my face toward him. "I want you to know Callie and I are over." He pulled his hand away and my body betrayed me, yearning to have his warm touch again.

"Why?" I asked quietly.

He sighed. "Emily, I'm a detective. That means I should be good at reading people and situations. I don't want to sound presumptuous, but I have a sense there's something growing between us."

My face burned from embarrassment. "Well, I—"

He cut me off. "It's not one-sided."

I stopped breathing. "What?"

He looked at me intently. "I can't deny I feel something for you. I'm not exactly sure when it happened or what it is but there's something about you that draws me in. I've kept it professional because of our working relationship on the case, but if Callie's visit showed me anything, it's that I care about you. I was livid when I found her there, hearing what she was saying to you. It felt wrong. I want to set the record straight.

"When I went off with her this afternoon, it was to re-iterate that we were done and there was no going back. We finally discussed some things I wasn't ready to talk about the first time around, but I was ready now. I'm certain that had something to do with you."

I gave him an earnest smile. "So what happened then?"

"She cried, of course. Pleaded with me that she made a mistake and she'd do anything to make it better. But like I told you the other day when she called, I'm finished with her. Seeing her confirmed that for me. It gave me the sense of closure I needed after months of being angry about it. When I looked at her today, I didn't feel that anger and resentment anymore. I just saw a piece of my old life." He gave a dry laugh. "It's funny, isn't it? How someone who was such a big part of you becomes a distant memory. It feels…" He paused.

"Freeing?"

He grinned at me, his dimple making a subtle appearance. "Yeah, something like that. As much as I hated her being here, it showed me I was ready to move forward."

"And the divorce?"

"After some arguing, she agreed to sign the papers. Knowing her, she'll probably drag her feet in hopes I'll change my mind. I'll push her on it though. She needs to let go too."

I grabbed his hand to offer comfort and was pleasantly surprised when he interlaced his fingers with mine. It felt electric.

"I'm sorry you had to deal with her today. I know it can't be easy," I said empathetically.

"About as easy as it is with you and Trevor during this case." His eyes followed as he traced his thumb lightly along the top of my hand. "But I now know for sure I've moved on." He looked back up at me and gestured between the two of us. "And perhaps now we can figure out what this is."

"I'd like that."

CHAPTER 18

The June sun seemed more vibrant today and the cheery songs of birds lifted my spirits. Everything seemed new as I made my way to the café this morning with Ben in tow.

Okay, so maybe the world wasn't in Technicolor, per se. But it felt that way, knowing that he'd be the one hanging out at Crafty today rather than the other officers. Nothing against them. They were good guys. But after our little chat last night, I couldn't help the excited flutters of butterflies in my stomach.

We stole glances most of the morning between the throng of customers. My heart skipped every time I caught him looking at me, especially when he gave me that dimpled smile reserved only for me. I felt like a lovesick teenager and I was okay with that.

Delores strolled through the door, sporting her usual uniform of colorful Lilly Pulitzer. Today it was a baby-blue dress with vibrant swirls of pink flowers.

"Long time, no see," I greeted her.

"I know. I feel terrible. It's wedding season and I've been swamped. All those bridal gifts." She let out a breath as if she was finally catching up. "Looks like I'm not the only one who's been busy."

"You're right. Joanna's treats are a sensation." I pointed over to the case. "Anything strike your fancy?"

Delores bent down to get a better look. "Oh my. Would you look at that," she said while pointing to the intricately decorated cookies. "That one damn near matches my dress. What a hoot! I'll take a couple of those, please."

"You got it." I opened the case, secured two of the prettiest ones, and bagged them up.

She gave me a mischievous smile as I handed them to her. "Looks like that's not the only thing keeping you busy," she commented as she dug through her oversized purse for cash.

"Huh?"

She nudged her head toward Ben, who was currently concentrating hard on whatever was on his laptop. Although deep in his work, I had no doubt he was listening to every word we were saying. He was a detective, after all. "That tall drink of water is looking mighty cozy here. Seems like you two have hit it off." She fanned herself for effect.

I waved her off. "It's nothing." She made a noise like she didn't believe me. I didn't blame her. With the way Ben and I were eyeing each other today, there was no doubt something was brewing between us.

"Whatever you say." She winked. "I'll stop in again soon. Give Joanna my love, will ya?"

"Yes, Delores. See you soon."

As she left the shop, Andy wandered through the front door with a pert-nosed, slightly husky cop. The pep in her step seemed to increase when she noticed Ben there. I glared at her when she wasn't looking.

"Hey. What brings you here?" I asked when Andy approached the counter.

He looked around the nearly empty shop and noticed Ben looking up from his computer. "Good, you're both here. I need to talk to you."

Ben got up from his chair and approached us. "What's going on?"

Andy rubbed the back of his neck. "Well, you know how I was trying to access the files on Melissa's personal computer?" he started slowly. The officer instantly looked bored. If she was the one supervising him, I didn't blame her. All that techie stuff bored me to tears too. She walked off to stand outside, giving us some privacy.

"Yessss," I said, trying not to yell for him to get to the point.

"I was able to get through all her security measures. Finally. After poking around, I learned Melissa had been married in the past and her relationship with her ex-husband didn't appear to be a great one."

I gasped. "Do you think he could have something to do with her murder?"

He looked between the two of us. "That's what I was hoping to uncover. I wanted to share what I found so maybe we can make some sense of it."

Ben crossed his arms and stood with an air of authority. "What did you find?"

"Melissa and a guy named Blake Sullivan were married for about three years in her early twenties. When she started getting serious about law, they had a pretty bad falling out, but it seems they still shared a joint account even after the divorce."

"That's strange." It had been nearly a decade. I would have figured they'd closed the account after all these years.

"Maybe they forgot about it?"

"I thought that too but then I saw daily account summaries from the bank in her email. I guess she set up some sort of alert."

"Yeah. I have that on mine. After my credit card was compromised last year, I wanted to make sure there was nothing suspicious going on. The quick summary of withdrawals and deposits give me peace of mind," I shared.

"Well, she was making some hefty monthly deposits to the account." He paused for effect. "Up until six months ago. And even more curious, those deposits would get withdrawn a few days after they cleared."

Ben grunted as he processed the information.

Andy slid his glasses up his nose and leaned in as if he was about to tell us some juicy gossip. "That's where it gets really interesting. Melissa's maiden name wasn't Maher. It was Collins. However, this isn't public knowledge."

I turned to Ben. "Maybe that's why we couldn't find any information about her earlier years."

"She must have had an expert hide any records for that part of her life then, because we weren't able to determine any other aliases for her. Even her birth certificate must have been altered."

"Andy, how did you find out about her maiden name?"

He looked uncomfortable. "That's the weird part. While I was in the system, it seemed like someone was remotely overriding what I was trying to do. The person was forcing me to different files on the computer. When I was able to get control again, I found a signature. Overwatch."

Ben and I exchanged a look.

Andy caught onto us. "Do you know something about this person?"

"Not too much, unfortunately," Ben answered. "Did

you find out much more about Melissa?"

"I haven't been able to look into it too deeply yet, but it appears she was paying off Blake to keep quiet about some things in her past. From an email exchange I saw, he threatened to expose her if she didn't continue to make the payments."

"Blackmail? Seems a bit extreme," I commented.

"Depends on what she was hiding," Ben challenged. "Wonder if it's a big enough secret to ruin her career? Now that we know her real name, maybe my team can find something."

Andy nodded. "I'm going to poke around more and see what else I can find but I wanted to bring it to you first. Figured you'd have an easier time pulling up records and whatnot."

"I find it weird that her payments stopped around the time she and Trevor were getting together." I bit my lip. "Do you think he knew about her ex-husband or her past?"

"Hard to say," Andy answered. "Speaking of Trevor, I saw that the trip he supposedly planned for Melissa was actually booked through her computer. It was all there in her browser history."

My eyebrows knitted together. "Why would she book a trip under his name?"

"Just because it was on her computer doesn't mean she was the one who booked it. Like I mentioned, someone was able to remote access in."

Ben shook his head and made a noise.

"What?" I asked.

"Just more and more pieces that don't seem to fit together. Speaking of which, I got an email from my forensics team a few minutes ago letting me know that the dirt samples from under Melissa's nails came back. Matched up with somewhere around Augusta, Maine."

"That's like an hour from here."

"I know. Someone went out of the way to take her there and bring her back for you to find."

Andy pulled a folded piece of paper from his back pocket and handed it to Ben. "Blake is still in the area. He plays in a local band that gets booked for special events and weddings. Looks like he has a gig tomorrow at the Mountain House on Sunday River. The Schultzman-Robbins wedding."

"We should check this guy out," I suggested.

"The wedding is going to be over two hundred people," Andy shared. "Should be easy to blend in."

"Crash a wedding?" Ben swiped a hand down his face. "Seems a little extreme. Let's go by the book and get a warrant."

"That will take a few days," I argued. "The wedding is tomorrow. Plus, people get tight-lipped when you throw a warrant in their faces. Maybe we can get him to cooperate in a different way."

Ben narrowed his eyes at me. "And how do you propose we do that?"

"I've got a plan. Trust me."

He shook his head and looked up to the ceiling as if asking the great beyond for some help. "Christ."

• • •

The next day, Ben and I made our way to Newry, Maine. The Mountain House on Sunday River was a beautiful venue, surrounded by breathtaking landscapes. The view went on for miles, and the ope• • •n space gave me a sense of peace. Maybe for once Overwatch couldn't find me out here.

The rustic venue utilized the land and nature surrounding it for decor. Chopped logs were made into benches for the wedding ceremony, and twinkling lights were strewn around a repurposed barn filled with tasteful decorations. The barn doors opened wide, leading to a dance floor outside that showed the spectacular views of the mountains nearby.

To keep ourselves under the radar, we hung back from the ceremony and waited for the hordes of people to make their way to the reception tent. We decided we'd tag on the back of a large group that would be walking by shortly.

"I'm not crazy about this idea," Ben admitted as we got out of the car. He ran his hands down his fitted charcoal suit to smooth out any wrinkles from the drive. The dark material was cut to perfection, enhancing his broad shoulders and lean legs. His forest-green tie, selected to match my dress, brought out the green in his hazel eyes. He'd cleaned up his normal scruff, which gave him a ruggedly handsome look.

Eat your heart out, James Bond.

I gave him a one-shouldered shrug. "It's the best plan we've got. He needs to let down his guard so he'll talk."

"This is a gray area. If we get caught, this isn't going to look good for me."

I looped my arm through his and led him in the direction of the barn. "Well, good thing I'll be the one doing the questioning. I'm not a cop and it's my plan. No one can hold it against you."

He shook his head. "I doubt my superiors will see it that way." He looked down at me from the corner of his eye. "I also don't feel comfortable with your strategy to get him to talk."

I rolled my eyes. "We'll be in a public setting. It's not like I'm cornering him in a dark alley in the middle of the night. What's he going to do?"

Ben's body tensed against me. "You'd be surprised. I've seen a lot in my line of work. Especially with the way you look tonight."

I'm sure it was a shock to him. In all the time he'd known me, I was either in yoga pants and fleece or my work attire, which consisted of jeans, a tee, and an apron. Tonight, however, I had kicked it up a notch. I chose a gorgeous dress with a sweetheart neckline that showed off modest cleavage. The dress came up in a V above my knees and tapered down to my ankles in the back, making it flow beautifully as I moved. My auburn hair hung in romantic curls around my shoulders, and the makeup I carefully put on caused my plain brown eyes to take on the color of warm honey. The soft-red lipstick accentuated my lips, making them look full and inviting.

I was pretty impressed with myself. And judging by the way Ben's eyes were devouring me, he felt the same.

"I promise I'll be safe," I assured him as we made our way into the reception area.

The sun was starting to set and happy wedding-goers took advantage of the free-flowing alcohol. Thankfully, this was a social bunch. Many people stood around with drinks in hand, mingling with one another.

I read up on the happy couple's wedding journey from their page on The Knot. They were avid campers, which was why they had chosen this venue. It made them feel in touch with nature and they wanted to put the camping flair into their big day. One area outside held a large bonfire where people were welcome to mingle, play music, and make s'mores. Despite the beautiful decorations and the lavish buffet and open bar, the couple wanted people to feel relaxed, hence the decision to go against the traditional seating charts. Without the name cards, it made it easier to blend in.

After some thorough Facebook stalking, I learned that the bride, Becky Schultzman, was a CPA consultant around my age. I also learned that she studied abroad in Spain her senior year of college, giving me a perfect backstory in case anyone asked who I was. Saying we met during that semester abroad seemed plausible enough without potentially running into anyone who could question it.

It was amazing how much you could find on the internet. After a quick hour of research last night, I had the lay of the land and enough information about the couple to seem like we belonged.

Becky and her husband, Rob, had a great group of friends. Despite having a range of different groups, everyone bonded as if they had known each other for a lifetime. Being the friendly bunch that they were, Ben and I answered questions and kept it short and succinct. For example, Ben was my boyfriend and Becky and I had kept in touch over the years. Although Ben and I now lived in Michigan, we made our way to Maine for the weekend to see my old friend Becky get married.

We tried to take the focus off us by asking the others in-depth questions. Truthfully, I was worried our lies would become too complex and we'd slip up. Thankfully, the band started playing, which cut the conversation short. Everyone had a good buzz at this point and felt courageous enough to let loose on the dance floor.

"There he is," Ben said into my ear, his warm breath causing shivers down my spine. "Lead guitarist and singer."

I took stock of the man. He had thick, short black hair with that just-rolled-out-of-bed look. He wore a tight black button-up with the sleeves rolled to his forearms, showing off a number of tattoos. He was the epitome of a hot rocker with a voice that could make a girl faint.

And I would have had I not known his backstory.

Blake Sullivan had dropped out of college his junior year to pursue music. His band had been bound for greatness but the wild lifestyle that came along with it had landed him and another band member in rehab for drug addiction. After two stints over the course of three years, Blake made a recovery but his friend wasn't so lucky, dying of a heroin overdose a year later.

Blake had joined his current band four years ago, sticking with the safe route of corporate events, fundraisers, weddings, and the like. Although the band was booked regularly, he relied heavily on the monthly payments from Melissa to live a modest life. Without those payments, he was barely scraping by.

It was a sad story, but it made me wonder how he got away with blackmailing Melissa all those years. It also made me curious to know why he wouldn't have secured a part-time job instead. Surely his commitment to the band wouldn't interfere with a normal job. Judging by the events he usually performed at, it was more of an evening and weekend gig. So why go through the stress and uncertainty of relying on someone else for money to get by?

A slow song started, and Ben interlaced his fingers through mine. "Would my lovely girlfriend like to dance?" I looked up at him, the dim lights causing his eyes to sparkle. "People are looking at us. If we're going be believable, we've got to play the part."

He pulled me to the floor and spun me around into his arms, placing a large hand on my waist and pulling me against him. He grabbed my other hand and I placed one arm around his shoulders. "Did I mention that you look beautiful tonight?" he complimented.

I blushed. "Ben, I don't think anyone can hear us. You don't need to say that."

"This is me telling you, Emily. I'm being honest. You look stunning. I'm not saying it for the benefit of the others."

My heart felt full as I looked up at him. Under the warm twinkle lights, I lost myself in his eyes, believing we were together as we danced slowly against one another. We still hadn't discussed what was growing between us but for a moment, I got a glimpse of what it could be. It was perfect.

I felt his fingers press a little more into the small of my back, as if he were feeling the same thing. "Thank you," I finally whispered in response.

As the slow music filled the air around us, everything else seemed to fade away. My hand reached up to touch Ben's face and I relished in the feel of his skin and scruff under my fingertips. I looked down at his full lips and my breath hitched as I was flooded with the intense desire to kiss him. Now that I knew he felt something for me, would it be so wrong to finally act on it?

Ben pressed his face more into my hand, his breathing becoming labored as he whispered my name and began to dip his head down to me. My heartbeat echoed in my ears as he came closer. I never wanted anything more.

But before he could reach me, a chorus of clinking glasses broke us from our trance.

"If you would all take your seats. It's time for the best man to make his toast," Becky announced as she addressed the crowd from her seat.

Ben looked back down to me, the look of disappointment clear on his face. "It's show time."

I nodded, leaving his embrace reluctantly. I grabbed a glass of champagne off a nearby table and made my way to the suites used for the wedding party to get ready. I knew the band would be hanging in that area while the toasts were given, so I walked in that direction until I heard voices coming from the farthest room.

I stumbled into the area, pretending to be overly tipsy.

"Oh!" I exclaimed while straightening myself, making certain to emphasize my cleavage. "This sure isn't the ladies' room." I flirtatiously giggled, eyeing Blake. "But I'm alright with this option instead," I added seductively, taking a swig of my champagne and batting my eyelashes.

Blake stood up and made his way to me. He leaned casually against the doorjamb, resting one arm above his head, and let his gaze rake over my body. "It's lucky for me that you took a wrong turn." He gave a charming smile.

I gave him a grin back. "You're pretty good up there. I'm surprised a music scout hasn't snatched you up with a voice like that." Stroking a man's ego always seemed to warm him up. I saw Blake's walls start to come down.

"Yeah, well, I haven't found the right offer yet," he bragged. I was sure it was a lie based on what I knew. "Why don't you come in and hang out with me for a bit? I don't have to be on stage for another half hour." He wrapped his arm around my shoulders and led me into the room before I could answer.

He grabbed a beer for both of us while we took a seat on a snug loveseat. "I could never say no to a good-looking rock star," I said as I took the beer from him, letting the innuendo plant a seed in his mind.

He gave a small laugh, still laying on the charm. "I think I saw you on the floor. You were dancing with your boyfriend?" he asked nonchalantly as he took a sip of beer.

I feigned surprise. "Boyfriend? God, no. He's just a friend. My go-to for events like this. He's gay," I added for effect. "Yeah, I actually broke things off with my fiancé a few months ago. Dodged a bullet with that one. Now I'm just keeping things casual. No attachments. No expectations. Just living in the moment."

Blake muttered something indiscernible before taking another drink of his beer.

He didn't seem too eager to open up, so I tried a different approach. "Plus, I wouldn't want to rub anything in his face if I jumped into another relationship. Poor guy. He worked at that law firm in Portland where that woman was murdered a few weeks ago. He was a wreck. Kept calling me when it first happened to talk. I didn't know the woman, but I couldn't imagine working somewhere and seeing someone every day and then have them gone so unexpectedly." I shuddered.

"I knew her," Blake admitted. I was surprised he shared that so soon. He shifted in his seat and I could feel the walls coming back up.

I acted shocked and earnest. "Oh. I'm so sorry! I didn't mean to upset you." I grabbed his hand and rubbed my fingers slowly along his knuckles, hoping to loosen him up again. Maybe human contact would bring him back from whatever dark place he'd gone to just now.

He took a long pull of his beer. "Yeah, I knew her way back before she became a lawyer. Before she was anyone worth knowing, really."

"How do you mean?"

"Let's just say she and I knew each other in a different lifetime when we were different people." He gave an acidic laugh. "Hell, she would have needed a lawyer back then judging by half the things we would get into."

"Funny how people can change like that."

Blake's eyes darkened as a faraway look overcame him. "Yeah, well, we lost touch when she started to take her life seriously. Guess people like me from her past wouldn't help her reputation when she became a fancy lawyer. I wouldn't exactly be a great reference." His disdain was palpable as his face started to turn red and a vein throbbed in his forehead. To his credit, he kept himself collected. "She said the best thing I could do for her was to keep my mouth shut. You believe that? After everything we'd been through, she wanted to stuff me back into the closet with all her other skeletons."

"What skeletons?"

One of Blake's bandmates appeared in the room. "We're on in a couple of minutes."

Blake drained the rest of his beer and turned to me. The sinister cloud that hovered over him was suddenly replaced with a flirtatious grin again. "I gotta get going but I'd love to see you on my next break." He gave me a wink. "Get to know you a little better. Less talk about exes."

"Wouldn't miss it."

I followed him out of the room and back to the reception area. He made his way to the stage as I made a beeline for Ben.

"Well?" he asked when I approached him.

"Well, I think I have an idea of what Blake was 'blackmailing' Melissa about. Apparently, she had an unsavory past. Something that would have probably prevented her from becoming a lawyer. She was paying him to keep quiet. Now the question is, what is it?"

"Maybe we'll find out more when we get intel on Melissa Collins. I'm hoping this will be the break in our case."

"With what we learned so far about her, I'm almost scared to know what else we'll uncover. If her recent activities were her on her best behavior for the sake of her reputation, I can only imagine what she did that would make Blake react that way."

CHAPTER 19

It was a quiet ride back home that night, both of us lost in our thoughts. Melissa's murder was more complex than I could have ever imagined. How could one person have so many secrets? From secret affairs and working with drug lords, to hidden husbands and unknown aliases. I wondered who Melissa Maher actually was. And until we figured that out, I had a feeling we wouldn't be any closer to finding the motive behind the murder.

Ben had requested a warrant before we left, and after a few days of waiting, the police were about to bring in Blake Sullivan for questioning.

It was a gray morning, with cool mist dampening the city. The dankness only seemed to exacerbate the already musty, dark precinct. We made our way to the back of the building prior to Blake arriving. I, of course, hid out of view in the interrogation room. I couldn't let him know our chat a few days ago was in connection to a police investigation.

The room was dark and cold, making the process seem more sinister than it was. Ben entered and took a seat across from Blake, sliding him a cup of crappy coffee.

Judging by Blake's posture, I worried that this conversation would go nowhere. There was a chance the little I learned the other night at the wedding would be the only thing we uncovered about Melissa. And with no new intel yet about Melissa Collins, we were desperate to get the firsthand information from him. His guarded eyes made me believe it was a lost cause.

"Yeah, I knew her when her name was Melissa Collins," I heard Blake say. "We grew up in the same neighborhood and our towns were pretty small, so it wasn't hard to know everyone's business."

Much to my surprise, Blake wasn't as tight-lipped as I expected. With Melissa gone and no incentive to stay quiet, he must have figured there was nothing to lose by being honest. He was singing like a canary. He shared more details about the small town they grew up in north of Portland and how they'd first met.

"When did you and Melissa get together?" Ben asked while flipping to a new page in his notebook.

"We hooked up a few times in high school but didn't start dating until our early twenties. She was back in town after her junior year in college and saw me playing at one of the local bars. That's how we reconnected. At that point, I had already left college a couple years prior to pursue my music career. Man, that was when I was really something. My career was starting to take off back then. I was on top of the world with her by my side," he said with nostalgia. "But things took a turn."

"How do you mean?"

"She was going through this phase in her life where she didn't know what she wanted to do. Thought college was a waste of time, especially because she didn't wanna spend her life slaving behind a desk. She took a year off to go on the road with me as my band started to make a name for itself." He smiled to himself. "She was wild and free in those years. Down for whatever. Always looking for an adventure. We had some good times."

He rubbed the back of his neck. "Truth be told, I think I was taking advantage of her."

Ben gave him a questioning look but said nothing.

"You see," Blake continued, "she was going through this rebellious streak. Stickin' it to her parents for some reason. I think it had to do with her ma cheating or something. Honestly, I can't remember. Those were some hazy times. Things got rough."

"In what way?"

"Guess we flew too close to the sun. We thought we were invincible. Got caught up in the rock star dream. It was constant late nights, drugs, spending money we didn't have, and hanging out with sketchy people. She said we had to fake it until we made it. That all big stars started out this way. The only way to get ahead was to blend in and rub elbows with the people who could open doors for me."

Ben gave a nod but didn't press anymore. He leaned back in his chair casually, sensing the floodgates opening. I, on the other hand, was sitting on the edge of my seat, about to jump through the two-way mirror. We were on the verge of something here. I could almost taste it.

"I learned the hard way that when you spend money you don't have, you end up running into some financial issues. When you hang with shady people, that's the support system you turn to for help when you're in a bind. We had to do some questionable things to get out of the hole we dug. Pushing drugs was one of the main things we had to do.

"Of course, when you work as a middleman, people expect you to take it with them. We took everything from coke and molly, to angel dust and heroin." He let out a breath as if he was surprised by his own admission. "That's some hard shit right there. It takes over your life. Before long, me and a couple of my bandmates would be so fucked up we would miss shows. And if we didn't miss 'em, we were a disaster on stage. My music career fell apart."

"Were you and Melissa married at this point?"

"Yeah but not for much longer. As my gigs and deals started to dry up, our marriage headed south. I blamed her for pushing me into the sex, drugs, and rock-and-roll life-style. Blamed her for ruining my career. She told me we wouldn't have been in this mess if I hadn't put us into debt in the first place. It was a fucking mess. A real shitshow."

"How long ago was this?"

Blake gave out a low whistle. "God, it seems like for-ever. About ten years ago? She was twenty-three when we ended things. I was twenty-five."

"I see." Ben took a note. "And then what happened?" I was impressed by Ben's voice. It was cool, collected, with nearly no inflection. I could see the benefit of it. Without the judgment there, it made it easy for Blake to air his dirty laundry.

"Well, a few months before we called it quits, a maid found us all doped up and passed out in our room. Our band manager forced me and Rob, my drummer, to check into rehab. Melissa went to rehab in a different state. Her parents chose it so she could be far away from me, I'm sure. They blamed me for her spiral even though it was their fault that she even started acting out to begin with.

"Anyway, she got out a hell of a lot sooner than me. Under her parents' influence, she asked for an annulment and told me she was going back to school. Said she wanted to put this all behind her and start over. Her parents had a good reputation and would be damned if Melissa's 'error in judgment' would tarnish the family name. People had already caught wind that little Melissa Collins sold drugs and went to rehab. Her college wouldn't even take her back. Said they didn't tolerate that kind of behavior.

"So her parents forced her to change her name, sealed the record of her true identity, put her through law school, and made me sign something that said I would keep my mouth shut." He shook his head and clenched a fist.

That would explain why we couldn't find any information on Melissa's past. Her parents must have sealed the record so it wouldn't affect her employment.

"There was a financial incentive," Blake added. "I was hurting for money and they backed me in a corner. I had no choice. My music career was over, and I had no degree or job to fall back on."

Ben flipped through his notes. "Are Melissa's parents still around?"

Blake shook his head. "They died a few years later. Some freak fire burnt their whole house down. It went up so fast that they were trapped inside. The police weren't sure what caused it or how it accelerated so fast. It was nuts. I don't think they know even today."

Although Ben's back was to me, I could see the tiniest flinch near his shoulder blades. No doubt he found that piece of information interesting. "So with them gone, how were you still receiving payments?"

"Melissa kept them going. Around the time her parents died, she was starting to gain momentum in her career. At that point, she was just paying me so I didn't ruin her chances of making partner one day. She was ambitious, determined to make partner in her mid-thirties. With lawyers, it's all about credibility. I'm sure her clients wouldn't feel secure if they knew she pushed drugs and did a stint in rehab. So she opened a joint bank account and took over once her parents had passed."

"I understand those payments stopped a few months before she was murdered," Ben pried. "Any reason why?"

"She didn't say. She wouldn't even return my messages and I couldn't stop by her home or the office either. I was in Ireland at the time, collaborating with some musician friends over there. By the time I got back, she was dead."

Ben paused, absorbing the information. He flipped back through his notes. "Last question. Do you know anyone by the name of Carlos Chakalos?"

It was if the air was sucked out of the room. Blake nodded tensely. "Yeah. I knew him. He was the one I owed money to. Melissa introduced us."

"We have reason to believe Melissa may still have been in contact with him."

Blake nodded again but said nothing.

"Melissa seemed pretty serious about her career, enough to pay to keep you quiet. Why would she risk her reputation by staying connected with him?"

"With Carlos, you don't have a choice," Blake answered as he leaned forward. "No matter how much she wanted to start fresh in this new life of hers, there were some things from her past—like Carlos—that just wouldn't let her go no matter how hard she tried."

• • •

"His story checks out," Ben said when we were back at my apartment that night. "We've got records and alibis for Blake during the time of Melissa's death. He wasn't in the same country." Ben scooped broccolini onto his plate. "That knocks him down on the suspect list."

"Damn," I said after swallowing a mouthful of steak.

"That would have been a perfect motive."

"A little too neat and tidy, don't you think? Doesn't seem like this case wants to be figured out so easily."

"If not him, then who? We're running out of people." I carved up my steak and took another heaping bite.

He took a sip of his beer and thought. "I think the next thing we need to look into is why she stopped the payments. She was moving up in her career and starting to get more high-profile cases, which meant keeping her past a secret was still important. Did someone force her to stop making those payments or was there some other reason? Was there someone from Melissa's former life who was still calling the shots?"

I twirled my hair around my finger as I considered what Ben was saying. "None of this makes sense to me."

"I know—"

"Really think about it," I said, cutting him off. "How many more of these clues are we going to chase after, Ben? We're getting information from God only knows who and why. Yes, the clues are helping us understand more about Melissa's life. And yes, they could all be credible reasons as to why someone would want her dead. But I'm really starting to wonder why Overwatch is feeding us this information. It's not out of the goodness of his heart. If he actually cared, why not just tell us who did it?"

"Well—"

"Unless," I cut him off again as I shot up from my seat and paced the living room. "Unless this is all a diversion from something else."

Ben looked at me, his eyebrow cocked up in amusement as he took in my outburst. "What are you trying to say, Emily?" He was patronizing me, but I didn't care. I was on the verge of something, I just wasn't sure what yet.

"What I'm trying to say is, what if Overwatch is actu-

ally the killer? And what if you and I are a lot closer to figuring out who that is than we think?" I stopped and tapped
my chin thoughtfully as I considered my next statement.
"Think about it. This person knew Melissa intimately
enough to know all these little pieces of her life that even
the people closest to her may not have known."

Ben stood, taking our empty dinner plates to the sink.
"We know this person is a skilled hacker." He shook his
head and rinsed the plates. "A hacker could find out anything about anyone if they're really good at what they do."

"But why her?" I grabbed the rinsed plates from him
and stuck them in the dishwasher before hopping up and
taking a seat on the counter near the sink. "She's made her
mistakes and has clearly done some questionable things,
but why her? If a hacker was investigating someone and
looking for revenge, what would be the reason for choos-
ing her unless there was some personal connection? She
had money, but she wasn't rich. It's not like they were
blackmailing her for payments like the Blake situation."

"Sometimes hackers just like to see the world burn
because they can. They don't need a reason, just a way
in. Maybe this Overwatch guy has nothing to do with her.
Could be he just found an easy way to hack her computer
and discovered something far too interesting to let her go
without having a little fun."

I made a face. "Do you always have to shoot down my
ideas?"

He laughed. "If you want to play detective, you have to
be open to other possibilities, Emily. Sometimes the truth
is way different than anything you could have guessed."

Ben shut off the water and looked at me again. My
heart raced as I realized how near he was, bringing back
the memory of our dance at the wedding a few days ago.
In a situation that was seemingly innocent, I couldn't help
but feel the air shift around me. It was thick with sexual

tension, and by the way Ben's eyes dilated, I knew he was aware of it.

I thought back to the way he reacted when my towel fell the other day and how he nearly kissed me while we were dancing. My skin flushed as I wondered what would have happened if there hadn't been those constant interruptions. Would I finally know what it felt like to have his full lips devouring mine?

My nipples hardened at the thought. He noticed.

"Emily." He leaned closer to me. His large hands gripped my thighs and pulled them apart slowly, wedging his way between my legs. He raised a hand, cupping my cheek, and leaned his forehead against mine. "I can't stop myself."

"So don't," I whispered, urging him to put me out of my misery.

Those two simple words were all he needed. Before I could blink, his lips were on mine. They brushed me tentatively, seeing how I would react. My pulse quickened and I gripped his shoulders, silently giving him permission him to kiss me harder. Begging for it.

And he did. God, he really did.

He deepened the kiss, sliding a hand from my neck into my hair, and held my head in place for better access. His tongue penetrated my mouth with slow, languid strokes, causing a moan to rise from my throat. His other hand was at the small of my back, his fingers caressing my bare skin. He pulled me closer and I could feel all of him between my legs.

It was a kiss to end all kisses. It was more than I could have imagined.

I gripped his shoulders, pressing myself harder against his body. I wanted to feel everything. All of him. My fingers were on the edge of his shirt, seconds from ripping it off his strong body.

That was when we heard a creepy jingle sound down the hall from my bedroom.

We both turned. "Wh-what is that? Jack-in-the-box?" I asked as I listened more.

Ben nodded as a small wooden box on mini wheels slowly rolled down the hall and came to a stop in front of us. He turned toward it and pushed me securely behind him. I peeked over his shoulder. The music stopped playing and a clown with a disturbing laugh sprung from the box, startling us both.

"What's in its hands?" I squeaked out. "I'm not sure." He walked over, grabbed the piece of paper, and read it out loud. "Time is running out."

"What does that mean?" I came up beside him and read the note. "Not to mention, how did this get in here? Someone was watching the apartment all day."

The jack-in-the-box gave a scary little giggle, causing me to jump back into Ben. He grabbed me and held me steady against him. "We need to get this out of here," he said quietly in my ear. Goose bumps pricked my skin, partially from the evil toy at our feet and partially from my adrenaline rush from that kiss.

My phone buzzed with an incoming message. I grabbed it off the counter and pulled open a text from none other than Overwatch.

Ben towered over me, looking over my shoulder at the video message. A dark figure appeared on the screen. "Emily Ayers," the disoriented voice started. "You have done well following my clues, but I fear you've become distracted by the detective." I looked up at Ben. "You've put your trust in him when it should have been mine," the person seethed. "It's time to take this murder more seriously and remember who's in control." A timer with large red numbers appeared on the screen, counting down the seconds quickly. "You have one week to bring the killer to justice, or I'll destroy your life. You've witnessed what I'm capable of. That was only the tip of the iceberg. Time is ticking."

"What the fuck," I cursed under my breath. Ben gripped my waist roughly, as if he couldn't contain his emotions. We focused on the last few seconds of the video.

"Melissa's ex-spouse may not be the killer but isn't it curious how the bribes stopped suddenly? Locate Remy Collins for the answers. You have seven days." And with that, the video disappeared.

We both jumped at the sound of the jack-in-the-box erupting into flames behind us, its creepy laugh becoming distorted as the plastic melted down. Ben rushed to put the flames out before it set the apartment on fire. After thoroughly taking care of the issue, he turned back to me, speechless.

I looked back to the melted heap on the floor, and the clown gave one last giggle before shutting down completely.

"If I didn't have nightmares already, that sure has done it for me."

CHAPTER 20

I was at a loss. I felt miserable.

I sat alone in my bedroom soon after receiving the message from Overwatch, needing some space. After Ben's team did a deep sweep of my apartment, swapped out my locks (again), and added more surveillance for my apartment and the café, I excused myself to my room, saying I was exhausted.

As I sat on my bed, I heard the quiet drone of the TV coming from the living room. The blue light flashed through the bottom crack of my closed bedroom door. Every so often, I'd hear Ben moving around to get a drink or something from the fridge. But other than that, he let me be.

Alone with my thoughts.

The video damned me for putting my faith in Ben. I had made a vow to myself to investigate and I was doing just that. Ben and I had become partners on this case along the way. Even so, we still followed all the leads we could. Everything Overwatch sent our way was handled, so what more could he want?

I wrapped a throw blanket around myself tightly. The eerie feeling of being watched washed over me again and I all but screamed into the nothingness, "What do you want?!"

What was I missing? Why were they so furious about my relationship with Ben? Had I said or done something wrong? I came up empty-handed.

Regardless, Overwatch had made it clear to me. Whatever was going on with Ben was causing an issue. I wasn't sure if us generally working on the case together was the problem or the fact that our relationship was turning into something more.

After my relationship with Trevor, I wasn't ready to jump into another one with someone else, especially under the circumstances. Could everything between Ben and me be the result of an adrenaline rush? That was a thing, apparently. What if the attraction between us was nothing more than that? Was I willing to risk whatever Overwatch was threatening, come hell or high water, to be with Ben?

I didn't know what would happen if time ran out and we still hadn't located the murderer. One thing was for sure though: I worried for my well-being. I saw how easy it was for him to pull money from our bank accounts. If he did something like that, I wouldn't just be out of work, I would be out on the streets. And if that was just a taste of what was to come, what would he stop at? I didn't think Overwatch was violent, but I saw what happened to Carmella's storefront. Thankfully, no one had been hurt, but she wasn't the target.

I was.

I bit my lip to stop myself from crying. With resolve, I decided I needed to take a step back from Ben and focus on my investigation. The thought depressed me, but it was the only way. I needed to end this once and for all.

I sighed and flopped down on my bed. We had been working through these leads for the last three weeks and still hadn't gotten any closer to the truth. I was beginning to worry that seven days wouldn't be long enough to find the person responsible for Melissa's death.

A knock sounded at my door. "Come in," I called out weakly.

Ben cracked open the door and stuck his devastatingly gorgeous head in. Keeping my distance would be a challenge. "Hey," he said, a look of concern on his face. "I'm going to bed soon but wanted to check on you."

I leaned up, adjusted the blanket on my shoulders, and wrapped my arms around my knees. I took him in. The look he gave me broke my heart. Every cell in my being wanted to reach out to him, to have his arms around me. Inviting him in was on the tip of my tongue and I struggled to keep the words from spilling out. How could we have started to get so close just to have it taken away?

Emotions raged inside me. I put up a wall for his safety and mine. I felt guilty giving him mixed signals.

"I'm fine, thanks," I replied lamely.

He opened the door wider and I almost thought he would cross the room to me. If he did, I wasn't sure how strong I could be. Instead, he leaned against the doorjamb, assessing me a little more. My skin flushed under his gaze.

"My contacts located Remy Collins. He's Melissa's younger brother."

My eyebrows shot up. "I take it that means your team was able to dig deeper into her life now that Blake shared more details?"

He gave a nod. "Remy emancipated himself when he was a teenager. Had a falling-out with his parents and distanced himself from the family. He didn't have contact with anyone from the family. Or so we thought."

"I wonder if he did it for the same reasons Melissa rebelled. The affair Blake mentioned?" I said more to myself. "Where is he located?"

"Quebec City. He's a chef at a restaurant in Old Quebec. We were able to get in touch with him and he's expecting us to come there for questioning."

"Us?"

"I want you with me, Emily." My heart rate spiked at the way he said it, unsaid meaning laced within those words. He cleared his throat and straightened. "For safety reasons. I'd feel better having my eye on you," he recovered. "With everything we've seen from Overwatch, I don't trust anyone but myself to protect you. It's about five hours away. You think you can get the next couple of days off from the café?"

"I have tomorrow off already. I'll just see if I can switch with Jo to get off on Friday too. She'll understand. She wants us to figure this out as well."

"Great. I'll make arrangements then."

"Great."

We stared at each other for a moment longer, the tension hanging between us. I thought maybe he'd want to discuss what happened between us in the kitchen. I secretly hoped he'd want to continue where we left off.

I chided myself. I couldn't even keep my distance for five minutes before I almost gave in to my weakness. My insides hummed as I looked at him. He was ruggedly male with his dark five o'clock shadow and broad build. He could be considered a bad boy at first glance with the way he had perfected brooding. But I knew underneath it all there was a kinder side to him. He was almost mine and I couldn't have him.

Finally, Ben spoke, unaware of the war raging inside

me. "Okay, right then. Well, I'll let you get some sleep. Goodnight."

"Night," I said softly to his retreating back.

I flopped back down onto the bed and let out an exasperated sigh. I lay there for an hour, festering in my thoughts. Why did things have to be so messy? All I wanted was to move on after things ended with Trevor. I was going to focus on building my business, rediscover who I was after the uncoupling, and get on with my life. Instead, I was tied up dealing with Trevor's affair, my business might be collateral damage, and my quest for independence had been derailed by the devastatingly handsome live-in detective who I couldn't be with.

Needless to say, things weren't going according to plan.

Aside from being the mistress of my former fiancé, Melissa was nothing to me. So why was I being sought out and essentially punished for her mistakes?

I slammed my fists into the pillows. It really was unfair. I was sick of being on edge and fearful of doing the wrong thing because of the repercussions. Now I was pissed. Where did Overwatch get off telling me what to do? I couldn't live my life as someone's puppet, even if he had the capability of taking everything away from me. I spent part of my adult life in an unhealthy relationship, one in which Trevor called the shots and I pretended everything was fine. In the end, what was I left with? A life in shambles and some psycho forcing me to investigate a murder that had nothing to do with me.

This was bullshit.

I stood up and paced my room, a sense of resolve washing over me. What did they say in *Fight Club*? Something about after losing everything you were free to do anything?

Yeah, that sounded right.

I had worked hard to make it in Portland and build a successful business. If I didn't cater to every whim of Overwatch, then all of that might come crashing down. But I was tired of being afraid, tired of being told what to do. And tired of this person using my business, my friends, my livelihood, and my apartment to control me.

Enough was enough. I was done.

This might be the stupidest decision I could ever make, but from now on I was going to do things my way. If I lost everything because of it, so be it. Everything in my life might be taken away but I still had me, and I still had the ability to choose what I wanted for my life. And I liked those chances.

With a new sense of purpose, I walked determinedly to the door. I was going to tell Ben our new game plan.

Find Overwatch.

I was certain Overwatch was at the center of everything. Screw the timer. And screw the fact that Ben's team couldn't find anything on this person. Once we got back from speaking to Remy, I had a new idea.

We were going to bait Overwatch.

As I stomped across the wood floor, a hollow noise sounded under my foot.

Confused, I stomped my foot down again. I heard the noise. How had I never noticed this?

Probably because I wasn't usually walking around with Hulk rage. But nonetheless.

I moved my foot and felt the board shift ever so slightly. I got down on my knees and dug my nails in the creases between the boards. It was loose but too tight to pull out.

I raced out to the kitchen to get a knife for some leverage. Back in the room, I jammed it into the crack and maneuvered it so the loose board would pull out. I grabbed it and put it aside. Using the flashlight on my phone, I lit up the dark space underneath the floorboards and saw what looked like a folder. Sticking my hand in, I pulled it out and inspected it.

Suddenly, a memory flashed through my mind of Trevor ransacking my room to find something Melissa had left behind. Could this be it?

I opened the folder and found documents about a man named Jason McFalls. There was no photo, and the files were limited. I read on and learned this person was in the foster system, but the last known foster family was when he was eighteen. That was five years ago. What happened since then? Did the state stop tracking information after someone became an adult or did something else happen?

I was perplexed. Was this a case Melissa was working on? If so, why was it so important that she hid it here?

In my gut, I knew Jason McFalls was important. I just didn't know why yet.

CHAPTER 21

Ben's experience as an undercover cop was apparent the next morning. He was thorough, to say the least.

We knew Overwatch had eyes and ears on us so he took extreme measures to ensure we couldn't be found. That meant leaving our personal cell phones behind (we still had our burners). Taking a beat-up undercover car that was so old, no GPS was available. The car predated me and left much to be desired. It also meant having someone else book our stay at the hotel. It was all very secretive and intense, but I was glad to know that maybe, for once, my every move wasn't being watched.

On the ride up to Quebec, I decided to bring Ben up to speed.

"Although I wish I had known sooner, I'm glad you waited until we were out of earshot of Overwatch," he finally said after I finished.

I gave him a guilty look. "Honestly, that wasn't the reason I didn't wake you up last night. I was having a moment."

He shot me a glance from the driver's seat. "What kind of moment?"

"The kind where I was certain it was in our best interest to pump the brakes on what's going on between us." He started to say something. "But after consideration, I decided against it," I added quickly. I looked out the window for a moment. "I want to go after Overwatch."

"We've been trying, Emily. I still have guys working on it."

I turned my gaze to him. "I have a different idea."

He frowned. "Why do I have a feeling I'm not going to like this?"

I gave an innocent smile. "Because you're not. We're going to bait him. And by we, I mean me. I'm going to offer myself up."

"Absolutely not. No." He was furious, glancing over quickly to see if I was serious but knowing he needed to keep his eyes on the road. "You're out of your mind if you think I'm going to let you do this." His hands tightened on the steering wheel, causing his knuckles to go white.

I held my chin up defiantly. "I'm going to do it whether you like it or not—"

"Like hell you will."

"Ben," I said, softening my tone. "I need you to trust me. If we don't do this, either it will never end, or it won't end well. We need to take back some control."

He glanced at me again, saying nothing. I knew him well enough now to know when it was time to keep my mouth shut. He was angry, that was for sure. But I could see the wheels turning. He was practical, even if what I was asking was anything but.

"Fine."

"Fine?"

"I don't like it," he ground out, the muscle in his jaw ticking. "But I'll do it. My way," he emphasized.

"Well, Detective Hunter, I think we have ourselves a deal."

• • •

The rest of the ride was uneventful. The endless rolling hills and mountainside were peppered with tiny towns and lulled me to sleep a couple hours in. It was probably the most restful sleep I'd had in weeks.

"Emily," I heard Ben say off in the distance, stirring me awake.

"Huh?"

"We're almost there. I just thought you might enjoy the scenery."

I rubbed my eyes and sat straighter in my seat, adjusting my eyes to the bright summer sun. I looked ahead and saw a town that looked like it was straight from Europe. Or a storybook. Either way, it was gorgeous.

We drove down quaint streets past the Château Frontenac and wound our way through the cobblestoned streets of Old Quebec. My mouth fell open as I took in the architecture that housed the charming shops and restaurants. I was in love.

Ben pulled up to Hotel 71 in Old Quebec and handed off the keys to a valet. A bellhop promptly took our bags while we checked in.

"This is my kinda place," I noted as I saw the wine stations in the lobby. Pour your own wine? Hell yeah.

Ben gave an amused smile. "Maybe you can indulge a bit *after* we do what we came here for."

I waved him off. "Yeah, yeah."

Remy worked at the Italian restaurant within the hotel called Mateo's. He'd be on later this evening, which meant we had some time to kill.

We followed the bellhop to the small elevators and smushed ourselves in, making our way to the seventh floor. He led us down the hall and stopped at room 724.

I looked around. "Is my room on this floor too?"

Ben gave a sheepish smile. "They didn't have connecting rooms. I got us a double."

I swallowed. Sharing a room with Ben seemed dangerous...or good? Either way, excitement and nerves coursed through me as I realized there wouldn't be anything to separate us. Sharing an apartment was one thing. Being practically in the same bed was another. I gave him a sidelong glance and saw his expressions mirrored how I felt. "That's okay," I replied breathlessly.

"Okay. Good." It was endearing to see how nervous he was about it.

He slipped the key card in and gave us access. The bellhop placed our bags in the corner before offering any other assistance. Ben waved him off with a tip.

The door closed with a resounding thud, announcing that we were in fact alone in our shared room. I spun on my heel to distract myself and took in the space. Once again, I was in awe. The room was impressive, with high ceilings, refurbished wood floors, and tall windows that overlooked the old town and St. Lawrence River.

"It's so beautiful here. I feel like I was transported to an old European village." I sat on the window ledge and turned to Ben, who was unpacking his things. "I bet this place is stunning during Christmas. Can you imagine all the stone buildings and alleys decorated with garland, wreaths, and twinkling lights? A light dusting of snow coming down on shoppers?" I let out a wistful sigh.

Ben grinned. I wanted to kiss his dimple. "Big on Christmas, huh?"

"Yeah. It's hard to be anything but happy and hopeful around Christmas." I gave a small frown. "Trevor always said I was over the top about it, but I never let that put a damper on it for me. I consider myself an eternal optimist during the season."

"Only during the season?" he asked skeptically.

"Well yeah. I'm not insane. Those people who are happy all the time scare me a bit."

He let out a deep laugh and I couldn't help but laugh along with him. The sound of his laughter soothed my soul in a way I was desperate for.

He placed the last of his clothes in the closet and turned back to me. "Maybe you'll get a chance to come see Christmas here this year."

"That would be nice." I smiled. Ben cocked his head and looked at me thoughtfully. "You seem different today."

"How so?"

"I'm not sure. Less burdened? More determined? I guess that's the best way to describe it. Either way, I like this side of you I'm discovering."

I bit my lip and grinned at him. "I guess we're both discovering it. I know we're still in the thick of the case but knowing Overwatch can't find us is liberating. This is pretty much the first opportunity for me to feel like I can move on."

I patted the ledge beside me, encouraging Ben to take a seat. He obliged. "Being here makes me realize how important it is for us to find out who Overwatch is. If I can feel this way within a few hours of leaving Portland, it's worth fighting for with everything we've got. We're going to find him," I said confidently. "Clearly this person lives nearby to be able to get into my apartment. I don't care if we have to scour every damn house and apartment in the city. It's time we turned the tables."

"I agree. I thought it over more while you were sleeping. Although these leads are helpful in getting the story behind Melissa, we're no closer to finding the killer. It's time to go to the source."

"Find the source. Find the killer." I jumped off the ledge and smoothed a hand over my clothes, straightening out the wrinkles from the car ride. "All right. Remy won't be in for another few hours, so why don't we actually enjoy ourselves for once? Maybe grab a coffee and wander around?"

"Works for me."

We made our way down to the lobby and walked to the Place Royale, where we stopped at a café for some coffees and enjoyed watching the tourists mill about, stopping to take pictures of the Notre Dame.

Ben nodded his head at the tourists. "You know this is where they shot that final scene for *Catch Me if You Can?*"

I looked at the beautiful stone church and squinted. "Huh. Guess you're right."

I leaned back in my chair and closed my eyes, basking in the summer sun. It felt good on my skin, and the vitamin D was already working wonders for my mood. "I know you haven't been in Portland long but how do you like it so far?" I asked Ben. Our conversations had been so focused on finding Melissa's murderer that it was nice to have a normal chat for once.

He considered the question and took a sip of his espresso. "You know, I thought it would be a temporary move. Maybe a couple years tops. I couldn't picture myself living so far north but it's growing on me. It's not a bad place to start over, and maybe that opinion will be even truer once I can actually take time to settle in and explore."

"Why? Is a murder investigation ruining your social life or something?" I asked with a laugh.

"Something like that." His smile reached his eyes and I couldn't help but stare. I loved the way his skin crinkled around them when he was truly happy. Although broody Ben was sexy in itself—at times—this was the best I'd seen him yet. He looked at peace.

I brought us back to the conversation. "Portland is really great," I replied earnestly. "It's part of the reason I ended up growing roots there with Crafty Café and convinced Joanna to move up."

He nodded. "I lived in a small town all my life where everyone knew everyone. It's good to take some time to be who I need to be."

I blew on my coffee before taking a tentative sip. "How do you mean?"

"After the whole thing with Callie and Grayson. Everyone kept saying things would work out. That I should forgive them. You know, small-town gossip and Bible Belt talk. They kept pushing and pushing. To be honest, they made me feel like I was in the wrong for being angry and cutting them out."

I took his hand and laced my fingers with his, giving him an encouraging smile.

"With small towns like Wilmington, there are a lot of expectations on people. Me moving away wasn't about being selfish or a coward. It also wasn't because I couldn't handle Callie and Grayson being together, which was hard, mind you. The truth is, I figured if they would go so far with an affair, then there must have been something more between them than just attraction. My relationship with Callie could never be the same after she got pregnant. I mean, how would that work? Would Grayson and I share Callie? Would we act as co-fathers?" He shook his head.

"I left because I figured maybe they would have a chance with me out of the picture. She wanted a family. My work wouldn't allow it right then. Grayson gave her what she wanted. No need for me to be there and make things harder for them."

I cupped his cheek with my hand and gazed into his hazel eyes. "You're a good man, Ben. You know that?"

He took my hand in his. "I tried. I feel horrible that she lost the baby but her coming to find me in Portland is going against what I was trying to accomplish. Grayson made her happier than me. I just want her to move on and be happy."

"You did your part. You can't control what she does."

"I guess you're right." He scrubbed a hand down his face. "It's been strange to go through it all. They were big parts of my life. They made me who I was. Now..." he trailed off.

"Now you get to shape the kind of person you want to be in this new chapter of life. And so do I."

"It's a little overwhelming going through this on my own."

I let out a laugh. "It's a lot overwhelming! I have Jo and I still feel like I'm lost, like I have no anchor holding me down and I might get washed away to sea."

He held my hand and we sat in companionable silence as we considered how our lives had changed and how similar our situations felt. "I guess we have each other," he finally said. "We'll keep each other grounded."

I gave his hand a squeeze, feeling at ease for the first time in the last few weeks. It was great knowing I had Ben in my corner.

We spent the next couple of hours wandering around the quaint streets of Quebec, popping into shops to pass the time. I made a point to stop by a sugar shack and one of the many chocolatiers in the area. For competitive research, of course. But I think Ben knew I simply was enjoying the ability to explore new culinary treats. I made sure to buy enough to take back for Joanna, Delores, and the girls, but I would probably sneak a bit before I made it to Portland.

Ben checked his watch. "We should head back. Remy will be ready to talk to us in about twenty minutes."

As much as I wanted to enjoy the rest of the day and pretend the issues in Portland weren't happening, I knew it was time to get back to reality. The sooner we sorted this out, the sooner I would have control over my life again and figure out which direction I was going to take. Hopefully, Ben would be part of that equation.

We made our way to the hotel and took a seat at the bar of Mateo's. It was just before opening, so the restaurant was quiet aside from the bartenders, kitchen staff, and waiters bustling around.

"We're here to see Remy Collins. He's expecting us," Ben said to the bartender. Gone was the easy-going Ben from a few moments ago. Now he was in detective mode. All serious. Hundred-percent male.

God, he was hot.

A man with curly strawberry-blond hair came out from the kitchen. He was lean, but not muscular like Ben, with piercing blue eyes. He greeted us warmly. "Hello, Detective Hunter and Miss Ayers, I'm Chef Collins. Thank you for making the trip to Quebec. We have a few big events happening this week and it was impossible for me to come to Portland."

"You mentioned. It's fine. We appreciate you squeezing us in."

"Of course. Melissa and I may not have had the most traditional family relationship, but I still want to do my part to help find justice." He gestured to a table in a back corner. "Follow me. This section should be quiet enough for us to talk for now."

Remy waited for us to be seated before taking his own. "So how can I help you, Detective?"

"We're hoping you could shed some light on Melissa's relationship with Blake, specifically in regard to money." He pulled out a notebook, poised to write down Remy's account.

Remy's eyebrows shot up, and he let out a whistle. "You know about that? Wow. I'm surprised Blake was so forthcoming."

"He was. He also mentioned that the monthly payments Melissa was making stopped a few months before her death."

Remy looked surprised. "She did? Melissa and I reconnected about four years ago but had only gotten closer over the last year. I'm savvy at accounting so she had enlisted my guidance for her personal bookkeeping. It was my first love before cooking," he added as a side note. "That's when I saw the monthly transactions to her ex."

"Did you advise her to stop these transactions?"

"I did. Although she was doing well in her career, her finances were taking a hit. The last eight months or so, she was struggling to maintain her lifestyle, almost to the point where she was worried about paying her mortgage. We looked at her finances and I told her to cut down on unnecessary expenses, including those payments to Blake. She seemed against it, but I didn't want to push her after we finally built that relationship." He gave a tight smile. "I was happy to have my sister back in my life."

I interjected. "I'm confused. Melissa had moderately expensive tastes, of course, but nothing so over the top to make her worry about money. I know how much Trevor made when he was a lawyer there, and we could assume

Melissa would have made the same. He wasn't exactly frugal about his spending and still had plenty to pay off his student loans and was saving for a down payment on a house in the city. She must had had some serious debt to make her worry like that."

"Any idea about that?" Ben asked.

Remy folded his hands on the tabletop while he considered the question. "I wish I knew. I had the same concerns but didn't see anything in her accounts that was out of the ordinary. No loan or debts that would drain her like that. She wasn't forthcoming about what put her in the situation and, once again, I wasn't going to push the subject."

"When was the last time you saw her?"

"About a month before she was killed. I was in Portland meeting with a chef I was doing a collaboration with for a wine and food festival. She and I met for dinner the night before I came back to Canada."

"Did she seem off-kilter? Say anything out of the ordinary?"

He shook his head. "Nope. Same old Melissa." He scratched his chin. "Well, except…"

I leaned forward expectantly. "Except what?"

"She made this comment. Something about how brave I was to stand up for myself and go through with the emancipation. She said it must have been hard to start over from nothing and become so successful. She said she admired my grit and it was something she wanted to live up to."

"That doesn't seem so strange," Ben commented.

"Maybe not, had we been talking about it. It came out of the blue. And then she had this face while she said it. Almost like she was lost or scared? I couldn't quite put a finger on it. Before I could ask, she excused herself to the restroom and then changed the subject completely when she returned. I talked to her one more time between that dinner and when she passed away. She called to wish me a happy birthday and we talked briefly but she said she had to go back to court."

Ben scribbled a few more notes in his small notebook. "Do you have any reason to believe Melissa was in some sort of trouble?"

"Melissa and I had a challenging childhood. It's part of the reason I left in the first place. But she was tough. Scrappy. She made the best of it. Adapted. And found a way to survive. If she was involved in something sketchy, I have no doubt she had a plan to make it out ahead just like she overcame her drug addiction."

I shot him a look. "This time she didn't though."

That sobered him. "No. This time she didn't." He gave a sad sigh. "Look, if she was in some sort of trouble, she never shared it with me. Melissa was a private person. She only let people know what she wanted them to know. We had gotten closer, but not to the point where she confided everything to me. I didn't even know she had stopped the payments to Blake."

Ben and I looked at each other for a beat. "I see," Ben stated. "We looked at Melissa's will and didn't see you listed. Do you find that strange that she wouldn't have her only surviving family member on there?"

Remy shook his head. "Like I said, we just reconnected. I wouldn't have expected her to include me."

"She had a charity listed instead." Ben flipped through his notes and read off the name. "We haven't been able to locate any information on it. Seems like it's a front for something."

"Never heard of it," Remy said while scratching his head in thought. "We went through her finances but that name never came up."

"Is there anything else you could add?"

"Not that I can think of."

"If you think of anything, please let me know. Even the smallest detail can make a difference."

"Will do, Detective."

"We'll be staying in the hotel tonight so feel free to ring us if something comes to mind."

Remy stood, signaling the end of the conversation. "Of course. And please, feel free to dine with us this evening. The meal will be on me as my gratitude for you coming all the way to Quebec. It's the least I can do."

• • •

Ben and I sat in our room, each on our respective double bed. "Well, that seemed like a big waste of time." I kicked off my shoes and slipped under the covers.

"Nothing is a waste of time. What might seem insignificant now could be a helpful clue later on." He eyed me as I was fluffing my pillows. "It's not even five p.m. What are you doing?"

"Just trying to get comfortable while I mull this over."

"Don't get too settled; you don't want to miss your early-bird dinner." He cracked a smile.

"Ha. Ha. Very funny. After all the sleepless nights lately, can you blame me if I really was settling in for bed?"

"I guess you're right." He rested back onto his own bed, feet still hanging off to the side.

I gave him a sidelong glance, mentally calculating the space between us. There were maybe three feet max between my bed and his. Lately, the distance between us in my apartment seemed too close, too tempting. Now here we were, practically in the same bed. It was going to be a challenge to keep my hormones and hands in check.

Ben turned to me as if sensing my thoughts. I could have sworn I saw his pupils dilate, overtaking those alluring hazel eyes staring back at me. He eyed the space between our beds, as if going through the same thought process as me, and slowly looked back at me. He let out a slow, shaky breath as I held mine.

This was going to be a long night.

I gripped the comforter in my hands as a way to release the anxiousness that overwhelmed me—and to stop them from reaching out to him. His eyes flickered to my hands, lingering for a second before holding my gaze again. He began to move, slowly sitting up, as if he was fighting the urge to come closer but couldn't stop himself. He stood, eyes never leaving mine, and started to take a step to my bed.

The blaring of the room phone between us broke our trance. I half wanted to smash it and see where this evening was going and half thanked it because I wasn't sure if I was ready to take the plunge. I wanted Ben and after that hot kiss the night before, I knew I needed more of him. But right here, right now?

I wanted the moment to be right. After weeks of things going to hell, I wanted to be in control of something. Something that could be perfect. I didn't want the stress of Overwatch or a dead body looming over us. I wanted to be clear-minded so I could enjoy all Ben had to offer.

A look of frustration flashed across his face as he hesitated to grab it. After the third ring, he snatched it up.

"Yeah?" He answered gruffly. He listened for a moment before telling the caller he'd be there and hanging up.

"Who was that?"

"Remy. Said he remembered one other detail that might be of use. He asked us to meet him downstairs."

"Ok," I said regretfully, hating the thought of leaving the exclusiveness of our room. But it was for the best. Maybe.

I slipped my shoes on, checked myself in the full-length mirror, and grabbed my purse before we made our way down the corridor to the elevator bank. I hit the down button. "What do you think it will be?" I asked Ben as we waited.

"He didn't say, but hopefully it gives us a little more to go on than what we got from him so far." We stepped on the elevator and rode in silence to the main floor, but the heat between us was still strong. I nearly jumped out of my skin.

Remy was waiting by the entrance of the restaurant, gesturing for us to follow him to the quiet table we had sat at only a few minutes before.

"After you left, there was something nagging at me in the back of my mind. I finally remembered what it was but don't know if it's of any use."

Ben looked at him expectantly. "Fire away."

"The last time I saw Melissa, she took a phone call. She walked into another room and kept her voice down, but I could hear bits of her side of the conversation. She said things like, 'I need more time' and 'You'll get it.' When she walked back into the room, she looked flustered and stressed. When I asked her about it, she said she was having some issues with someone at work."

"Did she say who it was on the phone or what it was about?"

"No. I didn't want to push. But she told me not to worry about it and she would get things sorted out with *him*. That it was just a misunderstanding. So I'm assuming it was a guy from her work."

"Could have been a case they were working on together," I suggested.

Remy regarded me. "Yeah, I thought that too. But something about it made me almost certain it was something personal. I couldn't hear much but I did catch two names. Jason and Trevor."

CHAPTER 22

"**S**eems like things are leading back to Trevor. Again." Ben said from the chair nestled in the corner of our room.

I paced back and forth, like I usually did when I was trying to piece something together. "Seeming and being are two different things, Ben. I thought we ruled him out."

"How could you be so sure it isn't Trevor? There's more than enough evidence stacking up against him."

"But not enough evidence to actually pin this murder on him. Don't you think that's significant?"

He gave a noncommittal shrug.

"Plus, I just know it couldn't be Trevor."

"How?"

I stopped in front of him. "I feel it in my gut."

"Could be indigestion," Ben muttered to himself. "Emily, you can't say a man is innocent based on a gut feeling. You just can't."

"Like you've never had hunches before?"

He just grunted in response.

"None of those facts have distinctly said Trevor is a murderer," I argued passionately. "What happened to innocent until proven guilty?"

He leaned forward in the chair and rested his elbows on his muscular thighs. "Emily," he started softly. "This case is unlike anything I've ever dealt with, and I've dealt with some crazy shit. We can't rule anyone out yet."

I looked up at the ceiling, trying to keep my emotions in check. Trevor was an asshole for what he did to me, especially how he treated me at the end of our relationship. But that didn't mean he deserved to take the fall for something I truly believed he didn't do.

"Then why was he so desperate to find out what Melissa was hiding at the apartment?"

"Ok, let's consider that for a minute. You found a folder with information about someone named Jason McFalls, who seemed to have disappeared after he turned eighteen—"

"Another ghost, just like Melissa's past," I interjected. After another one of my Google searches, I came up empty-handed. Hopefully, Ben's team would have better luck.

"Remy heard Melissa say the names Jason and Trevor during a tense phone call," Ben continued. "Maybe Trevor was covering his tracks. Maybe Jason was an accomplice and Trevor was trying to hide the evidence."

I shook my head. "Trevor said she had left a folder in our apartment but didn't know the contents of it."

"It could all be an act."

"Fine. Let's take this Jason person out of the equation and consider the theory that it was someone from Melissa's work," I said. "How many men work at their firm? There's Trevor and Fred, the partners at the firm who wield the most power. Then there's Joe Robinson and Mike Ellis, two lawyers at the firm. Then there's Jimmy McHale, a paralegal. Andy Anderson, the IT intern. And Clark De-Voe, the paralegal intern. Also, there's some new guy," I snapped my fingers as I tried to think of his name.

Ben flipped through his notebook. "Rob Ferraro, the accountant. Started three months ago."

"Right. That's eight guys right there. And that's if we take her words literally. Melissa said she was having some issues with someone at work. That doesn't necessarily mean someone who physically worked at the firm. It could be someone she's working with on a number of things. A judge, a client, a witness. It could be anyone."

"Not to mention we don't know what the issue was. It could have been a simple work problem or disagreement. Not something worth killing over."

"Right. And it's possible Trevor was helping with a case, which is why his name was mentioned, not because he was the one giving her grief." I rolled my shoulders and stretched my neck. "You know, I always thought being a detective was cool. Solving puzzles and having 'aha' moments. This is not what I expected it to be."

The corner of his mouth quirked. "It has its challenges and a lot of the time the 'aha' moments come quietly. Gradually."

"So you don't look at your crime boards and suddenly discover the missing link between the yarn?"

"I'm afraid not. It tends to be a lot messier than those perfect lines of yarn connecting one person to the crime." He let out a small laugh. "I wouldn't know where to begin with this one. It's getting more complicated as the hours go on."

I bit my lip as I tried to visualize what the crime board would look like for this case. Ben cocked a head as he assessed me from his chair. "What?"

"Nothing. You just surprise me."

I crossed my arms and raised an eyebrow. "What? Is my neurotic side showing?"

He shook his head. "You're strong, smart, and brave, Emily." His voice was thick with emotion. He stood up and crossed the room, taking my hands in his. "It's admirable. Most people would hide out until this was all over or crumble under the pressure. But you... well, you're determined and willing to do what it takes to find the truth. You dive right in with no fear."

I swallowed. "Maybe I'm a little selfish. I want Overwatch to stop sending me messages. I want to bring the murderer to justice. And I want to move on with my life like I was trying to do before Melissa ended up dead behind my coffee shop. I just want to know how my life will be post-Trevor like a normal person. Maybe that's the driving force behind my determination."

"Maybe, but it doesn't change the fact that you're still smart, strong, and brave." He regarded me a moment longer, searching my face. "And beautiful."

I sucked in a breath just before he dipped his head down, painstakingly slow, and captured my lips. All the near misses and interruptions we'd had over the last couple of weeks were being made up for in this one kiss, and before anyone could stop us again, I wanted to experience it all with him.

He wrapped his arms around my body, pulling me against his solid frame as he deepened the kiss. I rested my arms on his broad shoulders and shoved my hands in his thick hair, giving him more leverage. Easing his tongue into my mouth, he moved in sync with mine. The sound and feel of his masculine groan against my lips only stoked the fire burning within me. I moved my body against him, urging him to keep going.

All my nerve endings came alive with every movement and touch. I couldn't remember the last time I felt like this, if ever. I was coming undone. Almost out of control. And I didn't even give a damn. I needed him. Every inch of him.

He lifted me up and I wrapped my legs around his hips, feeling his desire growing for me with each passing second. His hands gripped my ass to hold me steady, his fingers massaging me and making me lose my inhibitions. If he could make me feel this good with such a simple act, I wondered what was in store.

His mouth moved from my lips, down my jaw, and to my neck, hitting erogenous zones along the way. I all but moaned at the sensation of his tongue teasing the sensitive spots of my skin. Delightful goose bumps rose in the trail he left behind with his mouth. He carried me to the edge of my bed and placed me down gently.

He broke the kiss, pressing his forehead against mine. "I want you so badly, Emily. I've wanted you for so long." His voice was ragged, as if he had just run a marathon. It turned me on to know I could cause this response in him.

"I want you too. Right now."

He pulled away slightly and looked me in the eyes. "Are you sure?"

"Absolutely."

A smile tugged on his lips before he kissed me again, pushing me down to the bed with one large hand. He rested on the side of me, enveloping me into his arms and pulling me against the length of his body. His hand snaked up the back of my shirt, and the feeling of his fingertips on my skin turned me inside out.

I was desperate to find out what it would feel like to be skin against skin, him inside of me.

I ran my hands up his chest and unbuttoned his shirt one by one. I was torn between the impulse to remove it in one quick tug and the desire to take my time and savor the moment. In the end, I found somewhere in between frantic and languid.

I pulled open his shirt to reveal an immaculate body. I knew he was fit but seeing it with my own eyes was something else. His rounded pectorals had a light smattering of hair. His stomach was made of rock-hard abs without being obnoxious. His hips dipped in, leading to…well, I was bound to find out.

I pulled his shirt off him and tossed it aside. To be able to rub my hands along the warm muscles of his shoulders and back had me going insane. But it wasn't enough to only have my hands on him. I wanted to feel it all.

As if sensing my needs, he pulled my shirt over my head, taking a moment to appreciate the view of me in my lacy black bra. He raked a hand over my ribs and dipped his head down to kiss the swell of my breasts.

"Please, Ben," I begged.

I needed to be naked. Now.

He moved a hand to my back and unhooked my bra, pulling it away and leaving me exposed to him. He wasted no time, taking a nipple into his mouth while massaging the other. My hands instinctively went to the zipper of his pants and tugged.

I was no longer thinking. All I wanted to do was live in this moment. To take it for all it was worth.

Ben matched my urgency, pulling his pants off quickly so he could help me out of mine. And within a flash of a moment, we lay wrapped up with each other. All tangled limbs, warm skin pressed against each other, and kissing so frantically I thought I would die.

And then his hands moved between my legs and my brain all but short-circuited.

I never knew a man could be so in tune with a woman's body, especially the first time together. There was supposed to be a learning curve.

But Ben was something else entirely.

Within a matter of minutes, he had me on edge and I wanted to give in right then and there. The pressure building inside of me was unbearable, but it wasn't the way I wanted to let go.

"I need you inside me. Right now," I moaned against his mouth, writhing closer to him.

He rolled to the side, grabbing his discarded pants from the floor and pulling out a condom from his wallet. He sheathed himself before turning back to me. I wrapped my legs around his waist, lining us up perfectly. He only had to make a small move and he'd be right where I wanted him.

He looked me in the eyes as he rolled me fully on my back and positioned himself between my legs. And with a slow stroke, he entered me, watching my face the whole time as my body adjusted to him.

After ensuring I was all right, the real show began. He moved in purposeful strokes back and forth, eyes still on me. That alone was enough to do me in. Knowing he wanted to see my reaction to him turned me on like no other.

And within a few strokes, I came hard around him. He moved in rhythm to let me ride it out, kissing me roughly while I moaned his name over and over.

As the aftershocks subsided, his pace increased. His muscles tensed as he worked his way to his own pleasure, deeper and faster as the moments went on. He grabbed my hips to get more leverage, sinking into me deeper.

His brow beaded with sweat and his face intensified. I bit his bottom lip as I kissed him, sensing he was just seconds away.

And so was I. Again.

And with that, we both came together. He let out a deep

groan that was so primal, I almost came again just from the sound of it.

After the waves of satisfaction slowed, he rolled onto his side, pulling me to him. I rested my head on his chest as he pushed back my hair, now stuck to my face from the sweat, and kissed my forehead.

"Wow," was all I could muster in between labored breaths.

"I second that."

I knew the connection I had with Ben was strong, but I never would have imagined the chemistry between us would be that mind-blowing. After having an experience like that, I didn't know if I could stop.

So I didn't. "Again?"

He gave me a sexy smile and pulled me on top of him.

• • •

To say sleeping that night was impossible would be an understatement but for once I didn't mind it. I had to give it to Ben to be able to keep up with my demands. But I was more impressed with myself. A sex goddess? After last night's escapades, maybe I did have it in me after all.

We fell asleep together at some point in the early morning. The darkness of night was starting to lessen, making me believe dawn was just about to break. I debated waking up Ben again for another round but seeing him there so peacefully asleep made me consider otherwise. This wouldn't be the one and only night we had together.

I hoped.

Ben gently shook me awake. "Emily," he called. "Time to get up."

I opened one eye a crack to see Ben fully showered and dressed. I must have been so zonked out that I didn't even notice he left the bed. He held out a cup of coffee and the aroma was enough to get both my eyes open. "Need coffee." I didn't care if I sounded like a zombie, I was a force to reckon with on this little sleep with no caffeine.

I grabbed the warm cup from his hand and took a healthy sip. "You are a godsend."

"Figured you might need it with how little you slept last night." He looked at me with smoldering intensity, making me want to jump him again.

But coffee won out.

He took a seat on the bed next to me. I pushed my rat's nest of hair out of my face so he could kiss me. "Let's get packed up and head back to Portland. We can grab breakfast from the buffet downstairs before we leave."

After a quick shower—which I was tempted to invite him to—I tossed the remainder of my things in my overnight bag. Ben had spent that time making calls to his team, giving them an update on our conversation with Remy, and letting them know we'd have to question the remaining men of the office again. He informed me they had no luck locating Jason McFalls yet.

Ben grabbed our bags as we made our way to the elevator. "You know, one of my gut feelings is nagging at me," I said.

Ben had the courtesy not to roll his eyes, even though I was sure he wanted to. "Go on."

"I truly think whoever is harassing me with details and clues about Melissa's murder might be tied to it somehow. I know I said it before, but I believe it even more now."

"Why would someone go through that trouble to give you information if they were involved? *Cui bono?*"

"Uh, what?"

"It's Latin for 'who benefits?' I thought with all your sleuthing research you would have come across that term by now."

I gave him a playful punch to the arm. "Shut up." I grinned. "But no, seriously. That's what's making me think it's all tied together. What would be the benefit for Overwatch other than framing someone else? We've been led down so many paths investigating people who would clearly benefit from Melissa's death. If it's none of them, then someone else must be reaping the biggest benefit of them all."

I followed Ben onto the elevator and punched the lobby button. "Could be that the person just wants to see justice," he challenged.

"Then why not just give us the facts outright rather than making us go on this chase with dead ends? There seem to be more questions than answers at this point. If this person really wanted to see justice done, why not speed up the process? Why go through so much effort?"

"Just because someone hands over a name and claims that he or she murdered someone doesn't mean it will stick. We need hard evidence to back that claim. As far as I see it, we have yet to get a solid piece of information that can concretely tell us who murdered Melissa Maher."

I gave him a sideways glance. "Otherwise, Trevor would be locked up by now."

He let out a sigh. "If evidence proved that Trevor was behind this, then yes. He would be behind bars."

We took the short ride down to the lobby as I continued to argue my theory. I knew Ben was playing devil's advocate but I still felt strongly about my idea. Maybe I didn't have the evidence that he wanted but something about it felt right to me.

The elevator doors opened up to a bustling lobby. The

smells of freshly cooked bacon and roasted coffee wafted from the restaurant, causing our debate to halt. My stomach grumbled loudly.

Ben paused mid-sentence and looked at me, bemused. "What was that?"

"My stomach. I'm starving."

He gave a hearty laugh. "I should have guessed. Come on. Let's get you fed."

As we made our way to the breakfast buffet, another nagging thought came to mind. "I still don't understand what my purpose is in all of this. Why is this person so adamant about involving me? None of these leads seem to have anything to do with me other than Trevor."

Ben scooped a heaping pile of eggs and sausage into a to-go container. He held up a spoon of breakfast potatoes in offering. I gave him a quick nod before he dumped them into my container. He eyed them and me before deciding to scoop another spoon for me. He knew me too well.

"Whoever is behind this keeps their cards close to their heart. When they want you to know your purpose, they'll tell you."

"Like I said yesterday, I'm done letting someone else dictate my life. I think the person behind all of this, the anonymous messages, *and* the murder is one and the same and is closer than we think."

Ben's phone chirped. He grabbed it from his pocket and frowned.

"What is it?"

He closed up our to-go boxes and grabbed our luggage. "We gotta get moving. A weather alert says a big storm is going to roll through Maine. I don't want to be stuck in that. Not in that hunk of junk we're driving."

We made our way to the car and hit the road back to Portland. We drove in comfortable silence for several miles before my cell phone broke the quietness of the car. Ben's head whipped quickly in my direction, eyeing the burner phone in my hand with a questioning look.

"It's Jo. I didn't feel right leaving her without a way to contact me," I said to Ben before hitting the answer button. "Hey, Jo. What's up?"

"Just checking in on you. There's supposed to be some nasty weather coming."

"Yeah. Ben just said the same thing. We're on our way back now. Should be there in about five hours. How's the shop?"

"Great!" she said cheerily. "I got the shipment from that new vendor you wanted to try out and people *loved* it. Their stuff is so fresh. Anyway, we sold out of all the new stuff within the first few hours."

"Wow that's awesome, Jo. We'll have to think of more new items with their stuff when I get back."

"Of course! Did you learn anything new from Melissa's brother?"

I worried my bottom lip. "Nothing overwhelmingly helpful."

She let out a disappointed noise. "I was really hoping this lead was the one to help you catch the killer."

"You and me both, Jo. Listen, I'll be back in town later today. Come over for dinner."

"Sounds good. See you then!"

"Everything good?" Ben asked from the driver's seat.

"Everything's quiet on the home front for once." I turned to look out the window and let out a long sigh.

"Penny for your thoughts?"

I gave him a sidelong glance. "How did you know I had something on my mind?"

He gave a small laugh. "I've been around you enough

to pick up on the subtle changes. I also know you live in here," he said, tapping his head. "Plus, that sigh wasn't exactly quiet. Might as well unload."

Ben seemed to know my small quirks better than Trevor ever did. I guess that shows how oblivious I was to how much our relationship was lacking. Either that, or how pathetic I was to not know that there was better out there.

"Everything seems to lead back to Melissa's work. We've followed all these other potentials between her cases, her ex, and her family, but even with that, we're circling back constantly to someone who works at the firm."

"Not Trevor, I take it?" he asked with a hint of sarcasm.

"Humor me, will you?"

"Make your case, Miss Ayers," he responded in his most judge-like voice.

"I know a lot is going against Trevor. That I can't deny, but I know Trevor better than the police do."

"Not that well, apparently," Ben murmured quietly.

"Low blow. Although somewhat true in regard to Melissa, so I'm going to let that slide. Anyway, before you so rudely interrupted," I teased, "I know Trevor. And I know he's a smart guy, but he's no genius when it comes to technology. I can't tell you how many times he asked me for help on basic computer and phone stuff. For someone who grew up in the technology era, he was helpless."

Ben tilted his head as he pondered for a moment. "So you're saying he's too computer illiterate to be hacking your devices?"

"Exactly."

"Maybe so. But who's to say he didn't hire someone to help him?

"Seems a little bit risky, don't you think? He'd basically be giving someone access to his secret."

"Enough money could keep the right person quiet," Ben countered. "It could be that this Overwatch person was hired by Trevor and now he's blackmailing Trevor too."

I shook my head. "Trevor made good money with his promotion, but he wouldn't have enough money to keep someone quiet like that and still maintain his lifestyle."

"So then what's your theory?" Ben frowned as the heavens opened up and doused the car with relentless rain. "Shit. I thought we had a little more time to beat the storm." He slowed his speed and kicked on the windshield wipers and headlights. The ancient car seemed to be no match for the storm.

"Whoever did this to Melissa and is doing this to me has to be technically savvy, right? He'd have to be an insanely talented hacker. We know that. He also has to be close to Melissa. Know her life. Know her routine. Really *see* her. I don't think someone could pull this off if they weren't physically close by, you know?" As I said the words, one face came to mind.

It couldn't be. It made no sense.

But I felt it in my gut.

I shot up in my seat. "Get your team on the phone. I think I know who's behind this."

Ben tossed me his phone. "I should concentrate on the road. The Portland precinct is under my favorites. Give them a ring and put it on speaker."

Just as I turned on the home screen, a loud pop and thud sounded as he fought to control the car. "Hold on!" he yelled as he eased his way off to the shoulder.

I put a hand to my heart as I tried to slow my breathing. "What the hell happened?"

"By the sounds of it, I think we busted a tire. Damn car," he muttered. We sat for a moment, gathering ourselves as we watched a sheet of rain pour down. Rolling thunder sounded around us. He looked around and frowned. "Looks like we're the only ones out here. Guess we can't flag anyone down for help. I need to check the trunk for a spare. Pray there's one in there."

"Don't you think it's a little dangerous to be changing the tire in this weather? Not only could lightning strike you but the visibility is horrible. What if someone hits you?"

"This storm isn't going to let up anytime soon. I'd rather take my chances than sit here in the middle of nowhere." Ben checked the side mirror for oncoming cars. When he saw he was clear, he jumped out of the driver's seat and popped open the trunk. A few seconds later, he was back in the car, completely soaked. His shirt clung against his body, giving me flashbacks of the previous evening. I almost suggested another round right there.

"Nothing's there. We'll have to call AAA."

"Here." I handed him his phone.

"Goddamnit," he growled while furiously pounding the phone's buttons. "It won't turn on."

"What do you mean? The battery was full when you handed it to me not even two minutes ago."

"Something feels off." No sooner did he say it than a knock pounded at my window, startling us both. Ben instinctively grabbed his gun.

A man's face appeared in the window. He held a hand to his forehead to shield his eyes from the rain. "You all right?" he screamed above the thundering storm. "I saw you stranded here on the side of the road and wanted to see if I could give you a hand." He pointed a thumb over his shoulder. "I got a tow truck."

Ben grabbed my arm to get my attention. "I'm going to talk to him. Stay in the car and keep your door locked. Get the precinct on the phone."

"Okay. Jeez." I released my arm from his death grip and shook off the pain.

While Ben braved the storm to talk to the Good Samaritan, I pulled my phone out of my purse to see if I could call the precinct from there. Despite being a basic flip phone, the burner thankfully had a way to connect to the internet. I did a Google search for the number and watched as the phone slowly pulled up the results. With cell reception in this remote area of northwestern Maine, it could take until next year to get the results.

I looked up while I waited to see what was going on with Ben and the tow truck guy. In the downpour, I could only make out one of them still on the passenger side. The trucker must have gone back to his vehicle to get us strapped up.

Just as the search results came up with the number to the Portland station, a tap on my window sounded. I assumed Ben wanted to give me an update on what was going on. I cracked the door open and found myself staring down the barrel of a gun.

I looked up slowly. Not Ben.

"Wh-What?" I stammered. I looked past the man to see Ben unconscious on the ground. "You killed him!" I shrieked in horror.

"No," he said with a rough accent I couldn't place. "Not unless he drowns while he's passed out." The man jammed the gun into my ribs, and I winced in pain. "Get out of the car and come with me."

Fear washed over me, making me feel faint. My wobbly limbs caused me to stumble as I rigidly pulled myself out of the car. My brain was foggy from terror, as if everything was moving in slow motion. Through the haze, one smart thought came to mind. With my cell phone still in my hand, slightly out of the view of my captor, I clicked the screen and prayed to God I successfully hit the right area to call the police. And if I did, that the service out here would actually connect me to them.

The man pushed the gun into my back. "Drop the phone."

I carefully tossed the phone onto the seat so the screen was facedown. Maybe the police wouldn't be able to hear anything, but I hoped the strange call would alert them enough to connect with a local station and check it out. Surely Ben let them know this number belonged to a burner for emergencies? I prayed they'd find us in time.

"Why are you doing this?"

"Shut up. Keep walking to the truck." His scraggly hair was plastered to his cheek and in between the rain, I could sense a sinister look in his dark eyes.

It's the guy who took Melissa.

Not a damn car was on this strip of interstate during this storm. Had it been any other time, maybe someone would have seen what was happening and called for help. I kept my mouth shut as I slowly made my way to the tow truck, trying to prolong the walk as much as I could. I knew my situation would get worse as soon as I got in that truck.

I slipped in the mud, dropping hard to my knees. He yanked me up by my arm and shoved the gun into my back, pushing me forward. Before I knew it, we reached the driver's side and he shoved me in, quickly jumping in after me while still aiming the gun.

Without the rain nearly blinding me, I was able to inspect my kidnapper. I didn't know him, but something seemed off. For a man who at first look seemed to be aging quickly for his fifties, things didn't add up. Maybe it was in the nimble way he moved, as if old age hadn't stiffened his bones yet. Or perhaps it was the skin on his hands, which seemed too fresh for someone who would have spent years doing hard labor. Where were the callouses? The sunspots? The scars?

He drove with the gun in his left hand, out of my reach in case I was feeling bold. But as we sat in silence, driving in a direction far away from Portland, I felt anything but. I worried about Ben, who was lying lifelessly on the side of the drenched road. I worried about me and the fact that I had no idea where we were going or why. And I had no clue as to how to escape alive.

We drove for an hour, passing by endless forest and broken-down towns. As the houses became sparser and sparser, I felt the dread overcome me. Even if I got away, where would I run to? Maybe this man wouldn't kill me but something in those woods surely would.

I was shaken from my thoughts as the truck pulled onto a dirt road hidden in the thick forest. With the rain-washed roadway, the truck struggled in the mud, jerking around as it tried to grip onto anything stable to propel it forward. After slipping and sliding for another few minutes, he managed to free us and turned onto another gravel road heading deeper into the woods.

Fright and shock seeped into my bones, causing me to shake uncontrollably. No one would ever find me. I'd be lost forever without a trace. I wondered if this is how Melissa felt in her last moments.

He slowed down as we pulled up to an abandoned cabin. Peeling paint covered what was left of the shutters, and several beams on the porch lay broken. A smashed window in the front was boarded up, and the bushes surrounding the property were nothing but dead twigs.

As I looked at the house through the thundering rain, oppressive trees surrounding it, a sinking feeling settled in my stomach.

If I went into that house, I knew I wouldn't come out again.

CHAPTER 23

The man pushed me up the rickety front steps and into the dank, dimly lit cabin. He slammed the door behind us, dead-bolting it shut. I almost gagged on the rancid stench in the air and worried it was foreshadowing my future. It smelt like decaying flesh. Was it coming from another person he had kidnapped? Were they dead? I prayed it was the smell of a dead animal he was planning on butchering for dinner and not the scent of a human corpse in the other room.

The small space of the main area felt like it was closing in on me. My chest tightened.

I gulped in air, forcing a breath through my constricted throat. I knew I was scared shitless, but I needed to stay focused if I had any shot of getting away. I took another breath, which helped calm my anxiety slightly, enough to pay attention to the details around me. From what I could tell, there was only one door in and out. I counted six windows in total, half of them boarded up.

There would be no quick escape. If I was going to make it out of here, I'd have to find a way to take him down.

He forced me into a wooden chair by the fireplace—the only source of light in this tiny cabin—and tied me up securely. The ropes he used tore up my skin with the slightest movement. I wouldn't be able to get myself out of this one even if I gave it all I had. My hope wavered as I realized the plan I was formulating was now useless.

"What do you want?" I demanded.

"You just had to go fuck this all up, didn't you, Emily?"

My pulse spiked. I eyed him again, squinting in the dark room. I definitely didn't recognize this man, but he somehow knew me.

The man paced in front of me, clearly agitated. His movements were sharp and jerky. "I gave you simple instructions," he said, waving his gun in frustration. "You had a week. You had all the details to point back to the person who deserves to be charged for this."

"*You're* the person that's been harassing me? You're… Overwatch?"

"Harassing?" He scoffed as if offended. "I've been *helping* you. I've been trying to make you see who needed to be brought to justice. Everyone in this little situation is being brought to justice in one way or another." He laughed smugly.

Fear bubbled inside me as the man's tone sounded more unhinged. The gun was still firmly in his hand, but it shook slightly with his irritation. His finger was loose on the trigger, but one small twitch could set it off.

"Who are you?"

He let out a sigh and pinched the bridge of his nose. "Well, I guess we came this far and you won't have a chance to tell anyone after today, so what's the harm?" He asked more to himself.

He used his free hand to pull off the expertly placed

hair and prosthetics on his face. The amount of detail and skill was impressive. If Ben had been able to see his face in the rain, he would never be able to positively ID the man unfolding in front of me. The sinking feeling came back when I realized they'd never know who took me.

As he finished pulling off the last of his facade, he turned to me, shocking me to the core. "Andy?"

The quiet IT intern from the law firm, Kaminsky and Miller, stood before me. "Not who you would expect, huh? Those cops are idiots. All I had to do was play the part of inexperienced intern and they just assumed I didn't have the right hacking skills to even be a threat. It's amazing how much someone can learn on their own. No trace of schooling or work experience on my background check, I made sure of that." He seemed pleased with himself and, to be honest, he should have been. He had managed to get away with so much.

"Why? How?"

His satisfied expression turned to something more sinister. His eyes grew darker, and the soft planes of his youthful face hardened from anger. "There's a benefit to being 'invisible.' I was barely acknowledged at the office unless there was an issue or someone needed something. Otherwise, it was as if I was never there. The good thing about people not noticing you is the stuff you witness when they think no one is around. I saw it all. Pair that with the fact that I knew our servers inside and out, including all the things they thought they were hiding so well, and I learned a lot.

"For years I had been planning this. And then I was finally in their inner sanctuary, with all the information I needed right at my fingertips. It almost made it too easy."

"But you had an alibi for when Melissa had been kidnapped and murdered. The police said you were at your apartment. They saw you on the complex's surveillance footage."

Andy laughed harshly. "Manipulating camera footage is simple, Emily, especially for someone with my level of skill."

"I don't understand. Why would other people's secrets matter to you?"

"It amazes me how people believe their actions won't have consequences. They think just because they're good liars, they'll never have to answer for their sins. Take my family, for example." He paced for a moment before continuing. "Do you know how I ended up in the foster system, Emily?"

"No one told me," I admitted.

He gave a nasty laugh. "Of course they didn't, because no one ever cared to ask. Not even my foster families. All four of them."

"What happened to you, Andy?" I asked softly. "What could have happened to lead you to this point?" I hoped showing empathy would be enough to get him to lower his guard and maybe let me go. It was clear he was hurting and wanted someone to care.

He pulled up another chair, scraping the bottom along the uneven wooden floor, and sat across from me. His leg bounced impatiently while he debated what to share.

"My real parents happened. When I was eleven, my mom found out that my father was having an affair with his client. So cliché, right? My mom was the sweetest woman. Biggest heart. Best mom you could ask for. Despite my dad's infidelity, she wanted to make it work. She loved our family so much that she was willing to put it aside. My dad promised to end it but months afterward, we found out he didn't.

"My mom was distraught. She didn't know what to do. You see, my mom suffered from chronic depression. She mostly handled it well, but this situation was beyond her control. It triggered her and she sank deeper into hopelessness. She became angry. She took to drinking. She was inconsolable. It was like I didn't even know her anymore. The sweet woman I loved was gone and all she left behind was someone who was so withdrawn, she barely recognized she had a family anymore. She stopped acknowledging me. I tried so hard.

"After a while, my dad didn't come home as often because of her. Which only made things worse because we knew where he was most likely staying. With *her*." He said the word with contempt. "And then…" He paused, taking in harsh breaths.

"And then?" I pressed. I shifted in my seat, making the ropes dig into my wrists. I winced.

"And then one day he did come home. And my mom… she was ready for it. She shot him in the head. Point blank. Right in front of me. I ran to his side to see if he was still alive, but he wasn't. The hole through his head made sure of it. Sure, he was a bastard, but I didn't want him to die. I guess my mom took it as I was picking him over her, so she shot herself too. There I was, just a kid, sitting alone in my kitchen with both my parents with half their heads blown off. It took me hours to stop shaking before I could call the police."

My eyes widened as I recognized this story. The day when we found Melissa's body, Delores had told us about the little boy who witnessed his family getting murdered. In the edge of my mind, I knew this fact had to be significant to what happened to Melissa, but I couldn't figure it out just yet.

"After that, I was put into the system. My first three families gave up on me. Said they couldn't connect with me. I was too distant, too quiet, too *weird*. I landed my last foster family when I was seventeen. They only kept me around because they were never home to care."

"I'm sorry that happened to you, Andy," I said sincerely.

"Yeah, well. I hated my dad for doing what he did. He ruined our family. I could have handled divorced parents. Not two dead parents. I had to deal with that and then being unwanted over and over again."

I paused for a minute as I considered my next question. "Are you Jason McFalls?"

He stared at me intensely, and I worried that the question would set him off. After a moment, he simply nodded.

My brain started to make connections. Melissa had a file on Jason McFalls. Did she suspect Andy and Jason were the same? If so, what did it matter to her? Who was he to her?

"How does Melissa fall into this? And me?"

"The reason why my foster families thought I was quiet and weird is that I was busy putting things into motion. You see, none of this would have happened if my father kept his dick in his pants and his whore didn't continue to allow it despite knowing he had a family at home." His voice became deep and menacing. He gripped the gun tightly in his hand.

"After some research, I discovered who the woman was. Theresa Collins."

He waited for a moment while I let that sink in. "Melissa's mother?"

"You know what else I found out? Melissa was my dear ol' sis," he growled. "My dad wasn't ending his affair with Theresa because he had a whole other family. The affair had gone on much longer than my mother and I even realized. How could we not have known I had an older sister? All those years..."

"But wasn't she married? What about Mr. Collins?"

He gave a disgusted laugh. "That bastard had no clue. He was too busy with country clubs and golf and God knows what else to realize his wife was stepping out for nearly two decades. For years he assumed Melissa was his daughter. But I saw to it that he learned the truth." The look of satisfaction returned briefly.

"So what happened?" The hard chair was making my ass go numb and my shoulders were aching from being pulled behind me. If I felt this way after only an hour, I could only imagine how I'd feel if he kept me tied up for the night.

His face turned stone cold. "Apparently he didn't value fidelity and family as much as he did his reputation. Of course, they fought about Theresa's indiscretions and he had a hard time stomaching the fact that the woman he believed was his daughter for twenty-two years was not his. But, like I said, saving face came first so he tried to pay me off to keep quiet." Andy shook his head. "The money was nice. It helped me buy the tech I needed to become the hacker I am today, but it wasn't enough. He couldn't buy me."

I took it in. This must have been around the time Melissa was rebelling with Blake. "Did Melissa know?"

"Not at the time. She thought her family was arguing about an affair but didn't know the specifics." He got up from his chair and stood by the fire, peering into its depths. "I waited and watched until Melissa was at her lowest before I contacted her parents again with new threats. Ones that made them worry for her life. The reason they changed her name wasn't because of her drug use and the impact on their family reputation. It was because they thought I wouldn't be able to find her. They sent her away to law school under a new identity." He turned to face me. "But it didn't matter. At that point, I knew how to find out anything about anyone."

I looked at him in horror and awe. "You were just a kid. Barely a teenage boy by then. How could you have been able to do that?"

He leaned close to me, face mere inches from mine. "It's amazing what you can accomplish with enough determination," he said quietly before taking a seat across from me again. "Like the house fire, for instance. That was retribution for trying to hide Melissa. For not acknowledging their sins...for letting my family die. They didn't want to face the music because of their precious reputation and lifestyle? I took that from them and, as for Melissa, I let her know what it felt like to lose both 'parents' in a horrible way."

"And me? How do I fall into all this?" I asked in a small voice, realizing how unhinged this person was. There was no remorse in his voice after admitting he killed two people. He was on a mission to find justice and it had blinded him from his own wrongdoings. To him, the end justified the means.

"I thought an eye for an eye would be enough for me but despite it, she thrived. She did well in school, she secured a great job. But when I lost my parents, I got discarded. Passed around from family to family. She got everything. Again," he screamed with rage. "What I did wasn't enough.

"When I was finally old enough to get a job, I worked my way to end up at the law firm. I needed to get closer to her to see what kind of person she was. I needed to understand what was important to her so I could take it all away. Instead, I found that she was much worse than expected, just as horrible as that whore mother of hers.

"I saw everything. I found out about Melissa and Trevor and how they kept up their affair for months before you found out. All his cover stories to you. All the snide remarks Melissa made about your relationship with him.

After a while, Trevor treated your relationship like a joke. A game, even. How much could he get away with? How oblivious could you be? How trusting were you to all his lies? It was disgusting. You didn't deserve it. I checked on you. You were trying to grow your business. You were a loyal fiancée. You supported his dreams even though he was such an asshole to you, to your face and behind your back."

"Andy…" I started but he continued on with his angry tangent.

"It set me off. It showed me the other side of my family's situation. Did my dad and his whore do the same thing? I finally had a chance to get justice for my mom— to do it over. Kill the bitch, frame the cheater for it. It was all going so smoothly. You just had to follow the clues that all implicated Trevor while showing the world how shitty Melissa really was in the process."

He pushed out of his seat, still gripping the gun tightly. "I was rooting for you, Emily. I saw myself in you. I wanted you to have a better ending than I had. Trevor and Melissa deserved their fate, and I wanted you to be the one that took Trevor down. But you had to complicate things. You stopped following directions and went off course. You were fucking up the plan I carefully crafted," he yelled vehemently.

"Andy," I tried again, looking for the right words to say without setting him off. "I appreciate what you were trying to do and understand why you did it. What happened to you was…there are no words for how terrible. You never deserved that. But I would have been okay if you hadn't gone through all of this for me. It hurt like hell knowing Trevor betrayed me. It killed me to know he was leaving me for her. But I would have eventually moved on. I would have survived. It may have taken some time and the pain would always be there even if it faded over time.

But people learn to let go and get on with their lives. All of this… just made it so much harder. Trevor didn't destroy me like your father did to your family. I would have started a new life."

"It was warranted," he repeated harshly, spit spraying from his lips. "I did this for you. For me. For all the people who have been stomped on by the scumsuckers of the earth and were forgotten about. For all the lies and secrets that ruin people. For the people who weren't strong enough to fight back." He focused the gun on me. "Why'd you have to do this, Emily? Why couldn't you just stick to the plan? Why couldn't you just take the evidence I planted and put Trevor behind bars?"

He looked distraught, like he was at the end of his rope. My heart pounded in my ears as I saw the barrel pointing at my head. The fire danced dangerously in his eyes, showing me his resolve. He was going to kill me. "Andy, you don't have to do this. We can get you help," I pleaded.

"It's too late for that, Emily. I have to tie up loose ends and disappear again." He placed his finger on the trigger. "I'm sorry. I didn't want it to end this way."

I squeezed my eyes shut, accepting the fate that lay before me. I'd never get a chance to say good-bye to my family and friends. I worried about Joanna and how she would handle the news. My stomach clenched at the thought of Ben and never knowing if he was a second chance at love or whether he was even still alive. I'd never know how far I could have taken my café or if I'd ever have achieved the things I wanted out of life. If I'd ever have my own family.

I heard him cock the gun. I fisted my hands, nails digging into my palms, as sweat mixed with tears streamed down my face. I couldn't believe this was it. My life was over because of this stranger's vendetta.

"What the fuck?" I heard Andy spew out. I opened one of my eyes to see him looking out one of the front windows. "No! No! No!" he ranted. He frantically paced the room, and I wondered what was wrong.

That's when I heard the sound of a car heading up to the house. For a brief moment, a glimmer of hope warmed me.

Andy stopped pacing and lifted his gun. "I don't know how they found us, but they did." He shifted from side to side as he debated whether to make a run for it or if he had enough time to shoot me beforehand.

The door pounded behind him. "Open up! Police!" Another voice called out my name and a shiver ran through me. They found me. They were so close and that could be all taken away in seconds if Andy decided to kill me.

"Please, Andy," I begged. "Do the right thing." My heart raced as I saw the darkness return to his eyes. There was no reasoning with him.

The door exploded behind him and bright floodlights filled the room, temporarily blinding me. I turned my head away and squinted, trying to make out what was happening. The silhouette of three officers with guns drawn pushed through the door. "Put the gun down and put your hands above your head!" the leader of the pack shouted in a booming voice.

Andy, in his last desperate attempt, pointed the gun at me again and pulled the trigger.

Something hit me so forcefully, I jerked back in the chair and fell over. My head hit the ground hard. I tried to blink away the stars. There were shouts and scuffling surrounding me. Flesh hitting flesh and groans of pain sounded throughout the small cabin. I tried to look back up to see what was happening, but it was too hard. My head felt like lead. I was so cold suddenly.

A single shot rang out and was followed by a rain of bullets. I heard an agonizing scream that ended abruptly. I wasn't sure what to make of it. All I knew was that there was searing pain in my body and I could feel the warmth of blood trickling down me. My head pounded and I thought my brain would explode.

And then everything went black.

CHAPTER 24

The faint sound of beeping echoed in my ears as I slow-ly came to. I could hear the shuffling of people mov-ing around me, their voices hushed. Wherever I was smelled sterile, as if someone drowned the area with as-tringent.

As my mind started to wake up, flashes of what hap-pened came back to me. Andy. The gun. The police. The shot. The pain.

Was I dead? I stirred at the thought.

"I think she's waking up," a woman's voice in the dis-tance said.

"Emily?" A man's familiar voice said. I couldn't place it.

I tried to open my eyes, but it seemed impossible at first. My eyelids felt like weights. I mustered up the energy and tried again, opening them up just enough to see blurry surroundings of bright white and light. My eyes focused and I opened them wider to see two familiar faces.

Joanna and Ben.

"There she is," Ben said quietly while taking my hand in his. He stroked it lightly and pushed hair away from my face. He looked down at me tenderly, and for a moment I felt like I was the only thing in this world.

Joanna handed me water and helped me take small sips so I didn't spill it all over myself. "Oh, Em. I was so scared," she said with a shaky voice, throwing her arms around me.

"Ow!" I howled in pain as she pulled me in tightly against her.

"Oh God. I'm so sorry. I forgot."

Ben kissed my forehead and looked into my eyes. "Hey, you. You're okay now. We have you." His smile warmed me. "Do you remember what happened?" His voice was soft and comforting.

"A little." My throat was dry despite the water, making my voice sound gravelly. I shifted up in bed, another strenuous process. Pain radiated up my arm. I looked down and noticed a large area of my left arm had been bandaged up. "What's this?"

"Andy shot you," Jo provided.

My breaths came fast as the memories came rushing in. What he told me. What he did. It was horrible. My hand moved to my mouth to stifle a cry. Tears misted my vision.

Ben stroked my face again. "It's okay. Breathe, Emily. That's the only place he got you and it went straight in and out. No arteries were hit. The doctors say you'll recover just fine."

I grabbed his hand again and looked up at him deeply for the first time. "I thought you were dead." A tear trickled down my cheek and Ben gently wiped it away with the pad of his thumb.

"I might have been if you hadn't made that call to the police. They pinged your phone's GPS and found me face down on the side of the road. With the way the rain was coming down, they were certain I would have drowned in the mud if they hadn't found me."

My heart ached at the thought.

"H-how did you find me?" My tears started to subside, but my stuffy nose made it hard to breathe.

"The tech help we had requested a few weeks ago from the neighboring precinct came through. He had spent the last couple of days trying to crack some of the stuff Andy said he was too inexperienced to handle. When the tech dug deeper, he found a calling card."

"What do you mean?"

"Many hackers leave a signature of sorts; it's a source of pride. An ego boost. Our guy found some hidden in the areas Andy had been working on. It took some time to crack it, but he figured it out this morning. It was Overwatch."

I sucked in my breath. "How did they find us out in those woods, though?"

"They searched for more signatures and got a ping on an IP in the area around the time Melissa had gone missing. Looking on the map, this was the only structure out there. A cabin registered under Patrick McFalls, Andy's— or Jason McFalls's—father."

"So, I was right. Andy Anderson is Jason McFalls?"

Ben nodded.

The realization of how close I was to being dead shook me to the core. "What happened to him?"

"He's dead. We fired when he shot you."

"We? You were there?"

"Who do you think broke down the door? I couldn't bear the thought of him hurting you." He kissed my lips gently. "I was so scared I was too late," he said in a low whisper that sent shivers down my spine.

I felt a squeeze on my right hand, and I turned to Joanna's worried eyes. "I'm so happy you're okay and this is all over."

"Why did he do it?" Ben asked.

"In a way to avenge his mother, I guess." I explained it all until I was exhausted and my throat was sore.

Throughout the whole story, I watched both Jo and Ben's faces transform from confusion to shock, rage, and finally worry. By the end of it, I felt my anxiety rise again. "Is it truly over, Ben?"

"My team said Andy was working alone, but I'll dig deeper to make sure that's a hundred percent accurate. You're safe now, Emily."

I bit my lower lip. "And now what happens?" Although I didn't outright ask it, the meaning behind my question wasn't lost on Ben. The case was wrapping up and I'd no longer need police protection. He'd move out and move on with his life.

"Now I get you home and make sure you're okay while you recover," he replied simply. "We'll take it one moment at a time."

• • •

A week later, I was on the mend. Crafty Café was bustling with summer traffic. Although I was still limited in what I could do with my bum arm, the community coming into the café was supportive and patient with me. When the girls weren't available to help me and Joanna, Ben or Delores would offer a hand if they had time. Things were starting to feel normal.

I enjoyed the peace and quiet of not having a crazy

stalker harassing me constantly. And Ben, true to his word, ensured I was recovering. Although the case was more or less closed and the officers assigned to watch me were long gone, Ben stayed with me even though he no longer had to be at my apartment.

Rather than staying in the guest bedroom, Ben spent his nights in mine. I wrapped myself around him each evening, loving the feel of his solid body and warmth. He made love to me gently, careful not to overextend my wounded arm. But gentle or not, the passion was undeniable. He made me feel secure, wanted, and desired. Most importantly, he made me feel loved.

I had worried that once the case was over, the connection that Ben and I shared would dwindle away. If anything, we were growing closer as the days passed. After all the insanity of broken relationships, crazy exes, murders, stalkers, and kidnapping, we had agreed we should take it slow.

Saying and doing were two different things, though.

On a Monday late in June, I woke up to an empty bed. I turned over to see it was just before dawn. Joanna was opening up today and I was due in a couple of hours.

"Ben?" I called out in a croaky morning voice.

A second later, he peeked his head in. His hair was mussed from sleep and I couldn't help but smile to myself. He was so genuine, it filled my heart. "Did I wake you?"

"How dare you leave bed before giving me a good morning kiss," I said in mock anger.

He walked in with two cups of hot coffee from the café. "I figured you would rather have this instead."

"Mmm. My hero." He sat on the edge of the bed and handed me a cup. I kissed him softly.

The corners of his mouth tugged up as he watched me take my first sip. It was always bliss. "Do you know how beautiful you are in the morning?"

I felt around the mess of tangles on my head. "What do you want?" I asked suspiciously.

He gave a hearty laugh. "Can't a guy give a pretty woman a compliment?"

"I've spent my whole life seeing myself in the mirror after I wake up. It ain't pretty." I laughed. "Spill it."

He shifted a little as if he were uncomfortable and rubbed the back of his neck. "Well, you know how we said we would take it slow and that I would stay until you recovered?"

"Uh huh." My arm was almost healed and with some light physical therapy, I would be back to normal. My stomach sank as I considered where this conversation was going. Being with him these last few weeks had been indescribable. I couldn't imagine not having him here.

But it was inevitable. He said he would stay until I was better. There was no promise for anything beyond that.

"And you know how you're pretty much recovered?"

"Yes…" The sinking feeling worsened.

"And that would mean I no longer would have to stay here?"

My face fell. "Ben, just say what you want to say."

"I don't want to leave you," he said quickly. "I know taking it slow doesn't usually include moving in with each other."

"I wouldn't say our circumstances were that of normal people."

"I agree." He hesitated, took my coffee, and put it on the nightstand, and then grabbed my hands and looked at me deeply with his hazel eyes. The ones I got lost in each night we spent together, worshiping each other's bodies. "The truth is, I couldn't imagine starting or ending my day without you. You're brave, beautiful, big-hearted, clever. You're everything. I came to Portland looking for a fresh start, not to fall for a woman I thought murdered another woman out of a jealous rage."

"Falling for me?" I sputtered out the words.

"I'm as surprised as you are. I don't exactly wear my heart on my sleeve, Emily. But I can't help myself when it comes to you. Something about you makes me feel whole. I feel right for the first time in a long time. Years ago, I was always excited by the thought of going undercover some-place new. Now, I can barely bring myself to leave your side. I don't want to take it slow. Not with you. I want you, right now...for always."

Tears filled my eyes.

"Oh God, was that too much?" Ben asked, swiping them away. He cupped my face in his hands, his gaze still intently on me, waiting for a response.

"Absolutely not. It was perfect." I kissed him deeply. "I feel the same about you. For a while now, truthfully. I tried to rationalize it. Tried to tell myself it was the adrenaline or rebound emotions. I tried to convince myself it wasn't right for me. But deep down I never believed it."

"So what are you saying?" Ben asked earnestly.

"I'm saying I want you to stay."

Wrapping his arms tightly around me, he kissed me fe-verishly. "I know this is also not taking it slow," he started to say when we came up for air.

"Hmm?" I said in post-kiss bliss.

"But I love you, Emily Ayers."

I smiled up at him and touched his cheek lightly. "I love you too, Detective."

CHAPTER 25

Six months later.

The case was officially closed. After a thorough investigation, the Portland PD learned the ins and outs of why Andy Anderson (AKA Jason McFalls) murdered Melissa and how he planned to frame Trevor. After they had uncovered hidden hard drives and cell phones, they ended up down a deep rabbit hole, which included his manifesto.

We learned that Andy had used his hacking skills to toy with Melissa for months, even to the point where she'd been forced to make hefty deposits to an untraceable account to keep all her damning secrets hidden, including the truth about her identify which was sealed in closed records. After some digging on the hard drive, the police had learned it was tied to the charity named in her will—a fake charity Andy had set up to steal her funds and put strain on the lavish life he felt she didn't deserve.

But in Andy's eagerness to destroy her life, he'd slipped up, prompting Melissa to start digging, where she found out about her half-brother. She had hidden the files for Jason McFalls at my apartment when she felt her life was in danger. And it was. She had been too close to the truth, so Andy hijacked Trevor's car, kidnapping and killing her.

He had spent years planning his revenge, putting everything in place to cause the ultimate damage. Seeing her life fall apart fueled his ego, causing him to deviate from his carefully laid plan. Had his ego not gotten in the way and had he followed the details in the manifesto, he may have gotten away with it.

For such a young man, he truly was brilliant. It was a shame he didn't use that mind for something good. I felt a pang of sadness for him—he was so young to feel so much rage and heartbreak. I couldn't imagine what he had gone through.

Andy's story about his birth parents checked out, as did his multiple stints with foster families. From the foster system's records and interviews with the families, we learned that he had shown some troubling signs early in his childhood, most likely as a result of his parents' murder/suicide and his plan for vengeance. When he turned eighteen, he left his last foster family and fell off the radar, emerging later as Andy Anderson.

The police confirmed that he worked alone. He was alone most of his life. After being passed from foster family to foster family, he withdrew into himself more and more, focusing only on his mission. He didn't have any real relationships, no friends, and no family to claim him. Not even a pet.

It was a sad existence.

But I believed despite life's circumstances, people still had a choice between good and evil. Maybe what started out as righting wrongs in Andy's eyes had ended up taking a dark turn. No matter how he tried to justify his actions, there was no compelling reason to have murdered Melissa

Maher. His half-sister. The only family he had left.

Although we learned a lot about Melissa's life, we were still left with so many unanswered questions. But in the end, it didn't matter. Melissa was gone. Andy was gone. And nothing was going to bring them back.

Life post-murder had been interesting, if not busy. I finally had an opportunity to get into my own groove after Trevor and I broke things off. And even though Ben was now in my life, he gave me the space I needed to make my own decisions and find a bit of independence.

He also let me indulge in my own little quirks. Like Christmas.

Our apartment was bursting at the seams with Christmas decor. Ben, remembering our time in Canada, also booked us a romantic weekend getaway the week leading up to Christmas before we headed back to Rhode Island to see my parents for the holidays. For such a tough man who had seen so much in his life, he always found a way to be thoughtful and caring.

And for once I felt like I could be myself.

Business at Crafty Café was booming with our new menu offerings—ones with extraordinary presentation. We were able to hire a baker to work with Joanna so we could keep up with demand. The extra hands also gave Joanna the time she needed to create something bigger and better as the weeks went on.

In fact, our holiday treats were so well-crafted and delicious that we had been featured in several "Best of Portland" lists these past few months. Because of it, we were seeing an increase in customers even in the slower winter months.

These past six months had opened up a whole new world for us. With more capital, we were now in the works of expanding our current location and considering catering services. I was so proud.

And with our business doing so well, Jo and I had been able to hire a dedicated manager along with our new baker. Seven-day work weeks were now a thing of the past, and for once I was able to enjoy what this new life of mine had to offer.

So what had I been doing with my newfound free time?

Well, I picked up photography as a hobby. When Charlie decided to finally go off to college, she gave me a crash course on how to photograph our daily specials. After investing in a better camera, I realized I really loved it. I was still an amateur, of course, but I got better and better as the weeks went by. I expanded beyond food photography and found a new passion for landscapes. There was something so relaxing about taking photos out and about. It gave me a new appreciation for the city I called home. Not to be cheesy, but photography gave me a new perspective.

I also saved enough money to consider buying my first place. Nothing large, but I'd been looking at small cottages up the road, still within walking distance to the café. The perfect one hadn't made itself known to me yet, but I believed it was only a matter of time and I was excited by the prospect of calling someplace my official home.

And perhaps the reason I hadn't found the perfect home yet was because a certain someone in my life—cough, Ben—apparently had some pretty strong opinions about the place he'd also be living in.

Yeah, the "going slow" thing didn't really work for us. In these past few months, our relationship had blossomed. Each day he proved to be such an amazing man. Sure, he had his quirks and maybe we didn't always see eye to eye, but I knew he was someone I could count on. He was in my corner. He would protect me, celebrate me, allow me room to grow, and always be there to provide unconditional love.

In the years I had spent with Trevor, I never felt this sense of deep love like I did with Ben. But when you knew, you knew. Or so they said.

Well, I did know. And I couldn't wait to see what the rest of my life would be like with him by my side.

ABOUT THE AUTHOR

When Sofia Sawyer's fifth-grade teacher handed her a journal, encouraging her to keep writing, she vowed she always would.

As a lifelong storyteller, Sofia writes contemporary romances featuring independent women who take charge of their destinies. Based in Charleston, S.C., she follows her wanderlust whenever she can to new and exciting places, often finding story ideas throughout her travels.

When she isn't reading, writing, or jet-setting across the globe, you can find Sofia playing with her dog, taking advantage of the amazing Charleston restaurant scene, hiking, or hanging at the beach.

To stay up to date with her latest work, connect with her on:

Twitter: **twitter.com/sofia_sawyer**

Instagram: **instagram.com/sofiasawyerwriter**

Facebook: **facebook.com/sofiasawyerwriter**

Tumblr: **sofiasawyer.tumblr.com**

Pinterest: **pinterest.com/sofiasawyerwriter**

Sign up for her mailing list at: **sofiasawyer.com**